THE FRAGILE HOUR

Further Titles by Rosalind Laker from Severn House

THE SEVENTEENTH STAIR
TO LOVE A STRANGER

THE FRAGILE HOUR

Rosalind Laker

*To dear Hazel,
with whom I have
shared so much laughter,
with love
Rosalind Laker*

*Christmas
1996*

This first world edition published in Great Britain 1996 by
SEVERN HOUSE PUBLISHERS LTD of
9–15 High Street, Sutton, Surrey SM1 1DF.
First published in the USA 1997 by
SEVERN HOUSE PUBLISHERS INC. of
595 Madison Avenue, New York, NY 10022.

British Library Cataloguing in Publication Data

Laker, Rosalind, 1925–
  The fragile hour
  1. English fiction – 20th century
  I. Title
  823.9'14 [F]

  ISBN 0-7278-5181-0

Typeset by Palimpsest Book Production Limited,
Polmont, Stirlingshire, Scotland.
Printed and bound in Great Britain by
Hartnolls Ltd, Bodmin, Cornwall.

To Inge and our family,
here and in Norway

My grateful thanks always to Joe Hotchkiss,
who first suggested that I should write
about the Norwegian Resistance.

Chapter One

Anna parked her car at the roadside, but made no move to get out. Instead she clenched her hands on the wheel, making her knuckles show white. The car radio was playing the latest hit by the Beatles, but she was not listening as she steeled herself for the ordeal that lay ahead. Through the windscreen her haunted gaze barely took in the vista of the great Norwegian mountains all around her.

It had been a private decision to come here. Nobody else knew of it. She had flown in from Heathrow at mid-morning, caught a connecting flight that had brought her within range, and hired a car to drive the rest of the way. All because a short paragraph in one of yesterday's London evening newspapers had caught her eye and hurled the past back at her in a way she could never have foreseen.

A policeman came across from the grass verge opposite to bend his head down at the open window. "You can't park here, *frue*. Drive farther along."

She stirred herself and gave a nod. "Could you tell me what's happening at the lake? Has the wartime fighter plane been brought to the surface yet?"

"No, there's been a last minute delay and it will be early evening before it comes up. It's ten days now since the off-shore company installed a crane on the bank and brought their working-boat up-river, but the aircraft is

1

lodged precariously on a rock ledge deep down. One false move and it could go plummeting into the depths and that would be it."

He thought she shivered, but that was impossible on such a hot August day. Stepping back, he waved her on and Anna drove past the long line of vehicles parked at the roadside to the first available space. It was not surprising that so many people had come here today, for the new road through to the coast had made this once isolated area easily accessible. By now the music had given way to a news-reader, who announced that Nixon had won the Republican nomination for President and, in the next breath, that mini-skirts had become so short that in London the dry-cleaners were charging by the inch. Anna switched it off and parked for the second time.

Everywhere else in the world life was going on, however important or trivial, but she had come to face up to the past, whatever the consequences might be. Yet she had never expected to visit this lake, even though what had happened there was an integral part of her relationship with a man who had torn her life apart. It was like coming to the opening of Pandora's box.

How easy it was already to picture how it must have been for the pilot of the fighter plane, a Mosquito, on the March night when he had to make a crash-landing here on the snow-covered plateau. That had been during the savage days of the German Occupation of this peaceful land. With his aircraft badly damaged by anti-aircraft fire and losing height rapidly, he had still hoped to save the special cargo that he carried aboard. If he had not been familiar with the area, there would have been no chance, but he watched out for the dark gleam of the frozen lake that the wind had made patchy with snow.

Anna shut her eyes tightly, seeming to hear the spluttering engines as the aircraft descended swiftly out of

2

the night sky. There came the vibrating thud of the crash-landing followed by the screech of metal as it careened wildly before finally coming to a standstill with its nose deep in a snowdrift. It was then that there came a noise like thunder as the ice, thick though it was, suddenly cracked and split into great glittering fangs that soared upwards as if to devour this unexpected prey. Briefly the Mosquito remained propped at a desperate angle, one wing high, a curious quiver passing through its fuselage as if it hovered like its namesake, until it began to sink slowly down into the churning water. The pilot, badly bruised and shaken, watched from the snowdrift where he had managed to crawl to safety. He uttered a long and despairing groan as his fighter plane disappeared from sight.

With an effort Anna forced her mind back to the present. She wouldn't go to the lake yet. It was better to be on her own while the final salvage preparations took place instead of being in the midst of all the other spectators. Deciding to leave her jacket on the back seat, she tucked a strand of her silky light brown hair back behind one ear and put on large-framed sunglasses before gathering up her handbag and binoculars from the passenger-seat. Slinging the straps of both over her left shoulder, she slid out of the car and locked it behind her.

Setting off up the slope, she walked through grass hazy with harebells and thick with clover, lady's slipper and stretches of wild pansies. Slim and lithe, dressed in a cool green cotton blouse and white trousers fashionably flared, her subtly expressive face, presently showing strain, had the kind of well-formed bones that would carry her beauty through all the decades ahead. Her mouth was wide and generous and, at other times, quick to laugh. She had inherited her fine complexion and azure eyes from her Oslo-born mother, but in being practical and level-headed

3

with a mind of her own, she knew herself to be exactly like her English Naval Officer father, David Marlow.

It was rarely that he had spoken about the tragic period in his life and hers when her Norwegian mother had died. Yet he brought up the subject when she spent a half-term from boarding school with him when his ship was in port. She was twelve and they were seated at a window table in one of Fuller's teashops.

"I've often wondered, Anna, how you really felt after we lost your mother and I told you of all the arrangements I'd made for your care in my absences at sea. After all, you were only seven."

She had looked up from eating a cream cake with its fresh strawberry on top. "I didn't like the boarding school bit at first, although it's all right now. But it was wonderful being able to spend every vacation with Aunt Rosa in Norway. My earliest memories are of Mother taking me there when you were away at sea, and I've always been bilingual."

When she was older and her aunt had confided in her, Anna often wondered if her father had known that his sister-in-law had had a passionate affair with a German count in her younger days. That was when Rosa's staid and tiresomely dull husband was still alive.

On the slope Anna paused to pick a harebell as she had done so often throughout her childhood. She smiled, remembering how her aunt was always on the quayside to meet her and how they had waved exuberantly to each other. Aunt Rosa's welcoming embraces were warm and bosomy and full of love. They had needed each other, the maternally-minded widow denied children of her own and the lonely child.

To this day a certain French scent could bring back memories of childhood and teenage days, for Rosa had always used it. Although sated by travel through the years

4

of marriage to a diplomat, Rosa Johansen had still made seasonal trips to Paris for most of her clothes. She had splendid hats too, and Anna remembered the hilarious sessions they'd had together when she had been allowed to try them on.

Those vacations had followed a regular pattern that had made everything so secure and reassuring. In spring there would be skiing from a cabin on Nordmarka, not far from Oslo, and Christmas was at Rosa's elegant apartment within sight of the Royal Palace with parties and a tree aglow with real candles. But the summers were best of all. Then she would disembark at Bergen and take a steamer up the coast to the lovely little Town of Roses as Molde was still called. There she and Rosa stayed at the old family home with its view of the fjord. It was a time of picnics and sailing and trips into the mountains, most of it with local children who had become her friends.

The grassy slope had become steeper now. As the forest began to take over. Anna entered its secretive, dark green shadows, the foliage of the sky-high firs so thick that only spears of sunlight could penetrate. She inhaled again the familiar fragrance of fern and bark and dry cones. In another such forest she had once been engaged in a gun-battle, and in yet another she'd had to run for her life.

She came to a standstill, pressing her fingertips to her temples. Too much was coming back to her, unwelcome visions of wartime events that she'd tried to keep from her mind. Then she reminded herself sternly that remembering was the reason why she had come today. The delay in raising the fighter plane was a bonus in which she could gather her thoughts together and prepare for the dreaded moment when she would see it.

There was a sunny clearing ahead where timber had been felled. Anna hurried to it, wanting to feel the sun's warmth fully on her again. There she found a comfortable place to sit. Wild flowers were growing here too and wild cranberries, not yet red, showed in the nearby undergrowth. Within reach was a patch of ripe blueberries and she reached out to pluck a sprig of them. One by one she popped the blueberries into her mouth, using the old trick of pressing out the sweetness with her tongue to avoid staining her teeth.

It was a trick she had practised in her teens when she had not wanted Nils Olsen to see her with blue stains around her mouth. Before that in childhood she had never cared. Everything changed when she realised at fourteen that her long attachment to him had become something much more. But he was older by four years with a wide choice of girls of his own age. It had taken him until she was just seventeen and he was taking part in ski-jumping contests at Oslo's Holmenkollen for him to see her in a new light. When the spring vacation was over they had to wait yearningly for summer when they could be together again.

It became a summer she could never forget. But then 1939 had stamped itself on the memories of untold millions of people in many different ways. Loving and being loved for the first time paled into insignificance beside all else that happened. She had returned home again to boarding school in Derbyshire on that first tumultuous day of September when Hitler's forces had stormed into Poland. Two days later Britain and her allies were at war with Nazi Germany.

Correspondence had still come through from Rosa and Nils. She was able to let them know when her father's ship was torpedoed and lost with all hands. Their replies comforted her in her grief, but those were the last letters she received. The next day Norway was brutally invaded by German forces and the contact with the two people she loved most was broken.

6

The day after final school exams Anna presented herself at the local recruiting office of the Women's Royal Naval Service, determined to become a Wren, the nickname given to those who served in it.

"I'm here to volunteer," she announced.

"Have you any connection with the Royal Navy?" the recruiting officer questioned briskly.

"My father was a Captain until he was lost at sea. I can't replace him in the service, but I want to close the gap a little bit."

She was trained as a radio operator. After a year she gained a commission. In the fitting-room of a naval outfitters she regarded her reflection in her new uniform of Third Officer, a single blue stripe on the sleeves. The old tailor, who looked as if he had been making uniforms for officers since Nelson's day, had done his work well.

She slipped on the greatcoat, fastened the blue buttons and grinned with a sense of achievement as she straightened the naval tricorn hat. Then she picked up her gloves and slung the strap of her gas-mask over her shoulder. Her new posting was to the south of England, not far from where her father had moored his sailing-boat before the war.

"Portsmouth, here I come!" she said under her breath. Then she went out into the busy street and returned the salute of two ratings for the first time before running for a bus that was about to draw away. Wolf-whistles followed her from a truckload of Canadian soldiers passing by.

Some months after her arrival and with the booming of anti-aircraft guns, Anna knelt in the choking dust amid the rubble of a bombed cinema, holding to her a fellow officer. It had been their last evening together before he rejoined his ship. Marriage between them had never been considered, but she had become very fond of him and he of her. The tears coursed down her begrimed face as he died in her arms.

She had to keep her grieving to herself, although she knew that many sympathised with her. Life was too difficult generally to allow private troubles to intrude on others. Outwardly everything went on as before until the day she was told the Commanding Officer wanted to see her.

"What happened?" one of her fellow officers asked when she returned to the mess.

"I've been posted!" Anna exclaimed in bewilderment. "But I don't know where! I'm to take all my kit with me and report in London tomorrow afternoon."

"It must mean promotion. Lucky you!"

Next morning Anna caught the train to Waterloo Station. There she took a bus to an address in Baker Street. She noticed that grass and some hardy wild flowers were growing in the gaps left by the Blitz. It was a comforting sight, seeming to show that normality could follow any nightmare.

Chapter Two

At an office window above Baker Street underground station a stern-faced man in his forties stood looking out, his rank that of major in the Free Royal Norwegian Army. He could see on the far side of the bomb-damaged street a young Wren waiting for a gap in the passing traffic before she could cross. Although he had never met her, he recognised her as Anna Marlow from a photograph in his files.

"She's here," he said to a fellow Norwegian, also in army uniform, tall and broad-shouldered, who came to join him at the window.

"If looks were all that counted she'd be OK," Karl Kringstad replied drily. He had read the file on her in this office less than half an hour before; it had given her age, birthplace, parentage and much else about her. "Let's hope she measures up to her Commanding Officer's report."

It had stated that Anna Marlow was intelligent, alert and conscientious in her duties. She had also kept a cool head in several emergencies during air-raids and once, at great risk herself from falling masonry, she had rescued and attempted to keep alive a fellow officer who had been trapped under rubble in a bombed cinema.

"I admit that what we would expect of her is specialised work," the Major agreed. "But it was your hunch that put me on her track."

"It was only based on what I heard said about her on one occasion."

"But Captain Gunnarsen had known her and her aunt in Norway and, as you said yourself, he's a good judge of character. Anyway, we shall soon know. She's starting to cross the street."

"I'd better go." Karl turned away.

The Major frowned, moving from the window with him. "Why not stay and make some judgement of her for yourself?"

Karl hesitated, his gaze darkening. "I'm not sure whether I'm ready yet to voice an opinion about any possible replacement for Ingrid."

The Major was apologetic. "I was thoughtless. It's too soon yet. I simply thought that, if the Marlow girl has the right qualities, you'll be seeing more of her for a while than anyone else."

He saw the tightness increase about the younger man's mouth, but there came a sharp nod of acceptance.

"You're right. I'll sit in on this interview for a little while as an observer."

"Good. But don't hesitate to ask the young woman questions if there's something you want to hear direct from her."

When Anna was shown into the office, she was surprised not to see at least one or two naval officers or even a board of them. Instead she was facing a Norwegian major, ribbons on his chest, who was seated at a desk in a rather bare office brightened only by the scarlet, blue and white of Norway's flag. Another man with striking Nordic good looks, whose age she judged to be about twenty-eight, stood by one of the two spare chairs. The only naval link was in the large photograph hanging on the wall behind the desk of King Haakon in his Admiral's uniform.

"I'm Major Andersen," the officer said at once in

10

Norwegian, "and this is Captain Karl Kringstad. You're not here on any naval matter, but to give me the chance to talk informally with you. Please sit down."

"Thank you," Anna said, also in Norwegian since that seemed to be the language chosen for this meeting. She took one of the seats in front of the desk, vaguely aware that Karl Kringstad had seated himself in the other. She was still bemused by this unexpected turn of events. Then, without warning, she was gripped by an icy fear of what she might be about to hear. "Am I here to receive bad news about my aunt in Oslo?" she demanded quickly, her hands clenched together in her lap.

Major Andersen was quick to reassure her. "No! That's not the reason! Not at all!" He rose from his chair to come round and perch his weight on the edge of the desk, facing her. "I regret causing you any unnecessary anxiety. We are all concerned about those whom we know in Norway. My own wife and children are there." Then, before she could say anything, he continued, "I believe you have been in the WRNS since the very day King Haakon and Crown Prince Olav and the Government left Norway in exile for England."

She gave a nod, wondering how he knew. "It was June, 1940. I was already eighteen and about to leave school."

While speaking she had felt Karl Kringstad's hard gaze on her from where he sat nearby. It made her feel uneasy and also intensely aware of him as an extremely physical man. In every way he was a contrast to the Major, who wanted her to be at ease. Glancing across at Karl she met a kind of dark look in his sharply intelligent grey eyes. It was not exactly hostility, but something equally turbulent and disturbing. She wished he were not in the room.

"So you were very eager to join up," the Major commented.

11

"I was. In fact, I thought I was coming here today for a special interview before promotion."

"It's nothing like that."

Karl chose to speak for the first time, his eyes never leaving her, and his voice held an oddly challenging note. "I can hear the west coast in your Norwegian."

Anna looked fully at him. He had a strong face, high-cheeked with a handsome Viking nose and a jaw to match, his mouth well-cut and his hair a dark wheat-colour. There was a self-assured ease in his whole manner combined with an air of confidence that normally she liked in a man, but in his case she felt an extraordinary need to assert herself in order not to be overwhelmed by the force of his personality. There was a curious undercurrent passing between them.

"As a matter of fact," she remarked smoothly, "I can tell that you're from Oslo."

"Correct." He raised an eyebrow. "So you've an ear for the nuances of the Norse language."

"I think I can pride myself on that." She turned again to the Major. "I believe that you, sir, are from Bergen."

"Yes, indeed."

But Karl Kringstad had not finished with her yet. "I'd like to know how you absorbed the county of Romsdal into your speech."

"There's nothing surprising about it. I was only a year old when my mother took me to spend my first summer near Molde and that set the pattern for many summers afterwards. I suppose it could be said that for a while every year I grew up with the local children."

The Major was not oblivious to the underlying terseness in the questions and answers being exchanged between the two seated opposite him. Karl was revealing an interest in the character of this girl, bringing her out in his own way and it was going well.

12

Karl, sitting back with one long leg crossed over the other, continued his selective questioning of Anna as he watched her closely. "You mentioned your aunt in Oslo. What is her name? Perhaps I know her." But when Anna told him he shook his head. "No, I've never met Fru Rosa Johansen."

"Whereabouts did you live in the city?" She was determined not to be beaten down in this extremely civilised battle of questions and answers.

"Grefsen. Do you know it?"

She smiled, more at her own pleasant memories than due to any softening towards him. "Yes, I went often with my aunt to visit the Möen family on Tonsenveien."

"I grew up in the next road. They're fine people. A bomb was dropped nearby on the first morning of the invasion and I went to see if they were all right, but they had only suffered smashed windows from the blast."

Major Andersen intervened at this point. "I'd like you to tell me who else you know in Oslo."

Anna's resentment soared. It had been obvious to her almost from the start that these men were questioning her about Norway for some inexplicable reason of their own and she felt it was high time that it was explained to her. But she obliged the Major by listing her acquaintances in the city, adding that her closest friends were those with whom she had shared her summer days. Just as she was about to make a direct request to be told what this interview was all about, Karl stood up to leave. He made his apologies for having to break away. He turned to her.

"Goodbye, Fröken Marlow. Perhaps we'll meet again one day."

It was a relief to her when he was gone. The room had been too full of his angry presence. She leaned forward and spoke forthrightly to Major Andersen, who was seated again at his desk.

13

"Why am I here? Have you been testing my Norwegian? It's obvious that you wanted to see me for a specific purpose. Is it that you wish me to transfer from the WRNS to be an interpreter for newly-arrived escapees?"

He compressed his lips briefly. "It's much more than that. But, before I explain, I want to tell you something of present conditions in Norway. The newspapers here print whatever they can, but I can give you an insight as to what Norwegians are having to endure in their daily lives."

He went on to list some of the hardships being imposed by Reichskommissar Terboven, the German commander in control of the country. She knew, as everybody did, of the thousands of young Norwegians escaping to join the Free Royal Norwegian Forces formed in England under their exiled king, but she had not known that the penalty for even attempting to escape from Norway was death by firing squad. The Major also told her that recently the fathers of the successful escapees had been taken as hostages, whatever their ages, and sent to one of the concentration camps in Norway. The most notorious of these was Grini near Oslo where hundreds of patriots, men and women, were housed in apalling conditions and subjected to brutal treatment.

"Hitler thought Norway would be easy to subdue. After all, there are only three and a half million of us among all those mountains and fjords, but from the start on what we call the Home Front we proved him wrong. German reprisals and arrests and even torture happen every day, but nothing has checked the people's determination not to be broken."

Anna looked down at her hands linked in her lap, moved by all that she had heard. "Occupied, but unconquered," she said as much to herself as to him.

"You've summed up the situation most accurately." He paused for a moment. "How would you consider the chance to return there in these troubled times?"

Her head jerked up and she stared at him, her heart beginning to thump heavily. A possible understanding as to why she was here had begun to dawn on her throughout all he had been saying. "How would I do that?"

He sat back in his chair. "This is the headquarters of the Norwegian Section of Mr Churchill's Special Operations Executive, which organises military sorties and sabotage by the Resistance in Norway, as is being done in every occupied country. Here we select fellow countrymen, who have escaped, to return to Norway secretly and to undertake extremely dangerous missions. Naturally they have to be of the right character and calibre to meet such requirements."

"You haven't mentioned women."

"We have many women in the Resistance and you have been highly recommended. The training would be hard and strenuous. I'd want you to have a week's leave to think it over."

"How soon could I start that training?"

His eyes showed his satisfaction at her query. "Just as soon as I see you again. But there is an important point for you to remember. There can be no reunions with your aunt or anyone else in Norway. That would be putting their lives at risk just because you yourself would always be in danger. Their ignorance of your presence in the country would be their safeguard."

The thought of being in Norway and unable to see those she cared about was a bitter disappointment, but she accepted that it was how it had to be. "Does anyone else except you and Captain Kringstad know why I'm here?"

"Only those within a closed circle."

"How did you hear about me?"

He gave a slight shake of his head. "I can't tell you that, but I will say that it came from a reliable source."

"I feel privileged to have been mentioned."

15

They talked for another half an hour. He could tell that already Anna had committed herself whole-heartedly to what had been asked of her.

"Come back a week today," he said as the interview came to an end. "I need hardly say that everything has been strictly confidential. Now enjoy your leave."

In the nearest telephone box Anna made a call to a good friend from her schooldays, Joan, with whom she usually spent her leaves. Joan, married to a bomber pilot serving overseas, and alone at home with a three-year-old, always looked forward to Anna's visits. Her voice over the line was warm and welcoming.

"Some unexpected leave prior to an overseas posting, Anna? No, of course I don't mind that you can't tell me where. Catch the next train!"

They had an enjoyable week together. Anna was able to wear her own civilian clothes, for Joan was looking after her personal possessions for the duration of the war, since she had no home now. By chance on their last evening together when they were listening to the radio, the BBC broadcast a recording of President Roosevelt speaking to the people of the United States. His slow, gravelly voice was clear and articulate.

"If there is any man who wonders why this war is being fought, then let him look to Norway. If there is anyone who has any illusions that this war is unnecessary, let him look to Norway. And if there is anyone who doubts the will of democracy to win, then again I say, look to Norway. He will then, in the besieged yet unconquered Norway, find the answers to all his questions."

Joan glanced at Anna, able to tell by her expression that her thoughts were with her aunt and Nils in particular. "It was a very fine tribute."

16

Anna gave a slow smile. "I've always liked that man. He and I see eye to eye about Norway."

When the time came for Anna to fold away her own clothes again, she kept back one item that would be useful in the future. It was a traditional *kofte*, a thick hand-knitted cardigan such as was worn by people of all ages in Norway. Hers was in grey and white and had been knitted specially for her in an intricate pattern by Aunt Rosa's housekeeper. She made sure that Joan did not see it go into her suitcase, not wanting to give any clue to her destination.

The following day, after a return visit to see Major Andersen, Anna travelled to her training centre. It was in a bleak and isolated area. There were other women on the course with her, one Dutch and the others bilingual in French. She was the only one not destined to cross the Channel when the course was over.

It was as strenuous as she had been warned. There were lessons in unarmed combat and self-defence, hours spent at a shooting range and in operating and repairing a radio transmitter. On her first parachute jump she did not release her harness in time and was dragged some distance across rough moorland before she managed it. She did not make that mistake again. The most strenuous exercise of all, apart from climbing high walls and going hand over hand along a rope strung across a river, was escaping in the countryside under real ammunition. The trainees became used to ending a day wet, cold, bruised and muddy.

While the others were given individual briefings on France and Holland, Anna received hers from a Norwegian, who was a veteran of several dangerous sorties back in his own country. It was he who prepared her fully as to what to expect there under Nazi rule.

When the course ended it was February. She had been

encouraged all the time to think herself into the new identity and background that she had been given. Her surname was to be Larsen, which was common enough in Norway, making it less easy for any inquisitive person, German or otherwise, to pinpoint anything about her. On all the forged papers she was given she saw that the German language had priority over Norwegian on her identity card, ration book and clothing coupons as well as on a travel pass. She thought how galling it must be for the Norwegians to have their language demoted to second place.

Apart from her pre-war Swiss watch, which was of the kind that had been available everywhere, and her hand-knitted *kofte*, one of which would have been issued to her in any case, Anna was unable to keep anything else of her own. Some photographs in a leather folder, a powder-compact that had been a gift and other small personal possessions had to be put into a box that would remain stored until her return. She demurred about the two spare keys that Aunt Rosa had given her long ago to the Oslo home and the west coast house. Since the invasion of Norway she had felt that the keys had become talismans and that by keeping them with her she could be sure of opening those doors again one day.

"If ever questioned," she said to the Norwegian who had briefed her, "I'll simply say that they're the keys of my old home and I'm keeping them for sentimental reasons."

He considered seriously before he gave a nod. "OK. They may help you to unlock entirely different doors in an emergency. Some members of the Resistance carry bunches of master keys and then they can get in anywhere. Now you'd better go into the other room and see the clothes that are ready for you."

All the garments had been made in Norway or were

accurate copies, even to the labels, and included a ski outfit and boots, not for sport but for any necessary cross-country treks that might come about in her new venture. She was to pack everything in a well-worn suitcase, which she guessed had probably been brought across the North Sea by an escapee. A false bottom had been added to it for any secret papers she might carry.

At first Anna thought that the handbag, which held appropriate Norwegian-made contents, was of crocodile skin. But closer inspection showed that it was dyed fish skin. It was the same with a pair of shoes with wooden soles that had also been provided. The ingenious Norwegians, faced with a leather shortage, were making use of natural resources wherever possible. There was a pair of stout brown leather shoes, still in a pre-war Oslo box, but these had been scuffed deliberately in order not to look new.

When Anna, again in her WRNS uniform, stood once more in Major Andersen's office, he congratulated her on how well she had come through the course. Another officer, who was also present, gave her a wad of Norwegian Kroner notes, for which she had to sign. Then he gave two pills into her keeping, one a stimulant and the other lethal. She would have preferred not to have received the second one, but the Major had told her that Gestapo interrogation could bring a captive to a point beyond human endurance.

Both men shook her hand and wished her well. "As we say in Norway," the Major added, "farewell for the time being."

Outside an army car was waiting for her and she was driven out of London. Contrary to her expectations she was not to be dropped by parachute into Norway. Instead she was to go by a very different route.

Chapter Three

Rain was slashing down as Anna left the RAF plane
that had brought her north to Shetland. A friendly lieutenant, who introduced himself as David Howarth, met
her. Being in WRNS uniform, she gave him a salute,
which he returned. Otherwise he wasted no time with
preliminaries.

"I've a jeep waiting. Let's make a dash for it!"

Anna turned up the collar of her greatcoat as they ran
towards the vehicle, rain-fountains dancing up about their
feet. She gave a mock sigh of relief as she slid into the
passenger seat and he took the wheel beside her. "Does
it always rain this hard up here?"

He grinned as he turned the jeep onto the road. "We do
get more than our fair share of rough weather, being north
of Scotland. Not that I mind it myself. But you should see
how beautiful the isle is when the sun shines on the cliffs
and bays and skerries."

"I like what I'm seeing now." She was gazing out
with interest. In spite of the downpour and heavy skies
there was a curious, sombre beauty to the oddly treeless
countryside with a sprinkling of sheep here and there. The
single-storeyed stone crofts were the only sign of habita-
tion, but sometimes even these proved to be derelict.

"Since I was first posted here I've grown deeply
attached to the isle and the good-natured Shetlanders,"
David continued as he drove along. "They were used

to a quiet life before the war, but they've accepted our naval and military presence, and none would give away the secret operations that take place from here. And it's not only us disrupting their lives, but many escaping Norwegians arrive on the east coast of the isle. It's their first landfall after leaving home waters. Not that they stay long. They're taken from here to London."

Anna glanced at him quickly. "Do you have the names of those arrivals? I'd like to look at any listed under the letter O." She was thinking of Nils. It had often occurred to her that it was highly likely that he was an escapee, but he would have had no idea where to find her.

"I'm sure that can be arranged. It may be a few days before you're able to leave on the Shetland Bus for Norway and you'll have plenty of time to peruse it."

"The Shetland Bus?" she queried.

He grinned at her. "That's the name we've given this route of Norwegian fishing-boats across the North Sea, because they come and go so regularly on secret expeditions. I don't know what is in the cargo you'll be travelling with, but it could be anything from weapons for the Resistance to German uniforms for various sorties against the enemy. They return with secret agents, such as yourself, who have special information to deliver or others who need to escape and so on. The demand on these Norwegian fishermen is endless and nothing deters them, whatever the cost might be. Before the war all they ever did at sea was to cast nets."

"I hope the toll on these brave men is light."

He shook his head grimly. "We've had heavy casualties in men and boats. Also nobody knows how many individual escapees have lost their lives through being gunned down by enemy aircraft in the North Sea."

She hoped that Nils had not been one of them.

Soon they came to the little village of Skalloway with

its narrow streets, small shops and old stone houses. She was given comfortable accommodation and liked the place and the local people from the start.

During the next few days Anna met several Shetland Bus fishermen, who were waiting between trips for passengers such as herself or for a particular cargo or even for the weather to improve. She soon heard of the dreadful gales that blew there and how sea-planes, as well as fishing-boats, had been lost. She thought the weather exceptionally rough already as the wind buffeted her whenever she went out and the waves lashed at the land enclosing the harbour.

The Skipper with whom Anna was to sail was a thin, wiry man named Skansen. He had made any number of the perilous voyages.

"You'll be safe enough on my boat, the *Noreg*," he promised with total confidence.

She did not doubt him, able to see that here was a natural leader, a man to whom danger was simply run-of-the-mill.

When Anna was given access to the lists of escapees she ran her finger quickly down the names under O, but, although she checked again, the name of Nils Olsen was not on it.

The rain was gusting down on the day of the *Noreg*'s departure, the clouds bruised and low. Anna changed out of her WRNS uniform for the last time. Warmly clad in a thick Norwegian sweater and trousers under borrowed oilskins and wearing a sou'wester, she went on board the vessel. It was about fifty feet long and everything was very cramped with the fish-hold amidships. The engine room lay aft of it and at deck level was the wheel-house and the galley. The six members of the crew had bunks below in the forecastle and the only available one for her was in the Skipper's cabin, which lay in the stern.

22

Anna went below with her suitcase. There were two bunks and also a table between opposite benches fitted into the narrow stern. It was here she would eat with the men. No concessions were being made for her as a woman and she was glad of it. These fishermen would be at the battle-front again as soon as the *Noreg* left harbour and she would be in the fight with them.

She had been told that another passenger was expected to join the vessel and heard him being greeted as she stowed away her suitcase. When she came up on deck again he was already in the wheelhouse with Skipper Skansen.

The *Noreg* was casting off. David Howarth, who had come to the quayside with her, was waiting to see the boat leave. It was his custom and that of any fishermen on shore to gather and shout their good wishes to a fishing-boat setting out on a sortie. The crew on board were in high good humour as if they were doing no more than sailing off to gather in a bumper catch of fish. They waved and exchanged joking remarks with those left behind. Anna joined in the waving. The strip of water widened between the boat and the quayside. Beyond the harbour the whitecaps warned of a choppy voyage ahead.

Anna stayed on by the white-painted bulwark. All the crew were busy with various tasks and she was careful not to get in the way. She thought to herself there was no sound in all the world like the comfortable tonk-tonk of the diesel-engined Norwegian fishing-boat. She had heard it so often on those summer holidays with Aunt Rosa and she associated it with all the little islands and skerries that studded the sea off Norway's coast like green and gold gems. Always there was the screech of seagulls too. She looked up at those noisily wheeling and dipping overhead. It came to her how homesick she had been for the country she was soon to see again.

Shetland was slowly gliding away into the rain-mist. She was reminded of when she had left Bergen at the end of that last holiday before the war. Nils had stood on the quayside to watch her ship sail down the fjord until he was just a distant speck when a spar of land finally hid him from her sight. The old yearning for him had never left her. Maybe, if luck was with her, she might glimpse him one day from a distance. Even though she would have to keep out of his sight, at least she would know that he was alive and well.

The swell was increasing and great fans of spray opened up as the *Noreg* ploughed on through the waves. When there was nothing more to see, Anna went below to the cabin and hung up her oilskins. Sitting down on one of the benches she took a well-thumbed Norwegian paperback from her pocket. Somebody had handed it on to her before she left and she settled down to read.

After a few pages the youngest fisherman, Harald, who was acting as cook in the galley, brought a pot of coffee and two cups into the cabin. Anna was grateful for the hot drink. He sat on the bench opposite her to drink his own, a good-humoured youth with a mass of curls so fair as to be almost white, his eyes a bright cornflower blue.

"I've made lots of these Shetland Bus runs, Anna," he said easily after they had talked a while, "but we've never carried a woman passenger *back* to Norway before. There have been women refugees as well as wives leaving from there with their children to join husbands already in England, but that's all. There must be something special about you."

"Indeed there isn't," Anna declared firmly.

He was unconvinced. "How long have you been away from home?"

She knew he meant Norway. "Since the summer before the invasion."

24

"That's quite a time. It wouldn't have suited me. I've got the best of both worlds – I can be home sometimes to see my family and friends as well as being in Shetland where I've a girlfriend."

Anna did not think that many would share his point of view, considering the perilous journeys in between. "Where's your home port?"

"Alesund."

She knew it well. A salty little town with cobbled streets where most of the shops seemed to sell oilskins and equipment for deep sea fishing. "I've taken the ferry from there over to Haröy and the other islands for summer picnics."

She had gone with Nils and a whole crowd of their friends. He had been an enthusiastic photographer, taking pictures of everybody and everything. It was a profitable hobby, for his work was good and he sold a wide variety of his pictures to a foreign buyer with a travel business. She had her own favourite photograph of him, which normally she carried with her, but that had had to be left behind with her other personal possessions.

"Do you know if our landfall tomorrow will be anywhere near Alesund?" she asked.

Harald had taken a swig of coffee and he lowered his cup. "We'll be farther south. You and the other passenger will be landed by night at the pre-arranged place along the coast. Then we'll stay in the fishing zone and sail into port with the fishing fleet at dawn. But it's different every time. There's plenty of variety." His tone was matter-of-fact and did not alter as he put his head on one side as he tried to see the title of the book she had put down. "What are you reading?"

"It's one of Sigrid Undset's. *Kristian Lavran's Daughter*."

"That's her best, I read it in my final year at school."

Anna held up the thick book with a smile. "It's going to last me ages."

His eyes twinkled in wry amusement. "I bet it is! You won't have much time to yourself once you get going with whatever you'll be involved in when we land. You watch out for the Quislings – they're the most dangerous."

She nodded. This was the name dubbed on Norwegian traitors who sided with the enemy. It had been taken from Vidkun Quisling, the leader of Norway's small Nazi party, who had betrayed his country by welcoming the Germans.

"I'll be on my guard, I promise you. Do you know, I hadn't heard of the Shetland Bus until I came north."

"We try to keep it secret in every way. That's one of the reasons we all admire the Shetlanders. They can be trusted never to let anyone else know about it either." He gave a deep chuckle. "But even they couldn't have kept it from my mother. She guessed when I came home from my first trip. Nobody in the family can hide anything from her! She knew both my sisters-in-law were pregnant before they knew themselves! But none of the rest know about me, except my dad."

"Do you ever see your parents?"

"Sometimes. I take my tobacco ration home for Dad – the home-dried substitute in Norway is foul! Mother gets coffee and whatever else I can bring. She can't understand why tea is rationed in England and not coffee, but I told her the English drink tea all the time."

Anna laughed, for his mirth was infectious. "That's right."

"More coffee now?" He picked up the pot.

"No thanks. That was a big cup."

"It's just as well. I'll be serving an early supper soon. There's a strong squall blowing up and when it's really rough, it's impossible to cook anything in the galley."

26

As Harald went out, another man had been on the point of coming in and they spoke in passing. Anna did not recognise the newcomer at first, for his dripping sou'wester was pulled down and his oilskin collar stood up. But when he uncovered his head and ran his fingers quickly through his damp hair, she saw that it was Karl Kringstad.

"Hello, Anna Larsen," he said casually, taking off his long oilskin to hang it up. He was like everybody else on board in wearing a *kofte*, his black and white, over a high-necked sweater. "I knew you were going to be on board."

"So you're the other passenger." She was irritated that his original attitude towards her did not appear to have mellowed. "I suppose Lieutenant Howarth mentioned me."

"Yes, but I had known already that you would be sailing with the *Noreg*." He came to sit facing her on the other bench and leaned forward, resting his forearms on the table. "I was lucky to get here in time. My plane was delayed by fog at Aberdeen. But I'd have caught up with you later in Norway."

He did not sound as if that would have given him any more pleasure than their present meeting.

"I don't see how you can be so certain about that," she declared with raised eyebrows. "I'm to follow initial instructions already laid out for me."

"But I'm to see you through your first assignment."

"Are you?" She was taken aback, unsure that this was news she wanted to hear.

He must have noticed the coolness of her response, for he gave a slight shake of his head in self-reproach and smiled slowly. "I owe you an apology. I can see that for some reason we didn't get off on the right foot from the start and I'm sure whatever the fault it was mine. Believe me, I admire you for volunteering to come and it's important for all of us in the Resistance to work well together." He held out his hand. "Let's start all over again."

She put out her hand with some relief. He had not let down his guard entirely, but he had made an effort and she had the feeling that privately it had cost him a great deal. "That's a good idea. I want to do my best and get along with everybody."

"I'm sure you will."

Their hands parted again just as a shudder passed through the whole boat as it hit a large wave. Anna adjusted her balance by gripping the edge of the table. "Harald, the cook, told me there would be a squall."

"It's not going to be the best of weathers for you."

"I've never been ill on a boat yet," she countered firmly. "Before the war my father took me out in some very rough seas when we went sailing together."

"So you can handle a sail-boat. Can you row too?"

"Yes. And read navigation instruments."

"I doubt if that ability will be needed, but you may need to make use of a row-boat at some time."

"What is our first assignment to be?"

He outlined it for her. The target to be sabotaged was a factory on the outskirts of Bergen and he intended that she should act as look-out, which would release one of the trio taking part to give an extra hand in carrying out the operation. Anna knew what would be expected of her from the training she had received.

"You'll hear all the latest details when we get to a certain venue in Bergen," he concluded.

"I used to sail home to England from Bergen after the summer holidays sometimes. I'm sure this assignment will go well, because I've always liked the old city."

He smiled. "So have I."

It struck her that it was the first time they seemed to have something in common. Maybe he felt it too, because he began to talk about first going there with his parents when he was a boy. Then he went on to tell her that his father had died a week before the invasion and his mother and sister, Kristina, still lived in the family home in Grefsen.

"Do they know you're in the Resistance?" Anna asked.

He shook his head. "For their own safety I have to stay away from them. Once in Oslo I saw Kristina coming along Karl Johan gate and I turned away to buy a newspaper just in time." He regarded her steadily. "I hope you realise the vital importance of keeping your distance from those whom you know."

"It has been drummed into me."

"That's good."

She sensed that he did not want to talk any more about himself and that perhaps he had opened up to her more than he had intended. "I heard a lot about Reichskommissar Terboven during my briefing in England. Have you ever seen him in Oslo?"

"Oh, yes." There was an edge to his voice. "Do you know what he said of us as a nation when we failed to collaborate as expected? 'If they won't love us then they shall learn to fear us!'"

"What Nazi arrogance!"

"I agree with you."

She gave him a quizzical look. "Good. We agree. That shows we're getting on better already.

He laughed. "I believe we are, although it would have been impossible to hold different opinions on that point."

"May I ask you a question?" she asked, encouraged by his show of good humour. "In London Major Andersen introduced you as Captain Kringstad. How did you obtain your rank?"

"I had served five years in the army when the invasion came. After we'd fought on for eight weeks against it we were finally overrun and disbanded. I had thoughts of getting to England and becoming a fighter pilot. I already had a licence gained when the army gave me leave to take a flying course."

His words caused her to remember Nils coming home to celebrate after he had gained his pilot's licence and giving her a glance or two in the first stage of noticing that she was changing in looks and figure.

There was no more chance to talk then as Harald came in with a large dish of *lapskaus,* a thick meat and vegetable stew that Anna had not tasted since she was last in Norway. The men not needed on board followed in Harald's wake, one bringing bowls and spoons, for it was the easiest way to eat with the increasingly sharp rise and fall of the boat. All ate heartily, including Anna. Afterwards the men left again to take over from Skipper Skansen and those who had yet to eat.

Before going to bed Anna went up on deck. The wind tore at her and she had to hold on tightly. The height of the waves astounded her. They bore down on the *Noreg* like black mountains, foam flicking angrily at the tips. But every time, just when it seemed that swamping was inevitable, the *Noreg* swept on through a valley of water in drenching spray. The squall had turned into a Force 10 gale.

"Get below! The Skipper's orders!" someone in oilskins shouted at her, making himself heard above the noise of the wind and waves. "It's not safe for you up here!"

Reluctantly Anna returned to the cabin. The clock on the wall showed that it was nearly midnight, but she was certain she would not sleep. Instead her eyes closed as soon as she lay down.

It was an enormous crash that awoke her two hours later, almost shooting her out of the bunk to the floor. She guessed immediately what had happened. A giant wave must have hit the *Noreg* beam on! In the same instant she realised that the throbbing of the engine had ceased.

She had not undressed except for her woollen jumper and shoes. Swiftly she made herself ready again. Sailing under her father's guidance had long since taught her to remain calm in any emergency. Some life jackets were stored under the benches and she took one of them. She was seated on her bunk, tying it on, when the door burst open and there was a blast of cold, spray-damp air as Karl entered. He was quick to slam it shut after him, his wet oilskin glistening. She had sprung to her feet.

"What's happening?"

"We're having to ride out the storm," he explained breathlessly. "In fact, the Skipper has no choice. The engine-room is flooded. That great wave broke through its door." They both lurched as the vessel twisted course helplessly at an angry whim of the sea and he caught her by the shoulders to save her from falling. "I'm going back to give a hand on the pump now."

"Is there anything I can do? I feel so helpless shut down here!"

He continued to keep a tight hold on her and they staggered together. "Your time will come when we've landed. You'll have plenty to do then." Releasing her, he paused as he was about to go out again, glancing back fiercely at her. "Keep that life-jacket on."

Left alone again Anna felt like a die in a box. She wanted to remain sitting, but slid about with every deep roll of the boat. Thunderous waves broke overhead and poured off again with such noise that it was as if everything on deck was going with it. Once she was hurled to

31

the floor and skidded about on her back until she managed to get up again. This time she lay down on her bunk, which was only slightly more comfortable in that she was rolled about without falling out. She could guess how very much worse it was for the cold, soaked men pumping out the engine-room.

Her watch told her it was four in the morning when, to her immense relief, she heard the engine start up again. Karl came down into the cabin some time afterwards. He looked chilled and tired, fronds of wet hair showing under his sou'wester and trickles of water running down his face. Out of his pocket he brought some bread and cheese wrapped in spray-dampened paper. "This is all there is until later."

"Thank you." She took the food from him. "Is everybody all right?"

"Yes, they are." He was reeling with the violent movement of the boat, but kept on his feet. "The fishermen say it's not the worse storm they have experienced and they're taking it all in their stride."

She nodded in admiration of them. "What will happen about our arrival being delayed?"

"A watch will be kept for us on shore."

"Is there any improvement in the weather?"

"Not that I can see. But, although the Skipper is continuing to hove-to, at least the engine is in order and operating the bilge pump again."

"Let me know as soon as I can go back on deck."

"I will."

The gale lasted many hours. It was only when it began to ease that the *Noreg* could continue on its way. After a while Harald was able to serve hot food again. When Anna went on deck once more it was like returning to civilisation. The terrifying mountains of water had subsided to rough waves that continued to drench the

32

deck with spray, but presented no danger to the *Noreg* in spite of some storm damage. She saw with surprise that the lifeboat had gone and she guessed that it had been torn from its davits by that first gigantic wave. Karl had kept that from her! No wonder he had been so insistent about the life-jacket. Not that anyone could have lasted long in that icy sea.

It was refreshing to be in the open air again, even though the sharp wind stung her face. The clouds were lifting, allowing glimpses of a clear, wintery-blue sky. But with this fresh change in the weather, everybody on board had become highly alert. She knew the reason why and joined them in keeping a constant watch for danger from the skies.

It was just before daylight began to fade in the late afternoon that there came a warning shout. "Enemy aircraft ahead!"

The Heinkel had come out of the clouds not far distant. The men rushed to their action stations. What Anna had thought to be an oil-drum on deck proved to be a hiding place for an anti-aircraft gun, which rose up on some cleverly constructed support that brought it to the right height. Bren guns had been snatched up from elsewhere, Karl grabbing one in his turn, and all were taking aim from various parts of the boat. Overhead Anna caught a glimpse of swastikas on the broad span of the Heinkel's wings as she flung herself down on the deck by the wheelhouse. It zoomed over like a great roaring bird of prey, its cannons spitting forth, and met concentrated gun-fire from the boat. The deck was gouged inches from Anna's arms covering her head and somewhere glass was shattered.

With danger momentarily past, she sprang to her feet again and hurled herself into the wheel-house. Skipper Skansen was still at the wheel.

"Oh, it's you, is it?" he remarked evenly, giving her a glance. "Why aren't you below?"

"There was no time." She saw that it was here the glass had been smashed and the cold wind was blowing in through the gaps. "This will be like driving a car without a windscreen."

"Never mind that. You look out for the broken shards and the splinters. Those can be dangerous."

In spite of her tension a little laugh burst from her at his dry humour. "I'll be careful."

Being at the Skipper's side, she was able to see the Heinkel flying round to come into the attack again, even lower than before.

"Get down!" he ordered sharply. "Now!"

She obeyed him instantly, crouching down with her arms covering her head once more amid the roar and thunder of the attack. But this time, unbelievably, it was followed by the sound of cheering. The Skipper, who had dodged down briefly behind the wheel, stood again to give a long triumphant whistle.

"They got the bastard!"

Springing up, Anna saw the Heinkel flying away, smoke pouring from one of its engines.

But the jubilation had ceased. There was a casualty. It was Harald, who had been badly wounded. Karl and another man carried him below, but although everything was done to try to save him he died within the hour. Anna held his hand the whole time. She did not move until Karl took her gently but firmly by the arm to draw her away. Skipper Skansen conducted the service for burial at sea and all the men stood bare-headed. When Harald's body was committed to the waves one man began to sing Norway's national anthem and all joined in.

As everybody quietly returned to their duties Karl looked closely at Anna. "Are you OK?"

She nodded, turning away in private sorrow. The shadow of grief lay over everyone on board as the *Noreg* sailed on as before.

Chapter Four

Although the *Noreg* was twenty-four hours late, a watch had been kept on land as Karl had predicted. Under the cover of the early darkness he and Anna were taken ashore in a row-boat by a farmer, addressed as Leif, who had shaken hands with them in whispered greeting. Other men in row-boats were silently fetching in the cargo.

Anna looked back at the *Noreg*, a black silhouette on the dark water. It would return to Shetland as soon as the cargo was discharged and the glass was replaced in the wheel-house with some that Leif could supply. The *Noreg* would be carrying two refugees and five escapees, who had already gone on board from the other row-boats. The vessel would be crowded, but nobody could be left behind.

On shore there was a thick blanket of snow. Anna had seen it glimmering on the mountains and rocky crags when the *Noreg* had hugged the coastline. It scrunched underfoot as Leif led the way in silence through a wood and on across a wide stretch that was probably a field. Before long a farmhouse began to loom out of the darkness, but with every window blacked out there was not a light to be seen. But when Anna entered the unlit hall she inhaled nostalgically the good aroma of pale timber floors, daily bread-making and fragrant juniper that seemed to permeate these old farmhouses. Abruptly a kitchen door swung open and she blinked in the light and the sudden encompassing warmth.

"Come in! I'm Leif's wife, Eva." The middle-aged woman, who drew back for her and the two men to enter, had neat, grey-streaked hair that framed a sensible, broad-cheeked face, her expression kindly. Her husband, short with rugged features, was clapping Karl on the back, the need for silence over. Anna thought admiringly that the couple looked exactly what they were, honest country folk who had worked hard all their lives. Yet now they were risking everything to help others.

Leif was joking with Karl. "When Eva began getting anxious about you and the young lady not getting here, I reminded her that you seem to have nine lives! So both of you'd be all right!"

Karl laughed and swung off his rucksack as he introduced Anna. Eva turned to her in welcome. "You were expected with Karl, although he's usually on his own. If by chance you were alone we would have passed you on tomorrow to another 'safe' house."

"That's what I'd been told in London. I don't think anything was certain about Karl then, but he managed to catch the boat in time." Anna was holding on to the back of a chair, for she could still feel the movement of the *Noreg* after so much rough weather. With her balance uncertain she had taken Karl's arm all the way to the farmhouse. "I'm sorry we're late in arriving."

"That doesn't matter. All that's important is that you're here safely. Now come with me. I'm sure you've had enough of men's company for a while." Eva picked up Anna's suitcase and led the way out of the kitchen, speaking over her shoulder. "If you want any washing done, give it to me. I'll have everything ready for you by the time you leave in the morning."

When Anna returned to the kitchen she had bathed, her hair soft and shining after its washing, and she was wearing fresh clothes. Karl, newly-shaven and equally

37

spruce, had just given Eva some coffee and sugar that he had taken from his rucksack. Her face was flushed with pleasure and Leif was already tamping down his pipe with the tobacco that had been his gift.

Anna was poignantly reminded of Harald, whose parents would never again receive such gifts from him. To her dismay Karl must have been watching her, for he broke into her thoughts.

"Is anything the matter?"

"No." She had answered him more brusquely than she had intended, but she did not want him taking note of her all the time. "I'm just tired."

Eva swept forward. "Of course you are! Come to the table. You'll feel better when you've eaten. At least on a farm we get enough to eat, not like the unfortunate people in the towns."

She would have made a pot of the new coffee for her guests, but Karl would not let her, saying it was for her and Leif to enjoy. So she served a jug of milk instead. There was home-made goat's cheese on the table, pickled herrings, farm butter and a delicacy known as *spekekjött*, which was dried and salted meat cut in thin slices. Only the bread was poor, being dark, tough and heavy, for as Eva explained all the refined flour went to the Germans, either for those occupying Norway or else to be shipped back to Germany with local livestock and other foodstuffs, leaving the Norwegians hungry.

Both Anna and Karl were able to have a few hours sleep, but they were up by five to be ready to accompany Leif to Bergen. He was taking a load of cabbages, which were surplus to German requirements, into town. With no petrol to be had, the lorry was fuelled by wood in a large stove fixed to the back. Anna and Karl said goodbye to Eva, who gave them a packet of food and wished them good luck.

It was a cold, crisp morning and they sat in the front of the lorry with Leif for a bumpy ride along a narrow country road that eventually brought them on to the route into Bergen. The lorry did not go far on a load of wood and twice another sackful had to be tipped into the stove before they reached the ferry for the last stage into Bergen. They were stopped before going on board by two German guards. One looked in the back of the lorry and the other came to the driver's window.

"Papers!" he barked. "All three of you. And what's your business in Bergen?"

"I've a load of cabbages to sell," Leif answered amiably. "My nephew and his fiancée here have been helping me on the farm since I became short-handed."

The papers were examined and returned when the other guard had confirmed that the lorry held only cabbages. Leif was waved forward on to the ferry, which sailed soon afterwards. Neither he nor his passengers showed their relief at getting through, for there were other Germans on board who might have been watching them.

Leif had certain small shops that he supplied and, as soon as he drew up outside the first one in a narrow street, people came as if from nowhere to start queuing for whatever was to go on sale. Housewives ran from their homes, putting on their coats as they came. Some called out to him as he lifted the first sack from the back of the lorry.

"What have you brought? Cabbages!" The word was passed quickly down the line. Nobody paid any attention to Karl and Anna as they left the lorry and walked away with rucksack and suitcase down the street.

"Are you still feeling the effects of the fishing-boat, Anna?" he questioned considerately.

"No," she replied cheerfully. "The sleep I had at the farmhouse settled that."

39

She was looking in the shop windows as they went by. Now and again there were some clothes on display, as well as shoes and handbags such as she had been given, but everything required clothing coupons. Long lines of people were waiting patiently outside any food shop that had something to sell. German military vehicles were trundling past, no shortage of petrol for them, and enemy soldiers and sailors were everywhere, for Bergen was an important port. The German Navy had bases for their U-boats scored into the rock at the sides of the fjord. It was from here that these submarines slid out to torpedo Allied convoys in the Atlantic.

Soon she and Karl came within sight of the old fish market on the quayside. She remembered it as being a busy place as the day's catch was sold from the stalls, the fishermen making jokes and laughing, for the Bergenese were renowned for their witty sense of humour. But today the fish left from German consignments were already sold out and the stalls were bare.

It was as she and Karl were passing these stalls that there came the sound of soldiers singing as they marched. Soon they came into sight, helmets gleaming, heels crashing down, their voices booming: "*We march against England . . .*"

"They sing it all the time," Karl muttered.

"Considering that the RAF stopped them getting there in the Battle of Britain, it seems a poor choice of marching song to me," she whispered back.

Karl looked quickly behind her to make sure that nobody had overheard her remark before giving her a warning frown. "You can't be too careful," he said sharply. "Remember that."

She thought to herself that just when things seemed smoother between them, something she said or did

40

promptly made him on edge with her again. "I knew there was nobody nearby, but sorry anyway."

He relented and gave her a half-smile. "That's all right. It becomes a habit after a time to watch one's words in any public place."

Leaving the fish market behind, they reached one of the main streets and a little distance ahead was a public hall with banners being displayed. She could see several young men, dressed in khaki-hued uniform, distributing leaflets to passers-by. They were members of the *Hird*, the small Norwegian Nazi organisation, under Quisling. Posters with his large, self-important face were prominently displayed. The hall was being used as a recruiting station.

As Anna drew nearer at Karl's side, she found herself focusing her attention on a tall young man with thick, light hair in civilian clothes, who was talking convivially with a high-ranking *Hird* captain and two German officers. Then, as she gained an uninterrupted view of him in profile, she recognised instantly the lean, intelligent face with the forceful nose, the moulded cheekbones with the attractive hollows under them, the firm-lipped mouth she knew as well as her own and the determined chin. All colour drained from her face. Abruptly she clutched Karl's arm in shock.

"I know that tall civilian! His name is Nils Olsen!"

Karl jerked her hand from his sleeve and crushed it in his own, bringing his face close to hers to speak in her ear as a lover might. "It's OK!" he said quickly, smiling for the benefit of any onlookers. "I know him too. He's with us. Nils is one of our best agents."

She felt physically weak with relief at his words, having feared for one terrible moment that Nils had lost his committed allegiance to Norway's independence, which he and his politically-minded friends had discussed so avidly in

41

the days before the war. Now she recalled thankfully that he had always been among the vast majority of people who had considered Quisling to be a bad joke, never dreaming then that after 1940 the would-be politician's name would give the world a new word for 'traitor'.

Karl kept up the pressure on Anna's hand, but she was scarcely aware of it. Joy was high in her that she had gained her wish to see for herself that Nils was alive and well. There he stood, lithe and strong, suddenly taking a step back as he laughed at something that had been said. She wanted to run to him, this man she had loved since her childhood when he had moved with his parents into the Molde neighbourhood and become the natural leader of her group of friends. It made no difference to her that it was four years since they'd last met. He was twenty-six now and married for all she knew, but time had changed nothing for her, no matter what it had done for him.

As he stepped forward again after laughing, he happened to glance along the pavement, his light blue eyes still full of mirth, and he saw her. Recognition flared and his gaze dwelt on her for a few telling seconds before he forced himself to look back at those he was with.

Karl spoke in Anna's ear again. "Just keep going."

"Don't worry. I'm in control of myself."

Every step was shortening the distance. Soon she saw that Nils held a handful of leaflets, which he must have been distributing. When she and Karl were almost level with him, he broke away from the other three men and blocked their path.

"You two look like good citizens," he said in a friendly manner, "but you're not wearing our party's badge. Why not come into the hall now and listen to our speaker of the day? You'd appreciate all he has to say on the theme you see written up behind me."

On the broad banner strung across the entrance was the slogan: *'Forward with Quisling for Norway!'*

Karl replied on an amiable note, "We haven't time now, but we'll try to come back later."

"Take a leaflet to read in the meantime." Nils handed one to Karl and then he turned to Anna. He looked deep into her eyes, his own full of pleasure. "You'll want to read our literature too, *Fröken*. It sets out our policy of full co-operation with our German friends for our country's benefit."

"Naturally I wish the best for Norway," she replied with a smile, taking the leaflet from him.

Karl had gone a few steps ahead and was waiting for her. She hastened to catch him up and they walked on together. She gave a long, satisfied sigh.

"That meeting seems to have pleased you," Karl remarked.

"Oh, it has!" she replied happily, turning her radiant face to him. "Since the invasion I haven't known if Nils was alive or dead. There's so much I want to ask you about him."

"I expect you do." He was so non-committal that she did not know if he would be prepared to answer her questions or not.

They had reached one of the city's many sloping streets. It was lined by tall wooden houses painted red or ochre, blue or grey. All were entered direct from the street and near the entrance of one Karl took a veiled, barely noticeable glance in both directions before he opened the door and they went in. There was no lift and it was divided into apartments on all five floors. It was a steep climb up the stairs to the top floor where he rang a doorbell. It was answered by a serious-looking young man, whose face closed warily when he saw that Karl was not alone.

"Relax, Lars," Karl said as soon as they had entered the apartment. "Anna is with us."

Lars did relax and his smile was wide. "Thank God for that! How are you, Anna?" To Karl he added, "I knew you'd get here in time. Everything is as planned. Only final details to be discussed."

"Good."

Lars was already taking a coat down from a peg. "Make yourselves comfortable. I'm going to fetch the others. There's coffee in the pot and more in the kitchen cupboard."

Anna had unfastened her coat, but she did not remove it for the room was chilly, all fuel being hard to come by for townspeople. "Do you think Lars can spare that coffee? I know it's on ration."

"We'll only use what's left in the pot." Karl went into the kitchen where he reheated the coffee on an electric plate. Anna found some blue-flowered cups and saucers on a shelf.

Together they returned to the living-room. It was simply furnished, but although there was a comfortable-looking sofa with cushions, they both took chairs at a round dining-table as if, by unspoken consent, they wanted to be ready for the discussion to come.

"Please tell me about Nils Olsen," she implored, unable to hold back any longer. "How does he manage to keep on good terms with the Germans and work for the Resistance at the same time?"

"He's not the only one. The majority of our country's police force do the same thing. They obey German orders, but tip off local people if there's to be a raid for any reason. Nils organises food and other supplies for the Germans. It enables him to travel freely throughout the country and gather valuable information at the same time."

"He's taking a great risk!"

"No more than you're doing by being here now," Karl remarked drily. "How long have you known him?"

She had flushed, resenting the comparison, because her rôle would always be a minor one. "I was eight when we first met, but it seems like forever." She had no intention of sharing any of her memories of Nils with him. Taking a sip of coffee, she made an involuntary grimace. "This ersatz coffee really is dreadful."

"I'm afraid that you'll have to get used to it. There'll be no other kind unless Reichskommissar Terboven ever invites you to dine."

Her eyes danced. "Wouldn't that be an achievement! Think of the German secrets I could discover! I'd be another Mata Hari."

He shook his head, his smile becoming serious. "No. I wouldn't want you to suffer her fate."

She shrugged ruefully. "I'd forgotten for the moment how she ended up. But even if she'd known, I don't suppose it would have made any difference." With a shiver she cupped her hand around the hot cup and sipped her coffee again. "I suppose all that happened when we were at sea was my initiation."

"In a way, I think it was. Two kinds of life-threatening danger and also tragedy in a relatively short span of time." He paused. "I'm afraid there'll be more of the same for you to face in the time ahead."

"I'm prepared for that. All I hope is that I'll never fail anybody."

"I believe there's little likelihood of that. Otherwise I wouldn't have endorsed Major Andersen's decision to recruit you."

She looked at him quizzically. "So you were in on that too, were you? I felt your gimlet gaze boring into me."

He threw back his head on a surprised laugh. "Did I appear that fierce?"

She thought to herself that he was fierce most of the time, although he obviously did not realise it. Maybe she would be the same when she had been working in the Resistance for as long as he.

There was so much more she wanted to know, but at that point Lars returned with two men in business suits, aged about thirty. Karl knew them well already and they were introduced to Anna as Gunnar and Olav.

They all sat down at the table and a map was unfolded and spread out, the target and lookout point ringed. Anna studied it carefully. The act of sabotage was planned for two nights ahead. Although the others had not expected her they welcomed her presence since she would take Gunnar's place. The destruction of the factory was vitally important; for the Germans had a great need of the ball-bearings being manufactured there.

It became clear to Anna as every tiny detail was discussed that this plan had been formed some time ago and Karl had been in on it from the start. She could tell that nothing was ever hastily undertaken, except in an emergency, for the enemy's strength and alertness must never be underestimated.

Everybody relaxed as the map was finally folded away again. Anna could see that there was no boyish excitement in any of the men, only a steely resolve to hit hard in this latest strike against the enemy.

Gunnar and Olav left soon afterwards, after declining Anna's offer to share Eva's package of food, for they had to return to their office. She laid the table, Lars helping her, and when the three of them had eaten, there was still plenty left. Carefully she packed it up again after leaving some for Lars.

Outside again Karl and Anna went to another part of Bergen and booked into two single rooms in a guest house. They had reverted to the roles they had adopted

46

earlier that day of being Leif and Eva's nephew and his fiancée.

"There's a curfew in this district at nine o'clock," the owner warned as they signed the register in turn.

"We'll be in before then," Karl said.

They were early to bed, having had only a few hours sleep the night before and almost none on board the *Noreg*. After switching off the light, Anna drew back the black-out curtains and looked out. It was snowing again. Large flakes were floating lazily down. Already it was gently muffling the thumping boots of a patrol passing by in the street below.

Chapter Five

In the early hours of the morning there was an air raid warning. It had stopped snowing and searchlights were playing across the sky. Anna and Karl went downstairs with the other guests to the cellar, everyone wearing dressing-gowns or coats over their night clothes. But there was no anti-aircraft fire and the all-clear soon sounded. Anna fell back into bed and slept again almost at once.

In the morning she was dressed and almost ready when Karl came to her room to take her down to breakfast. He found her standing in front of a mirror as she gave her hair a firm brushing, making it swing softly, thread-like strands shining in the glow of a pink-shaded lamp. She gave him a glance with one of her quick sun-burst smiles.

"Do you think the alarm last night was caused by a British plane dropping one of our people somewhere in the mountains?"

Karl was leaning a shoulder against the wall as he watched her. He was intensely aware of the intimacy of being in her room with the unmade bed as if they might both have risen from it. All too often he found himself dwelling on the sheer physical beauty of her. Yet he still found it impossible to banish entirely the smouldering anger he had felt when she had first entered the London office and he had looked fully on her for the first time.

All his senses had been thrown and he bitterly resented it. Resistance work and emotional relationships did not mix as he knew from experience. He had no intention of becoming involved again.

"Maybe bad weather took the British plane slightly off course on what we call a collection run," he said.

"Whatever is that?" Anna put down her brush and gave her hair a final pat as she turned to him. Her eyes, full of interest, were as bright as a mountain morning.

Karl straightened up, his reverie over. "Although the Swedes are neutral they ask no questions at a small airport within their borders where a British plane collects or delivers our people or, sometimes, an urgent package. It's not generally known and we like to keep it that way. When I've taken the controls on that route it's always because I've had an important message to deliver to London's SOE that I couldn't entrust to anyone else."

Mentally Anna stored the information away. Perhaps it would be important for her to know of it one day in the future.

After breakfast they went their separate ways for a while, arranging to meet later. Karl was going to Lars's flat in order to double-check some equipment needed for the following night's sortie, leaving Anna to go for a walk. She would have liked to stroll leisurely as she went along Tyskebryggen, for the ancient merchant houses with their steeply pitched roofs and mellow paintwork encouraged the eye to linger, but on no account could she look as if she were sightseeing. Instead she had to keep her pace brisk and purposeful.

After going as far as St Maria's Church where she had once attended a service with Aunt Rosa, she turned back to the centre of town. She soon found the public library where she settled down with a book on the origins of skiing in Norway in pre-historic times. She had read no more than a chapter when Karl took the chair next to her.

"There's been a change of plan," he said in a low voice. "Let's go."

They emerged from the library just as a commotion broke out. A middle-aged man had been sighted wearing a paper-clip in his lapel, a Norwegian invention that, although forbidden by the Germans, people wore as a symbol of unity. An irate soldier had snatched it away, only to discover too late that a razor blade had been concealed behind it. As he yelled with pain, his sliced finger dripping, the man turned away and lost himself quickly among other pedestrians.

Karl hurried Anna away, for other soldiers had come running to their comrade's assistance. "That trick has been played for a couple of years now, but the Germans never learn," he said grimly.

When they reached a park, he brushed the snow off a seat and they sat down together. Some children were building a snowman a little distance away, but otherwise they were on their own.

"What's happened, Karl?" Anna was impatient to know.

He rested an arm along the back of the seat behind her. "Nils Olsen sent an urgent message to Lars earlier today. The German guard was trebled on the factory last night and that it is to be maintained. A vulnerable part of the building is now covered. It means that weeks of planning have come to nothing, but I've worked out an alternative way. I'm going in alone tonight."

The colour drained from her face. She was appalled by his decision. "You can't go on your own! I'll come with you! Just tell me what will be different about this sortie!"

"Your coming is out of the question." His tone was implacable.

She was undeterred. "It was going to be dangerous enough with four of us closely co-operating, but on your own you wouldn't have a chance!"

He gave her a hard look that told her bluntly that he did not want any more expressions of her concern. "For God's sake, listen to me, Anna! Other arrangements have been made for you."

Anna bit back a retaliatory retort, recalling the old saying that Norwegians were as resolute as their mountains. She had enough Norsk blood in her veins to match him in that, but she was here to carry out whatever task she was given. "What are my new instructions?"

"A report has come in on the movements of a certain German battleship. The information has to be delivered promptly and you'll be the courier."

"Where shall I be going?" Anna was unaware that she was sitting stiffly, her back straight as a wand. She only knew that Karl's determination to sabotage the factory on his own had filled her with fear for his safety.

"To Alesund. It's in the territory you know best and that's helpful. It's unlikely that you'll meet anyone you know, considering you told me once that you only went there on day trips. Nevertheless, you'll still have to be careful wherever you go in that district."

"I will. Is the information to be conveyed by word of mouth?"

"No, it's written in code."

"Do I return to Bergen afterwards?"

He shook his head. "You'll stay in that area until you're instructed to go elsewhere."

"Do you have the coded message on you now?"

"No. For safety's sake, Lars will pass it to me later today after dark. It will be folded very small and easy to conceal."

"My leather shoes have heels designed for that purpose."

He nodded. "I'll give you one of the work permits that will show that you have a legitimate reason for travelling. In Alesund you'll go to the Ryan Hotel and ask for Fru Sande, who is a widow and owns the place. Her husband was an artist and drank himself to death years ago. The hotel will be full of Germans, but don't be put off by that. Greta Sande is a go-between for a Resistance group, some of whom I know, and she'll get the message to them without delay."

"What happens to it then?"

"It will be sent on to the SOE in London by way of the Shetland Bus. You'll stay on at the hotel in some minor capacity, establishing yourself, and it is from there you'll carry out future assignments for the time being." Karl paused, choosing the moment to break something else to her. "If you should go to Molde, don't expect to see it as it was the last time you were there."

Anna realised what he was about to tell her and quickly reassured him. "It's all right, Karl. I know that it was badly bombed and burnt to the ground at the time of the invasion. I read about it in the London newspapers."

"Well, as long as you know. I didn't want it to come as a shock to you, because the rebuilding that's been done doesn't match up to how the Town of Roses was in the past."

She smiled slowly. "I haven't heard Molde called that since I was there, but that's exactly what it was. It was thoughtful of you to try to warn me of the change."

"It should be some consolation that your family home on the outskirts escaped damage and is intact."

Her face lit up. "How do you know?"

He was pleased to have brought such radiance into her

face. "It happens that the county of Romsdal is as familiar to me as it is to you and I was in Molde only a few months ago. My grandparents had a house on the opposite side of the fjord."

"Oh, where?" she asked eagerly.

"Not far from Vestnes. It lies on a slope with a grand view across the fjord and was a place for holidays, but it's closed up now. When we get back to our rooms at the guesthouse, I'll draw a map to show where it's located. Then if ever you need a bolt-hole in an emergency you can lie low there for a while."

"Thank you for the offer," she said gratefully, "but, if I needed a place to hide anywhere near Molde, I could go to my own family home." She patted the fish-skin handbag that lay on the bench beside her. "I have the key to it with me all the time."

"Ah." Karl regretted having to spoil her pleasure, but he knew that the moment had come. "I'm afraid you'll have to wait a while before you can use that key again. I'm sorry to tell you that the house has been requisitioned by the Germans as an officers' mess."

Anna stared at him almost in disbelief before white-hot fury exploded within her. "How dare they!" In her outrage she clenched her fists and thumped them on her knees. "My God! That lovely, peaceful house! Their jackboots clumping about in it! And their hateful swastika on the flag-pole in the flower garden!"

Although nobody was passing along the path, he cautioned her, but not impatiently as he had done the previous day. "I know how it is, but take it easy." Leaning forward, he closed his arm about her shoulders. "Calm down, Anna."

She breathed deeply for a minute or two, struggling with her emotions and shaking her head furiously as if to deny what she had learnt. Gradually her hands relaxed in her lap and her eyes were dark and troubled as she met his gaze again.

"I've no moral right to be upset about a house when many far worse things are taking place every day. It was selfish and thoughtless of me. But I've felt a terrible, frustrated rage at every sight and sound of the Occupation since I've landed. It's a violation and rape of everything I've loved and respected all my life."

He was understanding. "It did you good to let off steam. Don't worry about it. We've all gone through that pent-up rage, but it has to be brought under control. It's only by keeping our heads that we can defeat the enemy in the end."

"You're right," she agreed harshly, "and I'll never let rip like that again. It just makes me wish more than ever that I could go with you tonight and be really active against those Nazis!"

She has spoken with such vehemence that he raised an eyebrow. "You know that subject is closed."

"How shall I know afterwards if you're safe?" she appealed.

"You'll hear if I'm successful. That's what counts."

Anna felt rebuffed, even though he took her hand in his as they left the park on their way to buy her a passage on the coastal steamer going north. On the way to the ticket office they were stopped twice by soldiers for their papers to be checked.

"Don't they ever stop bothering people?" Anna commented pithily after the second time. She was in no mood to be hassled even in a minor way.

"No, Anna. Just remind yourself that it won't be forever, no matter how much Hitler boasts that the Third Reich will last for a thousand years."

She grinned savagely. "That's a good tip. Each time I'm stopped I'll think to myself that it's one inspection less."

54

Just afterwards they were stopped for a third time. As they walked on she caught his eye. "Yes, I crossed that one off, Karl. I suppose there's a few thousand more to come."

He laughed, pressing her hand encouragingly. "You'll get through."

She hoped he was right.

At the ticket-office the clerk had only one berth left for a female passenger on the evening's sailing. It meant sharing a cabin with three other women, but Anna was pleased to get it.

As she put the ticket in her handbag Karl suggested they go to a cinema to while away some of the time before she went on board. The programme included a newsreel showing German successes on the Eastern Front with scores of Russian prisoners being rounded up. There were also shots of Hitler welcoming Mussolini on a visit and Luftwaffe pilots smiling for the cameras as they returned from a raid on London. After a cartoon Anna turned to speak to Karl and saw he was fast asleep. Since she knew he would be awake all night and probably on the run from the enemy for most of it, she did not disturb him. He did not wake until the last romantic clinch of the main film.

"Sorry about that," he said with a grin as they emerged into the darkness of evening.

"It didn't matter. It was good for you to have a rest. Let's find somewhere to eat. I'm hungry."

They went into a restaurant on a second floor that over-looked the marketplace. When seated they surrendered the necessary ration coupons required for a meal as they had done previously. This time Anna also handed over the two unpeeled raw potatoes that Eva had thoughtfully included, separately wrapped, in the food packet. With such a short-age of the potato crop left for Norwegian consumption, it was only by handing over raw potatoes that it was possible to have cooked ones served in a café or restaurant.

"This is a treat," Karl remarked when the potato arrived steaming with his meal.

Anna enjoyed hers equally. "I'll never take this humble vegetable for granted again when the war is over."

"Neither shall I." Karl raised his glass of water with a smile. "This should be wine, but let's drink anyway to Eva's generosity."

"To Eva." Anna sipped her glass, but although she lowered it afterwards she promptly raised it again. "I drink to you too, Karl."

He could tell by her taut expression that her anxiety about his safety on his forthcoming sortie had not diminished in any way. He was relieved that she did not suspect his concern was entirely for her.

It was when they entered the dark street leading to the guesthouse that Lars, coming from the opposite direction by pre-arranged timing, went past them without a glance. But Anna knew that the coded message had changed hands.

In her room Anna sat on her bed and removed her shoe to slide off the flat heel. Karl tucked the message into the cavity and slid it back on for her. She put her shoe on again.

"Now I'll fill in that work permit for you." Karl took it from a concealed pocket in his rucksack. "I'll give you a spare one and some extra travel-passes."

He had quite a collection of them. When he had filled in the permit for her she put it in her purse, but the extra passes went into the false bottom of her suitcase.

Karl glanced at his watch. "We'd better check out now."

He turned up the collar of his dark blue ski-jacket when they left the guesthouse. It had become much colder again and the night was milky with falling snow. He had selected a pass that enabled him to go right on to the quayside with her. There Anna brushed a snowflake from her lashes as she and Karl faced each other to say goodbye.

"I'm glad we met," she said huskily. She did not use his name as there was a different one on his present pass. She was also aware that two soldiers were on duty by the gangway and could overhear all that was said. "You know I wish you well."

"I wish you all the best too." Karl handed over the suitcase that he had been carrying for her. Although she took it, she made no move to go aboard.

"Thank you for all your help."

"It was no trouble at all." Karl withdrew slightly, ready to leave.

Anna knew she should delay no longer, but as yet she was unable to part from him.

"Is there anything else?" he queried on a hint of warning, puzzled by her deliberate extension of what should have been over by now.

Anna did not reply but, in a sudden upsurge of emotion at what he was shortly to undertake, she dropped her suitcase to throw herself forward and kiss him fully on the lips. Instantly his warm mouth opened to hers and his arms went hard about her, almost lifting her from the ground. It was an obsessively passionate kiss as if they were seeking the heart of each other in this brief, ignited moment snatched from the misery and brutality of war.

He released her slowly, staring down into her face. Removing his glove he trailed his fingertips tenderly down the side of her snow-cold cheek and then traced the outline of her lips with his thumb. "Take care, Anna," he said softly.

She nodded, too choked for speech. Snatching up her suitcase, she hurried away up the gangway. At the top she paused to look to look at him once more. He gave a single wave in final farewell.

Chapter Six

When it was sailing time Anna and the other passengers, civilian and military, had to be on deck and wearing life-jackets. There would be no going below until the mine-sweeper, sailing ahead of the coastal steamer, steered a safe way through the minefield at the mouth of the fjord. In the wake of these two vessels was one of the German brothel ships that went up and down the coast to serve the forces.

It was impossible to see the passing shore in the snow-laden darkness, but Anna tried to judge when she was level with the factory where even now Karl might be gaining an entrance. She was following him in spirit through the whole hazardous sortie, even though the details of his new plan were unknown to her.

"Cigarette, *fröken?*"

Anna was standing so tensely that she was startled by the German soldier holding out a cigarette packet to her. She saw he was young, not more than eighteen, a shy smile on his face. Inexplicably at such a moment she pitied him, far from home and in a country where he and his comrades had expected to be welcomed by a people they saw as fellow blue-eyed, fair-haired Aryans. Instead they had met hostility on all sides.

"I don't smoke." Anna glimpsed how dejectedly he lowered the packet as she edged her way deeper into the cluster of civilian passengers. She found herself with two of the three older women from her cabin. They promptly included her in their chatter, but must have found her poor company, for her concentration was directed elsewhere.

Beyond the minefield the coastal steamer was on its own as it sailed through the night. The voyage was without mishap, although at dawn a U-boat came alongside and everybody was roused from sleep or called from duty as naval personnel came aboard to check the identity of each person. It brought home to Anna how important it was for her never to think she was safe anywhere from a surprise check on her papers.

It was afternoon when Anna stepped ashore at Alesund, Karl still in her thoughts. At first sight, ignoring the presence of the enemy, the salty old port looked exactly as she remembered. Built on three islands and linked to the mainland by a bridge meant that around any corner there was water and dozens of fishing vessels at their moorings, a moving canopy of seagulls wheeling overhead. The old wooden warehouses, red, yellow, brown and green, hugged each other in rows and the lids of snow on their roofs added to their venerable appearance.

She paused outside a corner stationers. It still sold postcards with cut-out dolls and clothes that she had bought with her pocket money on shopping trips with her aunt. Otherwise in the vicinity of the harbour the shops continued to sell rope and tackle for deep-sea fishing, the glass floats for nets piled up in the windows like translucent green bubbles. In childhood she'd thought they were like magical crystal balls and would stop to gaze in on them, hoping to see something mysterious in their depths.

Her first act was to buy a newspaper in the faint hope that a late news column might report something about the Bergen sabotage, but there was nothing. She dropped it in a street waste-bin as she went on into the main part of the town.

There she came across a sight that had always delighted her in childhood and even now, in spite of everything, brought a smile to her lips. It was the great rock that seagulls had made their own from time immemorial, meeting there in their hundreds every season and always heedless of the passing traffic. They were coming and going around it now with a constant beating of wings and a discordant screeching. She found it comforting that in the midst of so much change the sea-birds had not been frightened away by gunfire or the tramp of marching feet.

She had noticed already that there was an aggressive military presence in the town and the abundance of official notices pasted up everywhere gave further emphasis to the iron rule. She saw one in particular prominently displayed everywhere: *'Anybody attempting to contact the enemy will be shot!'* She knew that it referred to those escaping to England and along this coastline with its hundreds of inlets and bays and islands as well as an abundance of boats it must be a nightmare for the Germans attempting to control the outflow of escapees. She despised their Nazi inability to grasp even now the resolute character of the Norwegian people.

There was no need for her to ask the way to the Ryan Hotel as Karl had given her full directions. She soon reached it and regarded it appreciatively. It was old, built of stout timber as were most buildings in Norway other than those she thought of as city structures. Ornamented with charming gables, it had a Hanseatic look about it as if it might be as old as Tyskebryggen in Bergen. She must have passed it many times in the past without noticing it, but the war and its terrible destruction of so much fine architecture had opened her eyes as never before to everything that had its own particular beauty.

After showing her papers to the soldier on duty by the

stone steps, Anna entered the lobby, which was hung with woven tapestries in traditional local designs. Three officers were talking together. The two younger ones glanced in her direction as she went to the reception desk. A girl with soft platinum-fair hair greeted her.

"I'm here to see Fru Sande," Anna said, explaining that she had come from Bergen to apply for work that a friend thought she could obtain here. She had used the exact words that Karl had instructed her to say, for it was an undercover introduction for anybody who would know.

"Your name, please."

Anna gave it and waited tensely while the receptionist left the desk. But the girl soon returned and showed her into Fru Sande's office.

Greta Sande, who was in her forties, sat at her desk in a pleasing room with shelves full of books and two eye-catching, strongly-hued paintings. Her looks were arresting in that she had accepted her lack of beauty and dramatised the fact. Her gold-tinted hair was pulled back into a coil that emphasised her angular features with the prominent nose and chin. But her deep-set eyes, one screwed up against the smoke of the cigarette between her lips, were a magnificent violet and her smile on a mouth wide enough to split her face had extraordinary charm. Anna could tell that she was a woman who had always lived life to the full, probably many men passing in and out of her affections, and it was likely that she thrived on the present dangerous rôle that she played.

"Come and sit down, Anna." The woman stubbed out her cigarette in an empty ashtray and indicated a chair with a graceful gesture. "Who sent you here?"

"Karl Kringstad. I've a letter for you." Anna handed it over.

Greta read it through carefully, leaning back in her chair

61

and swivelling gently to and fro. Then she folded the letter again. "What have you brought me?"

Anna was cautious. "I'd prefer your door to be locked first with those officers in the hall."

Greta smiled again. "Don't worry. I never lock this door on purpose, which means to them that I'm not concealing anything in here." Her tone mocked their ignorance. "Until barracks were built the Germans took over town halls, hotels, schools and any sizable building for their own use or accommodation early on in the Occupation and mine was taken almost at once. I soon made sure that they respected me, partly because I'd worked hard to build up this hotel and I was determined not to lose it. I also had wild plans about poisoning those who were staying here and other mad thoughts of revenge." She gave a wry laugh at her own folly. "Later, when things settled down and the Resistance became organised, I found a more practical way to hit out at them, especially as their presence under my roof gives me perfect cover."

Anna could believe that Greta would have carried out those original wild plans if they had proved feasible, for there had been a ruthless glint in her eye when she had spoken of the invaders. "I can understand your feelings, because I experienced a similar sense of outrage yesterday when I heard that my family home had been requisitioned."

Greta inclined her head sympathetically. "I'd like you to tell me about that later and also give me some news of Karl. He mentioned in his letter that you had an idea that would explain your presence here, because as he told you, I'm not allowed to take any civilian guests."

"I thought I could be here as a hotel trainee, if you're agreeable. That would enable me to come and go as a temporary member of staff. Then, if I have to leave in

62

a hurry, the Germans could be told that I've gone on to another hotel."

Greta narrowed her eyes as she considered the suggestion. "Yes, that should be plausible enough. You'd better be a trainee manageress. That will give you even more freedom of movement. As a matter of fact, that should work out very well, because I have contacts with two other Home Front hotel proprietors, one in Oslo and the other in Trondheim, who could take you in. But you'll have to get a condensed training while you're here if you're going to pass yourself off in that rôle if you're questioned."

"Are you sure about my being here? It does add to your danger."

"It also adds to my pleasure in deceiving the Germans even more." Greta sat back in her chair. "So you can be safely installed here. We can talk more later and you can tell me what background you've been given and so forth. I've known everyone in my present employ for a long time and all are patriots, although with the exception of the only man on my staff, Emil, they are all ignorant of my being involved with the Home Front. You've met my daughter, Margot, at the reception desk. Now let's deal with whatever you have with you."

"Yes, of course." Reassured by all that had been said, Anna slid the heel off her shoe and extracted the tiny, folded message. "This is to be sent off at once."

Greta took it and nodded. "Emil will deliver it tonight." She tucked it into the waistband of her skirt where she had a concealed pocket. "Now I'll take you along to the kitchen. Not all the staff will be there as some are part-time."

She swept ahead, straight-backed with a fluid grace, her black skirt swinging. On the way she explained the lay-out of the hotel, which was larger than had appeared from its frontage. Everything that she said was accompanied by a gesture that compelled attention to her beautiful hands, a gold wedding ring on her finger the only jewellery she was wearing.

The kitchen was as scrubbed and spotless as was usual anywhere in the country. The cook, who was in a crisp white overall and a cap, was preparing a large turbot. Another woman was piling up plates and a third was checking a cupboard.

Emil in green overalls was just coming into the kitchen with a screwdriver and an electric iron in his hand. Grey-haired with a ruddy face, he looked as if he might have been a seaman before some accident caused him to limp. He gave Anna a smile that wrinkled his face like a walnut as Greta made her announcement.

"Fröken Larsen," she explained, "has come to commence here as a trainee manageress and stay for a while. I know you'll do all you can to assist her. Please, Emil, would you introduce everybody. After-wards, come to the office. I think the lamp there is faulty."

Only Anna and he knew that the real reason was being covered.

After the introductions Edith, the cook, who had twinkling eyes, answered a question from Anna about the difficulties of catering on the rations. "I've become such an expert that I could make soup from the proverbial rusty nail."

Anna laughed. "Has rationing reached that stage in Alesund?"

"Not quite." Edith indicated the turbot. "That's how we can serve this for the officers' dinner this evening and there won't be any over. They like their food too much. But even they're having to tighten their belts these days. At least they get plenty of German wine and beer that's shipped in to keep the troops happy." Edith shook her head censoriously. "There are some noisy parties here sometimes, I can tell you."

As Anna was led upstairs she decided to learn as much as possible from Edith while she was here. It would be useful to gain a full knowledge of how Norwegian women coped with the food shortages, quite apart from adding substance to the additional rôle she was playing.

The room was small but comfortable. Left alone, Anna went to the window and looked out. Three floors below, a narrow division of the sea lapped at the rock on which this northern Venice of a town was built and on the opposite side, traffic was passing a row of small shops. She was thankful that her own part in the chain of the message's delivery to London had been fulfilled without mishap, not for her own sake, but for Karl's trust in her.

"Be safe, Karl!" she whispered fervently.

A tap on the door made her stir. Straightening up, she went across to open it. Margot Sande stood there smiling at her.

"I know I'm interrupting your unpacking," she said apologetically, "but I had the chance to hand over the desk for ten minutes."

"I'm glad you've come and I haven't started unpacking yet. It can wait a little longer. Do sit down."

She indicated the only chair, which stood by the window, and settled herself on the bed. Margot paused to look down at the water below before seating herself.

"You could fish from this window, Anna," she joked.

Anna was amused. "I suppose I could."

"That's about the level of entertainment here. Dances are banned as they are everywhere else, everybody boycotts the ski and other sports contests that the Germans organise and we can't see any films that aren't German. It's a bore."

She had something of her mother's vivacity, but otherwise there was no likeness, for her features were pretty and symmetrical. Anna liked her: she was natural and unaffected, a person in her own right in spite of her parent's dominant personality.

"I don't expect to have time for entertainment anyway," Anna remarked. "I'm here first and foremost for one purpose only."

"I realise that. Mother just told me how we're going to explain your presence to the Germans. It sounds all right to me. You're the first courier who's actually stayed here for any length of time. Mostly we hide them overnight or for a few days at the most. The Germans will never know if you're here or not, because Mother objects to any of them setting foot in the kitchen. Even the officers' batmen by-pass it to the boot-room by way of the staff hallway."

Anna was intrigued. "Do they trust her so implicitly?"

Margot made a dismissive little gesture. "Of course not. They don't trust anybody, but they've no reason to suspect that Mother is anything but a zealous businesswoman who wants to keep her guests comfortable and content while they leave the running of the hotel entirely to her. As for the staff, they believe that Mother is in the same position as themselves, which is that it's only by working for the Germans that a livelihood can be maintained. No patriot wants to do it and it's a bitter pill to swallow, but that's how it is for many of us these days. So," she concluded warningly, "just make sure you never run the risk outside this hotel of appearing to be sociable with the enemy, because you'll be marked as a traitor from that time onwards."

"I don't want that!"

Margot nodded and leaned forward. "There's something I've been longing to ask you. How did you get on with Karl? I knew from how you introduced yourself at the desk that he had sent you."

Anna considered carefully before she answered. "It took me a little time to get on easier terms with him, but I haven't known him long."

"Ah!" Margot sat back with a kind of regretful acceptance of a foregone conclusion. "He's still grieving for Ingrid."

"What do you mean?" Anna asked uncertainly.

"You didn't know? Well, of course not. He'd never discuss losing her with a stranger or anybody else for that matter." Margot shook her head sadly. "He used to be so easy-going and I'd hoped he'd be more of his old self again. After all it's over two years since since he lost her. They'd met in their last year at school, drifted apart for a while and then met up again to find that they meant everything to each other. They married on the very eve of the invasion. As the Resistance began forming they became involved in it together."

"What happened?"

"Ingrid was on an individual sortie, but she'd been betrayed. The enemy was waiting for her and she was shot while trying to escape."

"How terrible!"

"What made Karl's bereavement even harder for him was that it should have been his sortie. At the last moment he had switched their missions, believing that the one originally allocated to him was the less dangerous."

"Oh, poor man!" Anna's voice was distressed.

"I agree. As I've said, bereavement changed him and I'd hoped by now that he would be more his old self again."

"Have you known him a long time?"

"All my life. His grandparents and mine were old friends. He used to stay at the country house in Tresfjord."

"He told me that."

"I've had to adjust to being without someone too, although – pray God! – it's only for the duration of this hateful war."

"I noticed your engagement ring."

Margot sighed wearily. "Johan had to leave Norway at a moment's notice. He was in Oslo at the time and escaped into Sweden. I suppose by now he will have managed to get to England. We didn't even have the chance to say goodbye."

"Was he in the Resistance?"

Margot nodded. "He was with one of the 'cells' that were broken up last year through betrayal, probably when somebody was tortured. Since then I've carried on working here and also doing transcripts of the BBC news broadcasts to Norway. Emil delivers them to the underground free press."

"But listening to the radio is banned since the German confiscation of them. Where is your set?"

"People hide them in all sorts of places from a tin on a kitchen shelf to a bird's nesting-box. Ours is in a jewellery-case on Mother's dressing-table."

Anna's eyes widened and a laugh escaped her. "So much going on here under the noses of the Germans!"

Margot grinned. "What could be safer?" She stood up. "I must get back to the reception desk. It's surprising how busy it gets there sometimes. You'll soon find out for yourself."

"I'm pleased you came. I was feeling very much on my own when I arrived here."

Margot crossed to the door, but although she took hold of the handle she did not open it at once. "Your chief danger will come from the officers fancying you."

"Do you have trouble with them?"

"I deal with it. How old are you, Anna? I'm twenty-two."

"I'll be the same in ten days' time."

Margot opened the door, but looked back over her shoulder with a smile. "I'll introduce you to some of my friends and we'll celebrate your birthday somehow. We still manage to enjoy ourselves occasionally in spite of everything."

The door shut after her, but Anna remained seated and pressed the back of her hand against her mouth. Now she knew why Karl had responded to her kiss as he had done and why he had spoken so softly when he had urged her to take care. He had been remembering another woman and another farewell. It had meant nothing on a personal level.

Chapter Seven

Within days Anna had acquired a great deal of knowledge about hotel management, absorbing as much as she could, never knowing when she might have to move on. Several officers showed interest in her from the start, chatting to her at every opportunity. She was soon able to pick out one or two among the older officers who were not entirely brain-washed by Nazism and, in spite of their uniform, liked them as ordinary men. Yet she knew they would be as quick to arrest her as the rest and always kept her distance.

When asked by any of them to tell something about herself, Anna talked of her fictional home and background as well as her supposedly life-long ambition to own her own hotel one day. She always added, as cover for the future, that she hoped to move on to a larger hotel before long.

"You mustn't leave too soon!" was the smiling protest that invariably followed. Often she was invited out, but she always refused, using an excuse borrowed from Margot.

"Fru Sande doesn't allow anybody on her staff to associate socially with her guests." Privately Anna thought it a ridiculous excuse, since any one of them could have swept aside these rules at any time. So far this had not happened.

None of them suspected that when they were dining at

the hotel or were otherwise absent, Anna went into the rooms with a spy camera that Emil had brought for her from the local Resistance "cell". There, using keys that Greta provided, she went through any papers left in a locked drawer.

It had never been done in the hotel before. Although Greta and Margot could converse in German, they would not have known which papers would be most useful to the Resistance. Greta offered to act as lookout for Anna, but she refused.

"You're in enough danger as it is by harbouring me. If I'm caught it need be nothing to do with you. There are enough creaking boards in any wooden house to give me warning of someone's approach."

At first, although several of the files that Anna found were labelled *Top Secret*, the contents contained nothing of importance.

As Margot had promised, Anna soon met some of her friends, who were all about the same age and fun to be with. Yet circumstances prevented frequent meetings. Once, in a house that stood a far enough distance from a road to be out of German hearing, the gathering broke all the enemy's rules by dancing to a gramophone and listening to the London news on a little radio produced from its hiding-place of a hollowed out fire-log. It was unlikely that the chance of such a party would come again for a long time.

The following evening Greta told Anna that Major Schultz was dining at the mess as the officers usually did except when off duty. He had not been long at the hotel and seemed to be engaged in some military matter of his own. Anna was wary of him and this would be her first chance to go to his room.

Anna never locked a bedroom door when she carried out her investigations, her ears always keened for the

71

creaking boards. This time she was rewarded in her search. In the drawer of a bedside table she found a leather file with its own locked clasp. She had been taught how to pick locks during her training and she had it lying open on the bed in a matter of seconds. With an increase in her pulse she found details of a great gun that was to be shipped in and installed in the heights above the town that would give it a wide range over the harbour and the islands all around.

She used her camera. It became clear that Major Schultz had come to Alesund to be in charge of the installation of this great weapon, all the heavy work to be done by Russian prisoners-of-war. These unfortunate men, captured on the Eastern Front, had been turned into slave labourers and Anna, although she had heard of their ill-treatment, had not yet seen any of them.

Suddenly she froze. Heavy footsteps were approaching at a determined pace along the corridor. Swiftly she thrust the papers back into the file, clipped the clasp shut and pushed it into the drawer. But in her haste, after locking it, she dropped the key even as the door began to open, giving her no time to retrieve it. Almost blindly she began tucking up the puffy coverlet to remove the indentation caused by the file.

"Fröken Larsen?" There was surprise in the officer's voice.

With no sign of confusion Anna looked across at him as he closed the door behind him. "Good evening, Major Schultz," she said smilingly. "I'm just leaving. I've been checking that everything is in order as one of my duties." She had spoken in German.

He threw his cap and gloves on to a chair and began to unbutton his greatcoat. He was well built, self-assured and aggressively handsome.

"It's a pleasure to find you here. We haven't had a

chance to talk since I rescued you in that line-up outside the store."

Somehow she managed to keep the smile on her face, although it was an incident that had angered her deeply at the time. She had been in a long queue on Greta's behalf for some winter-stored apples, newly delivered. The Major had spotted her and taken her right to the head of the queue and into the shop, waiting until she was served. The hostile looks of those in the line had followed her as she left. Nobody dared say anything with the German at her side, but she was acutely aware of the general disgust.

"That's right," she said lightly, going across to take his field-grey greatcoat as he shrugged it off. As he thanked her, she carried it to the clothes closet and hung it away on a hanger. It gave her the chance to stroll back to stand by the bed again and to put her foot firmly over the fallen key as she smoothed a crease as if finishing her task.

"How are you settling into your new career?" he was asking, standing between her and the door.

"It's early days yet, but I'm enjoying it all so far."

He was regarding her assessingly. "Did you know that you speak German remarkably well? I compliment you."

She did not want his compliments, but forced herself to make conversation.

"I've noticed that your Norwegian is fluent whenever we've talked in my language."

"I've had plenty of opportunity. I was among the first to step on Norwegian soil back in 1940."

His arrogant assumption that she would approve his explanation made her anger flicker dangerously. Yet somehow she managed to keep an interested expression on her face as if it were a mask. "I suppose my Norsk

73

accent is as strong when I speak your language as yours when you speak mine."

He spread his hands with a smile. "Yours is very charming. So where did you learn my language?"

"I had a German friend in my childhood. She lived with us for three years. My parents were among others in my country who responded to an appeal after the Great War to take a German child into their home on a temporary basis, because Germany was starving then." Anna thought to herself that the false background she had been given in her training certainly covered all contingencies. "Naturally, as we played together I gained a good grounding in the language. I also had a good teacher at school." It passed through her mind that at least that last sentence was true.

"Your parents' generosity was highly commendable, but times like that will never come to Germany again. Our Führer has ensured a golden future for us all." He must have assumed that she was in no hurry to leave by her talking conversationally with him. "I have some excellent wine here in my room. Will you join me in a glass?"

"Thank you," she accepted, hoping that he would turn his back as he poured the wine. That would give her a chance to snatch up the key. "But soon I have to take over at the reception desk."

"Forget about that for the time being." He made a dismissive gesture, all his movements sharp and purposeful. To her disappointment he went to a cupboard against the same wall as the bedhead. It enabled him to keep his eyes on her as he stooped down to open its doors.

"I've been wanting to get to know you, Anna," he said, sparing only a glance to locate the glasses and setting them on the cupboard. "In spite of what you say, I'm sure you must find life dull with Fru Sande keeping you practically under lock and key."

"It's not like that at all. There simply isn't anywhere much to go these days."

He did not even look in the cupboard for the wine, but reached in and took a bottle by the neck from a selected stock. Then he poured the wine, never taking his gaze from her. "There would be if you'd let me take you around. At one of the larger hotels that we have also commandeered we have dances and parties. You'd enjoy them."

She took the glass of wine that he handed to her. "Who goes to them apart from your fellow officers and their girlfriends?"

"Sometimes we invite local dignitaries who are enjoying civil power under our command and their wives too, of course."

Anna had another word for these people. Quislings. As for the girls, there were always those unable to resist good-looking men, whatever their crimes, while others of a mercenary turn of mind wanted the extras and the occasional luxury item that a German could give them.

The Major had tasted the wine and was looking at her expectantly. "Well? What do you think?"

She took a sip to humour him. "It is very good."

"Come and sit down," he invited, taking a step in the direction of a sofa on the opposite side of the room. "You need to relax when you're enjoying fine wine. You're standing there as if you're glued to the floor."

It was exactly how she felt with the key underfoot. "I suppose I am," she acknowledged.

Giving a happy little shrug as if already the wine had broken down barriers between them, she promptly sat down on the edge of the bed, a flick of her foot sending the key skimming underneath. She continued to swing her foot back and forth as if it were an expression of pent-up energy. "It's a long time since I've tasted anything as delicious as this." She drank some more of the wine, wanting to finish it and then get away. "Thank you, Major."

As she had feared, he came back to sit facing her on the bed. "Do stop addressing me by my rank, Anna," he said with smiling impatience. "My name is Klaus."

"Very well, Klaus." She spoke casually as if his request had no importance, but he still seemed encouraged by it.

"As soon as I saw you I was certain that we had a lot in common. You have an enlightened attitude towards my presence and that of my fellow countrymen here in Norway. I believe you could do a great deal of good in influencing others towards this attitude as you make new friends here in Alesund. Will you do that?"

She gave him a slow smile. "Naturally I want the best for all my people. I'd do anything towards that end."

"I can see we're going to get on well." He put his hand over hers, which she was resting on the bed between them.

She drew it away and looked at her watch. "I must go now."

"Not yet. Let me fill up your glass again."

She shook her head and set her emptied glass on the bedside table. "No, there isn't time."

He put his glass down beside hers and went with her across the room. There he reached in front of her to take the door-handle first, but he held it, keeping the door closed as he looked into her eyes. "I want to see you often, Anna. Not just here in the hotel. We have to really get to know each other. There's a supper dance at the end of the week. I'd like you to come with me."

She wondered mockingly if he thought the promise of an off-ration meal might sway the balance, but knew that wasn't true from the way he was looking at her. Although she did not want any more of his unpleasant company, she did not want to throw away the chance of any useful information coming to light through it. "You seem to forget that I have to keep to the rules. In any case, I'll be working at the weekend."

He looked complacent. "You won't be. I'll speak to Fru Sande myself."

With a flourish he opened the door for her, bowed and clicked his heels. Her final thought as she walked away was that she would return to his room when he went out in the morning and retrieve the key. But then she considered his invitation. Perhaps she should turn into a Mata Hari after all. Pity she wasn't as glamorous as Garbo in the film rôle. Anna grinned to herself. She'd always fancied wearing one of those head-hugging caps a-sparkle with crystal beads.

In the morning Anna had to leave the rescuing of the key to Margot, because she had to go out early at Greta's request. Carrying a shopping basket, she waited in line for over an hour outside a bakery in the hope of getting some loaves. But no matter that she had Greta's and Margot's ration-books with her own, the bread was being issued fairly with only one loaf per customer.

Anna did not find the waiting hard as many older people and pregnant women did, only that it was time-consuming. Fortunately the March day was crisp and bright with a clear blue sky, the sun sparkling on the snow and making the icicles drip. Most of the women chatted together as they waited in a single line that stretched far along the pavement. It was only in line that more than two people could talk together in the street, for otherwise they had to keep on the move. The Germans never risked any group forming, even if it was a family meeting one another.

When Anna finally took her turn at the bakery counter,

she was remembering the warm and spice-fragrant aroma of such bakeries in peacetime. Now there was the pungent, sour smell of the dark flour that was used. She wondered how long it would be before the wonderful cream cakes, such a speciality in times past, would come again. This bakery probably had not made a cake since 1940. Then the newly arrived Germans had bought up all the rich delicacies they could get, eating slabs of butter on cakes and chocolate, having been long starved of it in their own country where *Guns before Butter* had been the Third Reich's decree.

Out in the street again she had a little time to spare before the appointment she was to keep. Greta had received word through Emil that she was to meet the leader of a local Resistance group at a newsagent's in one of the cobbled side streets. Anna passed the intervening time looking in the shop windows. One was displaying some paper sandals, probably having nothing else, which were in various colours, some plaited and extremely smart. It was like a promise of summer.

At the newsagent's shop she had to wait until it was empty of customers before she could go in and make herself known to the man behind the counter. He leaned forward, lowering his voice. "Go through the door behind me and up the stairs."

Anna went at once and found the man she had come to see waiting on his own in a stockroom. He looked like a Viking warrior with his white-blond hair and ice-blue eyes, a deep-chested man with a voice to match. He was casually dressed in a thick dark blue and white *kofte* and knee-length ski-pants with calf-length, home-knitted socks. Anna's hand was lost in his large clasp as he shook hands.

"I'm Rolf," he said quite formally with a bow. "I've been told that you know this area well."

"That's right."

They sat down opposite each other on ancient, ink-stained benches that were probably redundant from some old schoolroom. She explained how she had discovered the information about a large new gun and handed over the film.

"You've done well, Anna! Action will be taken on this, I can promise you!"

She was unable to hold back any longer from what she wanted to ask him. "Have you had any news about a sabotage attempt on a Bergen ball-bearing factory? I've read nothing about it in the newspapers."

"All news is censored by the Germans anyway and they don't always let sabotage reports go through. After all, these incidents can be humiliating for them when the saboteurs get away. But, yes, the factory was completely destroyed."

"So Karl escaped! Unharmed?"

"Without a scratch."

Relief overwhelmed her to such a point that she had difficulty in keeping her voice steady. "Do you know where he is now?"

"No. We don't keep track of one another's movements except when we're working together."

He considered the topic closed and went on to give her instructions on a new assignment in which she was to be a courier again. But what he knew he must keep to himself was the purpose behind what she had to do. She would be carrying coded papers for further distribution that were part of a plot that had been hatched in London. The code would not be difficult for the Germans to crack and Hitler was to be led to believe that the Allies would make an invasion attempt through Norway. The seed had already been planted by two Anglo-Norwegian commando raids on the west coast and previous undercover work.

Thoughtfully he picked up a smallish package that was lying on the bench beside him. As yet only a few leaders in the Resistance, such as himself, had been entrusted with this secret ploy and eventually the papers would be strategically placed for 'discovery' by the Germans. The very least he could do was to alert Anna to the extreme importance and danger of her mission.

"It's vital that this package is delivered to an agent who'll be waiting for you at Sylte in Tresfjord."

"That's not much more than an hour and a half's drive from here." Anna took the package from him.

"It takes longer these days along that winding road in a wood-fuelled bus. It's not like it used to be and you won't get a return trip the same day. Take your skis. If the worst happens, you must go up into the mountains and come back that way."

"That could take two or three days! Longer if the weather is bad!"

"It's that or walk the road and you don't want to be questioned. With luck nothing should go wrong and you can stay overnight at a safe house in the village after meeting your contact at the Haug farmhouse." After giving her the rest of the information she would need and the password of identification, his voice deepened with the gravity of a warning. "If you're caught with the contents of this package, it'll be the Gestapo who will interrogate you about it and you know what that means."

Anna did not flinch. As she put the package into her basket with the loaf, covering it with a newspaper that Rolf had given her, she told him about Klaus Schultz's invitation. Rolf pondered for a moment.

"It could be advantageous to be accepted by the enemy, but be wary, Anna. You'd be on your own. If anyone becomes suspicious or something happens you don't like . . ." He left the sentence unfinished.

"I've had to look out for myself in the past. I can do it again."

When Greta heard that Anna needed to have her absence covered for two days and perhaps four, she suggested a pretended illness.

"Perhaps a bout of flu, Anna?"

"No, that won't do at all. I can't tell you where I'll be going or what I'm to do, but I must be able to explain my absence if case one of officers from this hotel should catch sight of me returning."

"Yes, of course. What about a sick cousin in the country? Would that fit in?"

"Yes, but I'll make the person my mother's cousin. I used to know an old lady who lived in the place where I'm going, but she died before the war."

"That's it then. You can safely use her name if you're asked."

"I'm not sure whether I'll be needing skis. I'd like to borrow a pair."

"Take your choice. There are plenty to choose from in the cellar."

"Thanks. I'll need a rucksack too."

"There's some on a shelf near the skis."

Before going to bed that night Anna made everything ready for her morning departure. Not knowing if it might be necessary to make an escape during this assignment, she packed a compass as well as extra pass-papers. Lastly she sewed a pocket inside her ski-jacket in which to conceal the package.

81

Chapter Eight

As Anna put her skis into the ski-rack of the waiting bus, the soldier on duty came up to her. "Why are you taking skis?" he demanded.

"I'm visiting in the country and I can take a short cut on my skis when I get to Tresfjord." She was tense, thinking of the package hidden within her jacket.

"Your papers." He held out his hand.

He found them in order and she was allowed to board. The bus was almost full and she made her way to a seat at the back. Shouldering off her rucksack, which held an emergency supply of food, she set it down on the floor beside her. Soon an elderly man sat down next to her. Just before departure two soldiers entered the bus and took seats. Immediately the passengers next to them moved to other places. It was the pattern followed on every public transport. If no seats were left, people often preferred to stand rather than sit with the enemy. Anna watched anxiously, for she had seen one of the soldiers, a sergeant, glower ferociously when the seat next to him had been vacated.

The bus soon began filling up, although the two seats by the enemy remained empty. When the last three passengers boarded, they each saw the seats, but chose to stand. The driver closed the door and was about to take off when the sergeant rose to his feet.

"Wait! There are places that haven't been filled yet," he stated on a threatening note.

The driver twisted round in his seat to answer in defence of his passengers. "I don't object if people prefer to stand."

"But I do," the sergeant replied implacably. "I want the vacant seats filled."

Anna could see by the set expressions on the faces of the three standing, two men and a youngish woman, that they had no intention of giving in. The support of the whole busload of passengers emanated towards them. The other soldier rose to his feet and took his rifle into his hands. He and the sergeant, grim, helmeted figures, were all the more menacing for waiting motionless to be obeyed.

Anna could guess, as she knew others would have done, what the outcome of this present impasse was likely to be. The three standing passengers would be turned off and everyone else would have to follow them. She was desperate. If that happened, she would miss her contact in Tresfjord. It was vital that the package was delivered on time. Slowly she stood up, her movement heightening the tension that had become almost palpable, every head turning in her direction.

"I'd prefer to sit nearer the front, sergeant. May I take the seat next to you? Then somebody else could have my place."

A heavy silence prevailed as the sergeant regarded her with some surprise mixed with approval. Apart from appreciating the fact that she had a lovely face, he liked the steady fearlessness of her gaze that lacked the hostility coming from everywhere else in the bus.

"Yes, you may, *fröken*." He moved into the aisle to allow her into the window seat. As she gathered up her rucksack to move into her new place, she was conscious of the same contemptuous looks thrown at her as when Major Schulz had escorted her into the bakery. She thought wryly to herself that if she went on hobnobbing with

Germans in public much more she'd find herself having her head shaved by patriots marking her as an outsider, which had happened to a number of Norwegian women having close relationships with the enemy.

Under the sergeant's instructions, the soldier went to the front of the bus and stood with his back to the windscreen, enabling him to keep a watchful eye on the passengers. It was an act of intimidation, but it also left enough seats for everybody and the situation was solved. With a suppressed sigh of relief, the driver drew his bus out into the traffic and in the direction of the bridge to the mainland.

As Anna had expected, the sergeant made conversation. He was greatly taken with the beauty of the scenery everywhere he had been in Norway.

"I wouldn't mind settling here after the war," he said condescendingly. "There's no place like home, of course, but I can tell that life has been of a high standard in the past and it will be even better under the Third Reich. It would be more like that now if British propaganda hadn't poisoned the minds of your countrymen and women. It will take time to erase, but after we've beaten the Allies, everybody in Norway will come around to the same sensible attitude as yours."

He talked on, Anna saying 'yes' or 'no' according to what fitted in, but through the window she was absorbing the scenery. It was all familiar territory, with the spectacular Sunnmöre mountains in a final scenic blaze of glory before the even greater Romsdal range took over. A finger of the fjord, lapping saltily green and gold in the sunlight, followed the route until it drew away for the forests and the occasional ice-bound lake. All the tall firs were inverted cones of snow, a-sparkle as if decked for Christmas as far as the eye could see.

To Anna's relief, the sergeant was not going as far as Tresfjord. She had been worried in case she could not shake him off. Instead he and the soldier, as well as at least half the passengers, alighted at the village of Sjöholt. There was a quick refuelling of the bus's stove with logs. Anna watched the sacks being brought from a garage to the back of the vehicle. It had become such a routine that it took less time than putting petrol into a car would have done.

As the bus moved on to higher ground, the trees thinned out and on Örskog mountain the sweeping, whale-backed slopes, so perfect for cross-country skiing, stretched away into the far distance.

A stop was made at a café there. Everybody on the bus went into it for coffee, but Anna strolled back along the road to recapture the feeling of being on these wide slopes where, no matter how many skiers gathered, it was possible to get away from everybody else in the mountains and be totally alone. She seemed to see again the confetti dots of colour as people skied away, the families keeping together and babies carried on parents' backs.

The tooting of the driver's horn brought passengers back to the bus. Wood smoke rose from its stove from a top-up refuelling. Anna had gone farther than she had realised and had to run back. Ahead dark clouds were gathering again for snow.

On the bus Anna collected her rucksack and took a seat at the back again. Everybody on the bus deliberately looked away as she went past, making the atmosphere as chilly as it was outside. As the journey continued, small mountain cabins were to be seen, nestling deep in the snow. All of them were private holiday retreats for skiing at Easter or for weekends at all seasons and always for a long spell in summer. Anna wondered how many had remained shuttered and unused since all lives in Norway were turned upside down on that day in 1940.

By the time the road had levelled out for Tresfjord,

large flakes had begun gently drifting down and masking visibility across the great Romsdal fjord to Molde. Some clung to the bus windows like miniature stars as the bus followed the road along the small subsidiary Tresfjord to its village of Sylte where mountains enclosed it protectively. As the bus slowed to a standstill outside the dairy, two armed guards stepped forward to carry out the customary checks on arrivals.

The first passenger to alight was a middle-aged woman. Anna saw with alarm that it was not to be a mere inspection of papers. The woman had to remove her coat and stood shivering as one guard searched the pockets and even the lining, while the other rummaged through the contents of her small suitcase. All the passengers waiting to leave the bus had to remain on board and take their turn, none spared the humiliating search.

Anna welcomed the hostility she had aroused earlier, for nobody was looking at her. She slid silently down to the floor where she was hidden by the seat in front of her. The driver became impatient, having a parcel to deliver to the dairy. He was allowed off to be searched as throughly as everybody else. Anna was glad that he was out of the way and would not know that she had stayed on the bus. That would be an unpleasant surprise for him later, but she would face that crisis when it came. She would have to leave the bus before it was too far from Tresfjord on its continued journey.

At last the bus was empty. The driver had been waiting to get back on board and he entered to remain standing by the open door. The voice of one of the Germans echoed through it.

"Is there anybody else in there?" He sounded bored.

"No. See for yourself," the driver replied.

Anna crouched down still further in her hiding-place as she heard the heavy thump of military boots entering the bus. She could imagine the soldier's gaze sweeping the seats.

"Nothing left behind, is there?"

"I'll take a look for you. It's part of my job to check up anyway."

The driver came along the aisle, glancing to one side and then the other as he advanced. Anna jerked her face up imploringly as suddenly he was there, looming over her. A flicker of surprise showed in his eyes and he reached out a hand so swiftly that she thought he was going to grab her and haul her into view. Instead, to her wild relief, he gave her a slight wink as he picked up a forgotten newspaper from the seat and turned back with it.

"Only this left behind," he said casually, retracing his steps.

Anna closed her eyes and let her head sink forward against the seat by which she crouched, deeply grateful for the man's quick wits. As the soldier stepped out, the driver informed some people waiting to board that he would be back as soon as he had refuelled. By the speed with which he closed the door, she concluded that it was not his usual custom to let passengers wait in the cold.

As he drove away from the dairy, he looked for Anna in his mirror. "I don't know what you're up to, but you made sure of not being turned off the bus at Alesund and now you don't want the enemy to spot you. Whatever the reason, the sooner you're off my bus the better for you and for me."

She rose up from her hiding-place, but still made sure she could not be seen by anyone at the roadside. "Thank you for not giving me away. Is there anywhere I can leave the bus without being seen?"

"Keep down and come to the front. I'll draw up for a matter of seconds by the church. Jump off, don't stop for your skis, and get out of sight. There's some alert on and I couldn't find out why. If you want to hide in the church for a while, the key may be over the lintel if it's locked."

She nodded. "I hope to catch this bus back to Alesund tomorrow. Will you watch out for me?"

He made a comical grimace and chuckled. "All right. I must be a glutton for trouble."

The church was in sight, a small octagonal building of wood and painted white, located almost at the water's edge. The driver looked sharply about for any signs of Germans in the vicinity. There were some military vehicles approaching on the far side of the fjord, but they were too great a distance away to present any immediate danger. He slowed his bus to a standstill, but Anna was out before it had stopped.

"Good luck!" he called after her as she sped in the direction of the church gates. Although he looked for her in his side mirror as he drove on, she was lost from his sight.

The key was not where the driver had said, but Anna soon found it and let herself into the church, locking the ancient double-doors again behind her. She was in a vestibule with a stairway that would lead to a gallery, the timbers of the walls so time-darkened that she could not begin to guess at their age. A vase of snowdrops stood on the windowsill.

Slipping off her rucksack, Anna put it down on a bench. Then she opened the double doors and entered the nave of the old church. It was a sudden feast for the eye of age-mellowed colour. Long ago local craftsmen had used their talents to decorate it to the best of their ability, the wooden walls painted with drapery, the columns to marble and the ceiling be-starred. All of it set off an altar of simple splendour, enhanced by a most primitive carving in relief of the Last Supper.

Anna sank down in one of the pews. The church was warm, for there was no shortage of logs in the country, the heat coming from a large stove. She guessed that there had probably been a service that morning. Perhaps a wedding, for there were snowdrops in a vase here too. Although Reichskommissar Terboven had removed all authority from the clergy after their united denouncing of Nazism, couples still went to their churches for a full marriage service after the German-imposed civil ceremonies. Anna wished today's couple well in their future together.

She completely forgot her own circumstances amid the unusual beauty of the church, its quietness disturbed only by the rumbling past of a military convoy before it closed in again. It was only then that she had the sudden sensation of being watched. Someone else was in the church! It had to be a person of authority with his or her own key and, whoever it was, would know she was a stranger and be wondering about her.

The creak of a board on the gallery made her turn sharply to stand up and face whoever was there. In the shadows a man stood resting his hands on the balustrade as he stared down at her. In the same moment his voice rang out. "Anna!"

It was Nils! A sob of pleasure and relief escaped her. "What are you doing here?" she cried, running forward eagerly.

He was already on his way down the stairs. They met in the vestibule, throwing arms about each other, he crushing her to him in their exuberant embrace and kissing her long and joyfully.

"I thought it was you!" he exclaimed, laughing as he held her back from him and then hugged her again. "I was amazed when I saw you in Bergen! Now you've appeared again!"

"And you! How did you get into the church when the key was outside?" she demanded happily.

He led her across to the hall bench where they sat together, he still keeping his arm about her. "Up in the gallery I've a hat and overcoat that I was given yesterday by some people too frightened of the Germans to do more. I thought a change of outer clothes would be helpful, but I didn't know then that it would enable me to blend in with wedding guests at a marriage here today just when I needed to lie low for a few hours."

"You got the coat yesterday? How long have you been in hiding?"

"Four days in various places. I was involved with three others in an act of sabotage farther up the fjord, but the Germans surprised us and we had to scatter. I thought I'd shaken off pursuit, but I believe one of my colleagues must have been traced to this area, which is why this alert is on. I hope he's got away."

"Men and women were being searched on the bus that brought me from Alesund." She thought how strained and tired he looked. "Have you eaten? I've some food with me." She started to unbuckle her rucksack on the bench beside her, but he put a hand on her arm.

"That can wait. I haven't starved. Tell me why you're here and what has been happening since I saw you for those few minutes in Bergen. Are you in Tresfjord on legitimate business?"

"Not as far as the Germans are concerned," she said wryly. "I've a delivery to make. Fortunately I escaped questioning when I arrived on the bus from Alesund. That's why I took cover here for a while."

"That was my good luck! It's great to see you again, Anna. It was all I could do not to give away my surprise when I saw you again in Bergen."

"It was the same for me. I'd thought about you so

90

many times, hoping you were safe and not in any danger."

"You've rarely been out of my thoughts either, Anna."

She could see he meant what he said. "You did so much for Karl and me in Bergen. If you hadn't warned him in time about the reinforced guard on the factory, four of us would have been taken. It was to have been my first sortie."

"It was sheer chance that I found out." He frowned deeply. "Thank God I did! I heard afterwards that Karl went in alone. That took great courage."

"Indeed it did! There's so much I want to ask you. How are your parents? They were always so hospitable to Aunt Rosa and me."

"They moved to Trondheim after the bombing of Molde. Our home was burnt to the ground."

"I'm so sorry. It was a fine house. I remember so well all the parties there and how we danced on the lawn during the summer nights."

"I remember everything about that last summer we spent together." He took her hand in his.

Her eyes softened. "So do I, but it was part of another life, another world."

"That makes it all the more memorable. Tell me when and why you came back to Norway. How long had you been here when we met in Bergen?"

They talked on, she telling him how it had all come about and he able to give her news of all their mutual friends, but he knew nothing about Aunt Rosa.

"I have been in Oslo several times on various sorties," he said, "but, even if it had been possible to call on her, I doubt if she would have been welcoming. She never really approved of me." He made a mock-rueful grimace, his eyes amused. "I suppose she had cause until I came to my senses that summer with you."

"Then she became afraid that we were getting too committed to each other. I couldn't make her see that marriage was not in our minds."

"Wasn't it? You know that what we had that summer was special to us. It had to go on. I thought you understood that." He put his arms around her and kissed her lightly and yet lingeringly on the lips. Then he drew away slightly and they smiled at each other. "Welcome back," he said softly. "It's been far too long. I've never stopped loving you, Anna. Let's take up again where we left off. Nothing has changed for either of us."

Then he kissed her again, holding her tightly to him and this time his kiss was all she remembered, powerful and ardent, his mouth insatiable for hers. All she had ever felt for him surged through her and it was as if the time between had never been.

Yet when their kiss finally ended, the heady sensation faded as she remembered she was not the same person as she had been in the past. Then she had been light-hearted and carefree, lost to all else beyond their charmed relationship. But war had matured and weathered her, ripping away all her youthful notions about life. If they were to go on together, it would have to be on a different plane.

"My love for you hasn't changed, Nils," she said softly, stroking back a frond of his hair that had fallen forward over his forehead. "Nothing could ever do that."

"Anna darling," he said huskily, his eyes warm with intimate memories.

She saw he would have kissed her again, but she withdrew from his embrace. "We can't go back to how we were. That's impossible. We're not the same two people, no matter how it seems at this wonderful moment of meeting again. We have to get through this war first and then re-assess how things are between us. Maybe along the way we'll find something even better than we had before."

His gaze searched hers. "There's nobody else, is there, Anna?"

Momentarily she had a vivid image of those final moments with Karl, but it went as swiftly as it came. "No one," she replied reassuringly, her voice warm. "There's a bond between us. It was always there as far as I was concerned and now I know nobody could ever break it."

"I believe that within me I've always known it too."

Their eyes held in a long, quiet look and then she tore hers away and glanced at her watch. "I must go. How had you planned to escape from here?"

"I'll wait until dark and then row the short distance to Vestnes. There are a couple of boats tied up nearby."

"But it's almost certain that the alert is on for you in this whole area. You could be picked up as soon as you stepped ashore. Why not come with me? I'll make my delivery and then we'll go to the safe house where I'm to stay overnight. You could stay there too. The Germans are looking out for a man on his own, not one with a girlfriend on his arm. Tomorrow you can catch the bus with me."

"That's out," he said wearily, running a hand through his hair. "I haven't a travel pass. Normally I have all the extra papers I might need, but those were in an attaché case I had to toss into the fjord at a second's notice when I thought I was about to be caught with explosives in my possession. It's vital that the Germans don't become suspicious of me, or else I'll lose all my sources of information. That's why I can't risk being found in this area after what happened. At Vestnes I'm certain to find a loyal fisherman who'll sail me down the fjord to the coast."

She tapped him on the chest triumphantly. "Your troubles are over! I've a spare travel pass hidden in my rucksack. Fill it in and it will take you all the way to Alesund with me."

He shook his head regretfully. "I'd be grateful for the pass, but I'll not travel with you tomorrow. You'll be safer on your own. If I do take the same bus, we'll not know each other. But it might be best if I stay here until the following day. By then the search should have been called off in this district. I need to be as inconspicuous as possible."

She nodded, reluctantly accepting his decision. "Very well, but I'll leave you all my food and there's a vacuum flask of coffee too."

"That's great!"

She began unpacking the food. "I'll have to leave the church locked."

"I can get out through a vestry window.'"

They kissed once more, arms tight about each other. Then she left the church, locked it and replaced the key. She did not look back as she went out of the gate. Her life seemed to have become full of partings that tore her apart.

Chapter Nine

Setting off up the valley road away from the church, Anna entered the great cul-de-sac of the Tresfjord mountains. Three teenage boys went zipping past her on their skis and a woman came along with two little children, but she met nobody else as she walked past the widely scattered farms. Each house was a mellowed, paint-box hue and a thin blue column of wood-smoke rose high from every chimney, for there was not a breath of wind to disturb the air. The large, traditionally rust-red barns, which housed the cattle and sheep throughout the snowy months, stood out starkly against the white landscape.

After covering at least a mile, Anna began to wonder if she had missed her destination somewhere along the way. Hearing hooves approaching behind her, she stopped and saw one of the sturdy little Westland horses, the colour of rich cream, drawing a sledge driven by an old man. She hailed him and he pulled up beside her.

"*God dag,*" she said in greeting. "Could you tell me where I can find the Haug farm?"

"It's near the end of the valley. I'll be going past. Want a ride?"

Anna accepted his offer and expected to be questioned as she was a stranger, but he was taciturn and absorbed in his own thoughts. Neither of them exchanged a word as they drove another couple of miles up the valley. She gazed around at everything. A great waterfall, frozen into silvery splendour, sliced down through the fir-covered slopes to a river somewhere out of sight beyond the occasional house set far back from the road. She could imagine how the thundering of the water would fill this part of the valley when spring released its flow. The old man drew his horse to a standstill.

"There's the Haugs' place," he said, pointing a gnarled finger at a yellow farmhouse set with its dark red barn against a scenic background of that same waterfall and the forested slopes.

Anna thanked him and got out. He drove on without a backward glance and she went up the path that had been dug out of the snow. In the front porch she removed her ski-boots and went indoors in her ski-socked feet. She knew that nobody calling in the country ever waited to be admitted and she followed the usual procedure of tapping on the door of the kitchen. The sound of voices and the clatter of cutlery stilled within.

"Come in," a woman invited.

Anna opened the door and met the stares of seven pairs of eyes. A family meal was in progress. Two boys aged about twelve and three younger girls sat at a long table, their farmer father at the head and his wife at the opposite end.

"God bless the food," Anna said at once, remembering the old custom when interrupting a meal. "I'm looking for Eirik Haug."

"You've found me," the farmer replied. He rose to his feet, a tall, rangy man. "We'll go into the other room."

He led the way into a large sitting-room, the furniture old, but well cared for, the lace curtains as crisply white as the snow outside. One wall was covered with family photographs, many in sepia, of long-gone forebears.

"I believe I'm expected," Anna said by way of introduction as soon as they were alone.

"Yes, and I'm glad you've come. There's too much military activity in this area today for my liking."

"The hunt is on for a Resistance saboteur."

"So I heard. I'll fetch the man who's been waiting for you since yesterday."

Only a couple of minutes passed before the door opened again. Anna turned from studying the photographs and gave a surprised exclamation. "It's you, Karl! Of all people!"

He crossed the room to her, a broad smile on his face. "When I was told that a young woman was here, I hoped it might be you."

"But I can hardly believe this!" she declared, still taken aback.

"It's not as unusual for our paths to cross in this way as you seem to think. It happens frequently when Resistance cells are linked in a sortie."

"But this is the second pleasant surprise I've had in less than an hour!"

"What was the other one?"

"I met Nils Olsen hiding in Tresfjord Church." She explained in detail how it had come about. "He's lying low after a failed sabotage attempt."

He frowned at the news. "That's bad luck. Things don't always go right."

"I'm so afraid for him!"

He tried to reassure her. "Don't worry. Nils knows what he's doing."

"I realise that." Anna remembered the package she was carrying and took it out of her inner pocket to hand it over.

"You'd better take this now and not delay. Are you going up into the mountains from here?"

He nodded, tucking the package away inside his ski-jacket. "Will you be all right?"

"Yes, I've all the papers I need to get safely back on the bus tomorrow. Which route shall you take?"

"I'll go down to the river beyond this house and then up through the forest by the waterfall—" He broke off as they both heard the front door crash open, his hand whipping to the revolver in his hip-holster. But he did not have to draw, for it was not the enemy, but a boy who shouted as he ran through the hall into the kitchen.

"Father! The soldiers are coming! They caught one man in somebody's barn and another at the church! Now they're looking for a girl who had been in the church too! They're searching every house and barn all the way up the valley!"

Karl flung open the door of the sitting-room and rushed into the kitchen. Anna followed, blaming herself entirely for this new turn of events. Somebody must have reported seeing her going in and out of the church. If only she had hidden somewhere else Nils wouldn't have been found!

"How near are the Germans now, Jan?" Karl was demanding of the boy, whom he was gripping by the shoulders. Anna recognised him as one of the teenagers who had passed her on skis. He was eager to tell what he knew.

"Two houses away! They're swarming everywhere and when I looked back on the way home, I saw truckloads of them loading up!"

Karl released him and turned quickly to Anna. "Get your skiboots on! You'll have to come with me now." He turned to Eirik Haug. "Anna had to leave her skis on the bus."

"There's a good pair in the back porch. She can have those."

Jan had forestalled Anna by running to fetch her boots. When she had taken them from him, his father sent him back into the hall to keep watch from the window.

Anna paused, boots in hand, on her way out to the back porch to put them on. "What of our ski-tracks coming from this house?" She did not want anyone else to fall foul of the enemy because of her.

"Karl took care of that already this morning in case of an emergency," Eirik Haug replied. "I sent all the children down to the river with him on skis this morning and I went up and down myself several times transporting logs with my horse and sledge. You'll not be on virgin snow until you're beyond the bridge."

Jan came skidding back into the kitchen. "Hurry! There's two truckloads of soldiers coming up the road!"

As he dashed back to keep a look-out again, Anna darted out to the back porch. Karl had already put on his boots and was shouldering on his rucksack which had been left ready there for his departure.

"Are you armed?" he questioned sharply.

"No," she answered, stooping quickly to tie her boot-laces. "It's easier to hide papers than a gun."

Fru Haug was thrusting a package of food into her rucksack. "There! I gave Karl his earlier. Now you won't go hungry."

Her husband had gone back indoors and he returned with a rifle and ammunition, which he gave to Anna. "Take this. Most of us hid our guns when the Germans told us to surrender them after the Occupation."

"Thank you," Anna said gratefully, looping its strap across her body as he added the ammunition to her rucksack. Then she took the skis he had selected for her. "You've all been so kind."

Stepping out of the porch, she snapped on the skis. Karl had already put on his and he took his ski-sticks into his gloved hands as he waited for her. She was ready in seconds.

Jan came running out to the kitchen porch. "One of the trucks is stopping outside!"

Karl and Anna thrust with their sticks and sped away towards the shelter of the trees. Fru Haug was ashen-faced, but she had her wits about her and turned to shepherd her children back to the table, all having left it in the general excitement.

"Sit down and start eating again! All of you! If you're questioned by the soldiers, you've seen and heard nothing unusual."

They took their places quickly. Her husband had just seated himself when the front door burst open and soldiers stormed into the house. She saw his mouth twist in a grimace of dismay as whistles were blown outside. The escaping couple had been sighted.

Both Karl and Anna had heard the signals, but neither spoke. He was leading the way, she close behind, and they swished down a curving route that led to the river, snow flying up from their skis. They followed the old tracks, but theirs would be easy to trace now that their direction had been located. Then came the excited barking of dogs being released.

Anna had not thought that her fear could be greater than it was, but it increased now. She had seen handlers with those dogs, great savage beasts that snarled and leapt with fangs gleaming whenever anyone else came near.

The bridge across the river came into sight, a narrow wooden structure just wide enough for a horse and cart. They shot across it and into the fir forest on the opposite side. Then the slope began to rise so sharply that they would have to climb.

"Follow the waterfall!" Karl ordered as they snapped off their skis. "I'll catch you up. Go!"

The first dogs had streaked out from the trees like grey wolves with fangs bared and they were making for the bridge. Anna, running up the hard snow, her skis over her shoulder, heard him fire a revolver six times in quick succession and then there came the shouts of soldiers hoping at least one or two of their dogs had escaped the bullets to reach their prey.

To her relief, Karl was already catching her up. "Don't slacken your pace! Some of the soldiers are on skis and very near! Be ready when I tell you to stop."

She knew what he meant and steeled herself for the moment when it came. Even now their pursuers would be crossing the bridge. Yet everything was curiously still, all sounds of pursuit lost as the fir forest closed in like a screen in their wake.

Karl was keeping close to the great waterfall for some reason of his own, although neither of them had eyes for its frozen magnificence in their flight. Anna could feel trickles of sweat running down her back and her skis grew heavier on her shoulder with every fresh step. The only sounds were the crunching of snow underfoot and their hard breathing in the effort they were maintaining.

Suddenly the stillness was broken by bullets zinging through the trees and some orders were being shouted out. Anna gasped and stumbled, but Karl hauled her upright with his arm under hers.

"Another few yards, Anna! And then lodge your skis and rucksack with mine in the rocks jutting out over the waterfall."

Her leg muscles were pulling agonisingly, but she joined him in an extra spurt of speed. As they brushed past low branches, the disturbed snow plopped down on them, one lot slipping inside her collar. It seemed to be getting darker and she realised the sky was losing light under the threat of a fresh snowfall. More rifle fire came, bullets wide of their mark, and a startled hare in his white winter coat sprang out from under a bush and leapt ahead out of sight. Anna envied him his speed.

"Now!" Karl snapped.

She tossed her skis and ski-sticks down beside his. After filling all her pockets with the ammunition, she threw her rucksack down too before flinging herself flat on her stomach behind a large fir tree. Pulling off her gloves, she loaded her rifle swiftly and aimed it in readiness. Karl had taken cover behind a neighbouring tree. They looked across at each other once and the meeting of their eyes at such an intense moment had a profound effect on her. It was the unique experience of total empathy with another human being, a losing of self that was also discovery. If she came out of this situation alive, she would remember it to her last day.

Now Germans were appearing amid the trees below the vantage point that she and Karl held. They had discarded their skis to follow unhampered at speed. One slithered and tumbled to his knees, but he sprang up and came on again. Anna took careful aim.

She and Karl fired almost simultaneously. Two of the enemy fell, one only wounded, but groaning and writhing where he lay. She fired again and again, picking off those who kept appearing, getting some of them even as they threw themselves down to fire back. Still the soldiers came, gaining more control of the situation. Anna reloaded her rifle again, but her ammunition was running low. Karl shouted at her as more and more bullets zinged in their direction amid the large snowflakes that had just begun to fall.

"Go! But stay by the waterfall all the way! I'll cover you!"

Anna ran almost blindly as she darted on up the forested slope, but she had no intention of going far. To her dismay she stumbled into a widely cleared area where trees had been felled and sawn through into great logs that were stacked up, supported at the base by two low stumps. Anna doubled up to avoid any chance bullet and plunged across the clearing to take shelter behind the stack. She did not have to wait long before Karl appeared sprinting low across the clearing while she covered him by firing in quick succession. He slid down on his knees beside her.

"I told you to get out of this!" he said fiercely.

She dodged down as counter-fire came again. "I'm not leaving!" she gave back angrily. "But I haven't much ammunition left."

"Neither have I." He looked about and snatched up a thick stake-like length of wood sticking up out of the snow. "But keep firing until I tell you to stop."

Instantly she understood his intentions. The snowflakes were falling faster now and they settled on her lashes, face and hands as she continued to shoot at the enemy. But it was becoming difficult to see clearly. Karl was levering the stake up and down, grunting with effort. Then the trigger of her rifle clicked uselessly.

"Take my revolver," he instructed. "I can't let go of this stake. But don't fire unless it's absolutely necessary."

"All right." Quickly she removed his revolver from its holster.

"Now take that package from inside my jacket and bury it under the snow by that tree behind you."

Everything was done in less than a minute. Visibility was getting worse all the time in the thickly falling snow. When the enemy's firing ceased, she could discern shadowy figures moving out cautiously from behind trees and rocks.

"Are they in the clearing yet?" Karl asked quietly,

his knuckles whitening as he tightened his grip on the stake.

"Not yet," she whispered.

An order was suddenly barked at them in German. "*Achtung!* Throw down your weapons and come out with your hands up!"

Neither Anna nor Karl moved. She could hear her own heart hammering and Karl's strong breathing in his suspense. The same harsh voice came again.

"If you don't come out, grenades will be thrown!"

She could see that Karl's last desperate plan to save them both would come to nothing if the Germans did not move nearer, but they were suspicious, uncertain whether she and Karl were only holding fire.

Then came the final threat. "This is your last chance to surrender! I'm counting to ten! One! Two! Three! . . ."

Anna moved quickly. Karl's agonised shout did not halt her as she darted to the side of the stacked timber into the Germans' view. She flung both the revolver and the rifle on to the snow in front of her and threw up her hands.

"My comrade is wounded!" she bluffed desperately. "You'll have to move him yourselves."

"Come forward!"

She saw that they were not going to come out from their cover until she was in their grasp. Keeping in a direct line, she went down across the clearing. Two soldiers seized her and struck her viciously before forcing her to her knees and keeping her arms twisted behind her. But she was left in charge of only one of them as the other joined those running forward to take Karl, about a dozen of them in all. Her head was down and she watched through her hair until the moment was right. Then she raised her head and shrieked out at the top of her voice.

"Now!"

There came a tremendous crack as the great logs were

released to come tossing and tumbling down towards the soldiers. Anna took quick advantage of her captor's horrified astonishment to lunge herself upwards in a trick she had been taught and butt him in the groin. As his hold on her fell away, she sprang to her feet and struck him another blow from her training days that sent him off his feet. Darting away, she raced back up the slope to where Karl was waiting for her, the package retrieved. He broke into a run at her side and they kept going until the thickly falling snow shut away the screams and yells and the crashing of the great logs against the trunks of trees in an unstoppable descent down the mountainside.

At that point both Karl and Anna slowed their flight by unspoken agreement and dropped sprawling on their backs in the snow, their breath rasping. Neither spoke, but after a while, they looked at each other in overwhelming relief that they had got away.

Karl sat up first. "Are you OK?"

She nodded, sitting up. "Yes, all thanks to you."

He dismissed this with an impatient gesture. "I'd seen that a snowfall was on its way and had counted on that for cover, but it held off longer than I'd expected. It was sheer luck that we found that stack of timber in the nick of time."

"What now?" she asked as they stood up together. Although they brushed some of the snow off their wet clothes, more was settling on them. She could just see part of the frozen waterfall, but the far side was veiled completely in the falling flakes.

"We'll get going." Karl looked purposefully ahead in spite of the poor visibility.

"I know all the survival rules and walking blindly about in a circle is not one of them, Karl."

"As I told you once, I know these mountains. That's

why I was insistent that we keep close to the waterfall all the time and then we wouldn't lose ourselves later when the snow came." He took her hand into his. "Keep close to me."

His clasp was as cold as hers, for their gloves were lost. Anna thought to herself that it was a measure of her trust in him that she was venturing deeper into this white wilderness at his side when all her mountain training for such weather dictated otherwise. Maybe she was too tired to protest in any case and her legs had become as heavy as lead.

After a while Karl released her hand and put a supporting arm about her waist, for which she was grateful. It was not long before the ground levelled out, but with the layer of new snow every step was a physical strain, for they plunged calf-deep each time. Mostly she kept her eyes closed, weary of brushing away the snowflakes, which were coming straight down, for the air was perfectly still. All around complete silence reigned.

Just when Anna thought she must drop, Karl took his arm away from her and gave a triumphant shout. "We're here!"

Swaying on her feet, Anna opened her eyes wearily to see that a mountain cabin had loomed up before them amid the flakes. "Did you know this was here?" she cried thankfully.

"Yes, I knew we should come to it by following the frozen river after leaving the waterfall." He made no attempt to search for a key, but put his shoulder to the door and burst it open.

As he disappeared inside, Anna lurched forward into the cabin after him and stood slumped against the wall in exhaustion. The windows were shuttered and it was pitch dark, no warmer than outside, but Karl lit a match and grinned at her in its golden glow.

"We're safe now, Anna!" he proclaimed before glancing about until the match burnt his fingers, making him swear. For no reason at all this struck her as extremely funny and she laughed weakly, letting her back slide down the wall until she was sitting on the floor. He struck another match and this time he lit a large candle set in a wooden candlestick and it illuminated the cabin with its soft light. "That's better," he said with satisfaction.

When she did not move, he came across to her and raised her up by her elbows to her feet again. Now that there was time to think, she felt numbed by the impact of Nils's arrest and all that had happened in the forest. He saw the need to get her busy.

"See if you can find coffee," he urged, "and there'll be a coffee-pot somewhere. I'm going up on the roof to take the snow-lid off the top of the chimney and then I'll get a fire going in the stove."

He went out again, taking with him two large saucepans from a shelf to get some snow to melt for hot water.

Anna was thankful to have something to do. She moved, stiff with cold, across to a cupboard. The furnishings of the cabin were typical in their simplicity; a wooden table and chairs, a bench with a single cushion striped blue and green, and red gingham curtains at the windows. Plates stood in a fretworked wall-rack, and fishing tackle took up one of three shelves with books, a vase of dried lavender and a collection of smooth river stones, pink and grey and pearl-like. There were several spare fishing rods stacked in a corner by the entrance with a snow shovel. A door at the opposite end of the room would lead to the sleeping quarter with bunks and somewhere outside was a privy. Aunt Rosa's skiing cabin had been far more luxurious, but Anna had no complaints, liking everything about this small haven.

Opening a cupboard door, Anna saw a jar labelled *Kaffe*

waiting there. She had known, as Karl had, that even in these days of ersatz coffee, no cabin would be without some. Whether applying to family or friends, it was an unwritten rule of the mountains that whoever took coffee to a cabin would leave what was left as well as replacing a stock of dry wood and matches for the stove.

She looked to see what else might be in the cupboard. There were plenty of candles and the usual container of salt left permanently, this one of pottery shaped like a comic troll with his bobble-topped red cap as a lid. Beside it was a bottle of oil and a pre-war Christmas biscuit tin containing homemade *lefse*, which was a kind of dry pancake. Most surprising of all was a shop-bought tin of fish-pudding. It was like finding gold in present circumstances.

"Look what I've found!" she exclaimed to Karl when he returned with both saucepans piled high with snow.

"Splendid! We won't starve." He stopped down in front of the stove and drew out from under it a box full of small logs and strips of birch-bark, which would ignite instantly. Soon the stove was crackling noisily as the flames leapt onto the tinder-dry fuel, their brilliance flickering through the grating.

Anna sat down on the floor beside him and tried to unfasten her ski-boots, but her icy fingers fumbled with the laces. Karl removed his own and set them by the entrance door, which he had bolted. He had also hung up his ski jacket before she had taken off one boot.

"Let me," he offered, kneeling down to do it for her. Already warmth from the stove was making a difference to the chill air, and he took her hands between his in turn to rub the circulation back into them. "Is that better?"

"Oh, yes," she said, flexing her fingers. "I can feel them again now."

"All you need now is that coffee."

108

He helped her to take off her ski-jacket, but left her to hang it on a peg as he put coffee ready in a pot. Anna took two cups and saucers from the wall-rack and put them on the table.

"Do you think there are any spare clothes here?" she asked. "After all that kneeling and sprawling in the snow, my own are damp right through."

"Let's see what we can find." Karl took up the candle and led the way into the little bedroom. There were two bunks, one on either side, and each with a pillow and a rolled-up sleeping bag. A large old chest of drawers stood by the wall in the middle. "Take a look. Nobody would mind after what you've been through."

There were caps, scarves, socks and gloves in the top drawer, some woollen jerseys in the next and three clean, but well-worn, ski garments in the last one. He took a pair of the trousers and a jersey and left her alone to put on those she had selected.

When she emerged, Karl was seated at the table waiting to pour the coffee. After hanging up her own clothes to dry out on pegs beside his, Anna sat down on the opposite side of the table. Her expression was strained and serious as she looked across at him over the cup of coffee that she held in both hands.

"You hoped I'd find this cabin when you tried to send me on ahead, didn't you?"

He inclined his head. "Yes, I thought you'd use your intelligence and guess I'd given you specific instructions for some reason."

Anna looked down at her coffee, too moved to speak. When it had seemed as if they had no chance as the Germans began to close in, he had wanted her life to be saved. Gaining control of herself again, she looked at him once more. "You wouldn't have been here or been nearly killed in the forest if it hadn't been for me."

109

He looked puzzled. "How have you worked that out?"

"It's obvious. Somewhere I messed up everything by going into the church instead of taking a chance and coming straight up the valley. If I'd done that, Nils wouldn't have been caught and you'd have taken the package from me and left without any trouble."

"For one thing," he answered patiently, "the bus driver knew what he was doing when he advised you to hide where you did. There must have been patrols everywhere. If you'd been picked up with that package, the Gestapo would have taken you into their charge. And what would be worse," he added bluntly, "that could have meant the destruction of a most secret plan and the loss of countless lives." Then to needle her out of demoralising remorse, he continued: "So drink up your coffee and let's have no more self-pity."

"It's not that," she retorted on a flare of anger. "I was taking the blame for whatever mistakes were made and I'm more than ashamed of them."

He shook his head wearily. "We all make mistakes sometimes. It happens. But in this case you're as blameless as anybody else, believe me."

She fell silent, remembering what Margot had told her about his tragic error over his late wife, and yet he had acted in her best interests. Her own outburst had revived painful memories for him.

"Do you think Eirik Haug and his wife will be interrogated?" she asked in a quiet tone. It was another thing that was worrying her.

"They'll be questioned, but we were far enough away from the house when we were sighted and could have been coming from any direction. But it means that for his sake and that of his family the Resistance can't make use of his safe house again."

She took hold of the coffee pot and refilled his cup

and hers. "How are we going to get out of here, Karl? We can eke out what food there is for three days at the most, but without skis we can't go anywhere. The German survivors in the forest will know that."

"But they won't know that this cabin is here and it's unlikely they'll be told. Yet we can't take a chance. I left my skis jutting out over the rocks by the waterfall and I hope to retrieve both pairs tomorrow if the snow eases."

"You make me feel a total amateur," she said simply, almost at a loss for words that he should have used his initiative at such a time of danger.

He shook his head. "You're far from that. It was an horrific moment for me when you stepped out from behind that stacked timber."

"It was the only chance we had. We were lucky that when the Germans gained the upper hand, they wanted us for interrogation."

"That makes it all the more important to get you safely away. I'm afraid you've no choice but to come with me again."

"No, I must return to Alesund. There's no need for anyone to connect me with anything that happened here as long as I return as arranged. After all, I was working at the Alesund hotel when the sabotage attempt took place."

"But that wouldn't have helped you today, because the Germans would still have arrested you in any case for being connected with Nils."

They went on talking, he shifting the conversation away from all that had happened. Soon they were on lighter topics, telling each other amusing incidents in their lives and generally filling in gaps about themselves. She learnt that he could play a saxophone and he that she once climbed the Romsdal Horn with Nils, who was an experienced climber, and a team of his friends.

111

"Not right to the top, of course," she said. "Only Nils and a couple of others did that."

"It was still an achievement."

After a while, in a serious moment, he told her about losing his wife. Anna was deeply touched, for she knew him to be a very private man, not given to revealing his innermost feelings. In silence she reached out her hand and linked her fingers with his across the table in compassion and understanding. All they had been through together that day had brought them both closer than she could ever have imagined possible. She had not known that facing death with another person could create a union of spirit that was unique and she was awed by this discovery.

Chapter Ten

Karl and Anna prepared their supper together. They used only a third of the food they had found, not knowing if the weather might keep them isolated in the cabin for another day. They made it a leisurely meal by sitting on over their coffee. It gave them both the chance to unwind after their traumatic experience in the forest. The strain of it still showed in her face, although she was unaware of it. For that reason he kept the conversation on an easy level.

After everything was washed up and put away, Anna felt sleepy in the warmth of the room. "I'd better get to bed," she said, smothering a yawn.

"You go ahead," Karl said, sitting with his long legs stretched out in front of him. "There's a box of tools by the door and I'll mend the lock I broke before I take the other bunk. Good night, Anna. Sleep well."

"That will be easy. 'Night, Karl."

She took a candle on a saucer and a jug of hot water into the little bedroom where she bathed herself down. Alone and no longer distracted by talk or small domestic tasks, all that had happened earlier came tumbling back darkly into her mind. She had found a man's clean shirt in one of the drawers and put it on, but she did not get into her bunk. Instead she sat on the edge of it, her elbows on her knees, her head resting in her hands and tried to get her thoughts into perspective.

Unaware that she was shivering uncontrollably, she

saw again the enemies she had wounded and killed. She tried to hang on to the fact that otherwise it would have been Karl's life and hers, but searing her memory was the spurting blood, the shock of faces in the seconds before death, the helplessly upflung arms and the dropped rifles skeetering away across the red-stained snow. Abruptly she clapped her hands over her ears, seeming to hear again the yells and screams and groans that were running through her head. Inevitably it led to a sudden image of Nils being tortured by the Gestapo. A moan escaped her.

Karl, who had just finished mending the lock, dropped the tools he had been using into their box, and went quickly into the bedroom. He saw immediately that she was suffering from delayed shock and he sat down to pull the unrolled sleeping-bag around her like a blanket, holding her close.

"Listen to me, Anna," he said drawing her hands down into her lap. "It was a bad experience, but it's over. You did what had to be done. It wasn't just our lives that were at stake, but those of others whose names the Gestapo would have tried to torture out of us."

"That's what will happen to Nils!" Anna buried her face against his shoulder, the violent shivering of her body passing into his.

"He'll not talk, but it may not come to that. He's built up strong German contacts and he's bluffed his way out of a tight situation once before. I'd put my money on Nils getting through somehow."

Anna took hope from his words, but the nightmare was still with her. "Hold me tight," she implored, needing the comfort of his close presence a while longer.

He pressed her still closer to him, stroking her hair, his lips a breath away from her brow. Her physical nearness was devastating to him. He had wanted her from first seeing her in that London office, not recognising at first

114

that all he felt was so much more. Every sighting of her since then, every meeting and every word they had ever exchanged had made him fall still more deeply in love with her. Today, when she had stepped deliberately into the range of German bullets, he had been struck to the bone by the force and depth of all she meant to him.

"Maybe you should try to sleep now," he suggested, trying to keep the thickness of desire from his voice.

"Not yet! I couldn't! Please stay a little while longer!" As if she feared he might still decide otherwise, she threw an arm about his neck, half-lying across his chest, her breasts pressed against him. He found the bouquet of her skin irresistible and her hair had flicked softly across his chin.

"Anna," he breathed, kissing her brow. Then, unable to restrain himself any longer, he raised her higher and crushed her to him as he buried her mouth in his.

To Anna it was like a warm wave sweeping over her. She had the impression of floundering mentally as if the day's events would not let her go, but then his passionate mouth drove all else away. Nothing existed any longer except his arms about her and the wild hunger for each other that they were sharing in a kiss that was setting her free.

For a few moments only they drew apart breathlessly to look into each other's eyes in the pale candlelight, as if scarcely able to believe what was happening to them. Then he swept her to him again, becoming her whole world.

"I love you, my *elskede*!" he exclaimed almost harshly when drawing breath again, angry with himself even as he rejoiced in loving this woman, pliant and eager in his arms. None of this was what he had planned, not to love again in the midst of war or to love so totally in the knowledge that he had found in her the other half of himself.

"I love you too," she whispered joyously, feeling as if all her life had been directed towards this moment in this place.

He unbuttoned her shirt and, drawing the garment from her, found her totally beautiful. She caught her breath as his palms passed deliciously over her breasts until, his face full of love, he buried his fingers in her hair and bore her backwards in a kiss on to the bunk. She watched as he left her briefly to discard his own clothes and then return to her, his muscled body pale and gleaming in the candleglow.

Anna arched her back as his wonderful mouth moved over her breasts in passionate exploration, his stroking and caressing hands changing the chilled shivering of her limbs into a trembling of the flesh in highly awakened desire. She cupped his head lovingly in her hands as he continued his own glorious discoveries of her entire body, every touch of his tongue and fingertips overwhelming her in sensual delights. Finally the moment came when she welcomed him with her entire being as he plunged into her, vibrant with energy, to transport her with him to such a peak of ecstasy that she threshed beneath him at its force, he holding her lovingly captive in his embrace.

In the blissful aftermath he stroked her tumbled hair away from her face and kissed her softly. They murmured tender words to each other until they made love once more. Afterwards they drifted into sleep, her head on his shoulder. Outside the falling snow dwindled away, the clouds shifted and the moon came out.

When Anna woke the room was in darkness, the candle having burnt out, and she was alone. Sitting up, she brushed back her hair with one hand and parted the gingham curtains over the window. Although it was shuttered from outside, a penetrating glimmer of light told her it was day. Yet she did not move. Resting her arms across her updrawn knees she thought over all that had happened between Karl and her in the night, her mind crystal clear.

It was no surprise to her that nothing had changed her feelings for Nils. She loved him gently and steadfastly as she had always done, cherishing the thought of him. Whatever happened, that would never leave her and was not to be belittled in any way for springing from her youth and inexperience in summers long gone by. Subconsciously she must have known it had relegated itself already to the past when she had said to him that nothing could be decided until this war was over.

In contrast, what she felt for Karl was wholly adult. Yesterday had been a revelation to her in their relationship. She understood now what had compelled her to kiss him as she had done when they parted in Bergen. Already in her heart she had been finding her way to him. Last night had been one of discovery in many ways. She hugged her arms in joyous recollection, marvelling that happiness could come at such a time and in a totally unexpected way. Whether her life should end soon through some trick of war or if she should live for many years to come, she would hold to Karl's adoring words that had made tears of joy trickle from her eyes.

Yet this morning the harsh reality of Nils' predicament was lying heavily upon her. She had to know soon where he was and if it lay in her power to help him in any way, no matter at what risk to herself. It would be the same at any time in the future. Nothing in life was without its complications, especially when a new love did not mean a severance with the old.

Holding back the curtain again, she held her wrist close to the glimmer of daylight and saw that it was almost eight o'clock. She sprang out of bed and went to look into the main room. Karl was not there, but a candle gave light

117

and the table was laid. The coffee-pot and saucepans of hot water stood on the stove, Best of all, was the sight of her rucksack propped with Karl's against the bench, pools of melted snow bearing witness to his salvaging of them. She ran across to hers in her bare feet and took from it her toothbrush and a change of underwear she had packed. Then she gathered her polo-necked jersey and ski-pants from the pegs where they had dried overnight. She saw that those Karl had borrowed were on the neighbouring pegs, soaked by snow from his salvaging expedition. He had probably slithered most of the way down to where their possessions were lying.

When dressed and ready, Anna went to look outside. As she stepped onto the cleared threshold, a brilliant, sun-sparkling scene instantly dazzled her and she flung up an arm to shade her eyes. The sky was as vivid a blue as a butterfly's wing without a single cloud to be seen. Karl, wearing his own ski clothes, was waxing a ski, the other three stuck upright in the snow beside him. He greeted her with a loving grin.

"Hi! I was just coming to wake you. We must get going as soon as we've had breakfast."

"You've rescued all our belongings! You must have been up at the crack of dawn."

"That's when I set out. In spite of our haste yesterday, we'd left the skis jutting far enough over the waterfall for me to find them. Then I burrowed for our rucksacks."

"Recovered treasure! Isn't it a wonderful day? Just the kind of Easter weather that I remember."

"It should set in for some time now. Have you sunglasses for your trip?"

"Yes, in my rucksack."

"Good." He glanced down in the direction of the valley, which was out of her range of vision from where she stood in the doorway. "I've been keeping watch, but so far there's no military activity in the valley."

"Why is that? Do you suppose they think we lost ourselves last night and are now only mounds in the snow?"

He shrugged. "Maybe. But it's most likely yesterday cost them too many casualties when they had already caught the two men they wanted and you were only small fry. Whoever ordered the pursuit must be regretting it. He'll have questions to answer from his superiors."

"But they must be wondering about you."

"I could have been your husband helping you to get away."

"With a revolver?"

"As Eirik Haug said yesterday, many hid their guns and that includes those of us in the army who fought the invaders. The Germans found that out to their cost some time ago." He stuck the waxed ski back with the others. "That's done."

Anna waited for him in the doorway. When he reached her, they kissed happily with their arms around each other.

"Do you know what I'd hoped?" she whispered.

"I think I was hoping for the same thing. Another day of heavy snow?"

She laughed softly. "Yes, although a week would have been preferable."

"A whole year wouldn't have been long enough."

Inevitably their loving looks and words led to their making love once more. By then the minutes were running out fast for them. The food in their rucksacks had frozen during the night and they breakfasted hastily on the same menu as the night before. Afterwards she washed up the few items they had used while he raked out the stove, having already restocked the wood supply

119

in the box beneath it. His last task was to replace the chimney-lid.

When they were ready to leave, everything made as tidy as possible, Anna left some food coupons under the coffee jar as well as some for clothing as both she and Karl had taken a pair of the knitted gloves to wear. Karl added some money to cover the cost and also that of two pairs of the spare ski-sticks the owner had kept there as he had only found one of their own.

Anna was sad to leave this simple sanctuary where she had found love and she took a last look around her before blowing out the candle.

"Come on, darling," Karl said, waiting to lock the door, for he had found the key earlier that morning.

She went out into the sun and snapped on her skis. As they left the cabin behind them, she gained a full view of the valley stretching away as far as the church by the blue water of Tresfjord and then on across the great fjord to Molde many miles away. Everything was clear and sharp in the pure morning air.

"Let's come back here one day," she said, lost in the beauty of the scene.

"We'll do that."

They both knew that chance might never come their way, but it comforted her to hope for it.

They skied together side by side and kept up a good speed, for there was a crisp crust to the new snow. They were completely alone among the glittering mountains, the endless slopes lying unmarked before them. It would have seemed like any day of carefree cross-country skiing, except that the imminence of their parting was hanging over them. Finally they came to the place where they had to go their separate ways.

"This is it!" he said, as they came to a halt. "Are you sure of shelter tonight?"

"Yes. I showed you the map I was given by Rolf before I left Alesund. All the *saeters* are marked and I have my compass."

"I'll try to send you a letter if I get an opportunity," he promised.

"I'd be content with a verbal message from someone just to know you're safe."

"I'll remember that." He enfolded her into his embrace with a groan of love and for a few moments they stood with their cheeks pressed together, he almost crushing the breath from her. "Always remember that I love you, Anna."

He had spoken with such tenderness that she could hardly answer him, but a lover's parting in war was no time for reticence. If words of love were left unspoken, the chance to say them might never come again.

"You're taking my heart with you," she whispered.

Then they kissed so long and deeply and lovingly in farewell that afterwards she felt mildly surprised that the snow had not melted under their feet and spring flowers blossomed around them.

He saw she was smiling and was glad. "What is it?" he asked. When she told him, he smiled too. "Didn't you see it happen? You must have had your eyes closed."

"I always do when you kiss me." She was as thankful as he that they could part with a smile to help the anguish that was in them. "*Farvel*, dear Karl."

He watched her ski away. She paused once to exchange a wave with him. Then he turned in the opposite direction.

Anna kept to the higher slopes from which she could sight the enemy far in the distance should that arise, but it was unlikely. She had no difficulty in getting into the cabins, the key to her aunt's country home coming into unexpected use.

It took nearly three days before she came down the

121

mountains at Sjöholt. It was where the bus had been refuelled on the way to Tresfjord. There were a few soldiers about, but none took any notice of her. She was still some way from Alesund and it would be curfew-time before she reached it unless she could get transport. A garage hand gave her the telephone number of a taxi-driver. He was already booked for the same trip, but would take her if she was willing to share with another woman passenger.

She agreed immediately. Her fellow passenger proved to be an elderly woman, well pleased to halve the fare, who chatted about her five beloved grandchildren all the way. Anna was content to listen, for it was so normal and domestic after what she had been through. The flow of talk did not stop even at the bridge check point where their papers were examined. The guard, young and amiable, gave Anna a sympathetic wink as he returned them.

Chapter Eleven

Entering the hotel, Anna went through the staff-lobby into the kitchen, a ski-boot in each hand. Dinner was over and only Emil and Cook were there, chatting together. At the sight of Anna the woman widened her eyes. "*Store verden!* You've caught the sun!"

"I had time for some skiing during my visit," Anna replied with a smile, padding across the tiled floor. "It was perfect weather for it."

"Lucky you! I haven't skied since that Easter the Germans came."

Emil looked inquiringly at Anna. "Are your skis outside, *fröken?* I'll put them in the cellar for you."

"Thanks."

As Anna was about to leave the kitchen, Edith called after her, wagging a finger dramatically. "Wait until you hear what's been happening here while you were away! Fru Sande will tell you."

Anna raised her eyebrows, wondering what it could be. She had intended to find Greta in any case to let her know she had returned.

When she entered the office Greta called from her private sitting-room beyond. "I'm relieved to see you safely back, Anna," she said, stubbing out a cigarette in an ashtray almost full. "You look so healthy with that tan and I'm a nervous wreck today. Sit down. You'll never guess what occurred here."

"Cook mentioned that something had taken place." Anna sat back on the cushioned sofa.

"You know that batch of young officers who moved in last week? They had a party here last night with a consignment of French girls from the brothel ship in port. If Major Schultz had been here, he would have intervened, but he had gone to Kristiansund for a couple of days. Cook put on the buffet that was ordered and there was so much alcohol being consumed that most of the men were soon drunk. Then, when supper was over, the trouble started."

"Did they start smashing things up?"

"No, nothing like that. The girls simply refused to go up to the bedrooms. Tempers were lost and there they all were, the girls fighting and struggling on the stairs with the drunken officers and screaming out that they would never serve the dirty *Boche* and much worse. I know enough French to have understood that."

"Those girls were courageous!"

"They were a new consignment flown in a few days ago. I've heard since that as soon as they went on board, they all rebelled. As with all the prostitutes brought from Nazi-occupied territories for these vessels, the Frenchwomen had been given no choice about leaving their own country."

"Weren't the officers warned of their attitude?"

"Apparently not. The girls were pleasant enough to their German hosts when they arrived at the hotel. It's my belief that they came for the food, which would be better than their rations, and some wine. But – obviously – nothing more."

"What happened in the end?"

"Soldiers were called in and there was such confusion. The girls were rounded up and shoved in the back of an army truck. They went off shouting '*Vive la France'* and singing the *Marseillaise*. But not to the ship. Today Oberleutnant Werner, looking bleary-eyed and with scratches down his face, told me they were being sent to a concentration camp."

"Oh no!" Anna spoke in dismay.

Greta let her hands rise and fall in a gesture of sympathy for their plight. "I shall give Major Schultz a full report when he returns tomorrow and I'll speak up for those unfortunate women."

"Please do! I will too."

"He might listen more to you than to me." Greta did not speak with much hope for either of their appeals before her voice took on an apologetic tone. "I've been going on about all the troubles here and I haven't asked yet if you had a successful trip."

"There were a few problems, but in the end all went well."

"I'm relieved to hear it."

"Now if you'll excuse me," Anna said, getting up out of the comfortable sofa, "I'm going to have a hot bath and go straight to bed."

"You must have something to eat first."

"I really don't need anything but sleep. I'll say good night and see Margot in the morning."

The next day was uneventful until early evening when Klaus Schultz returned. Having been told by Margot that her mother wanted to see him at once on an urgent matter, he went straight to Greta's office. He was shut in with her for twenty minutes.

Anna caught a glimpse of him when he emerged. His face was livid with rage, a muscle working in his cheek, and he went at once to his room. Anna could tell he would be a dangerous adversary if crossed and made up her mind to be extra careful in all her dealings with him.

125

Soon afterwards Margot informed her as to what had happened. "He was so angry and is going to reprimand all the culprits. I wouldn't be in their shoes!"

Dinner passed without incident. Afterwards all the officers went as usual for coffee in the comfortable *peisestue*, so named for the open corner fireplace where logs blazed in the evenings for their comfort, for they denied themselves nothing. It was after one of the waitresses had carried out the cups and emptied coffee-pot that the officers not involved in the French fiasco left the room. Although the last one closed the door after him, the snap of heels was heard as Klaus Schultz's angry command brought the rest to their feet. From the lengthy rumble of his tirade it was clear he was showing them no mercy.

Anna had taken over the reception desk and she saw them file out, some flushed, all of them looking disconcerted, and in turn they went to present their apologies to Greta. Not for the first time Anna thought what a contrast there was in the violent brutality the German troops committed under orders and the strict discipline that forbade them any personal laxness of behaviour off duty. It was Klaus's respect for Greta that had outraged him on her behalf.

When Klaus himself emerged from the room, he saw Anna at the desk and his stern expression softened into pleasure at seeing her. "You're back. How did your trip go?"

She had her answer prepared. "I'm sorry to say that the old lady I'd hoped to visit died a while ago. I took advantage of the time I'd been allowed off work to go skiing."

"What a good idea! Are you going to the ski-jumping on Sunday?"

"I'll be on duty." It was the perfect excuse. Any sports event sponsored by the Germans was boycotted, a measure of the contempt shown by people who had once crowded to Holmenkollen and other ski events in their enthusiastic, flag-waving thousands.

"That's disappointing. But I hope nothing has arisen to prevent you coming to the party with me."

"No. Nothing at all." She hoped her smile was not becoming fixed. He was leaning his arms on the reception desk between them, looking directly into her face as if intending to create a more intimate atmosphere between them. Little did he know that while he was at dinner, she had examined the file he had brought from Kristiansund. Unfortunately it only showed that he had been organising the bringing in of more prisoners, Yugoslavs this time, to work on the immense task of installing the great gun. "Fru Sande would never renege on a promise to let me off duty."

"I'm sure she wouldn't." He paused for a moment. "Fru Sande has been most gracious over the disgraceful upheaval that took place here while you and I were away."

"I've been told about it." Anna had been waiting for the moment when she could bring up the subject and now he had done it for her.

"Your employer has always been most gracious. She has never objected to drinking parties for officers only and those can be extremely noisy and destructive at times. What happened here the other evening was inexcusable behaviour on her orderly premises. If there were more people in this country as co-operative as Fru Sande our task here would be an easy one."

"She's very fair in all matters. What of the French-women? Are they to be treated fairly for their protest against being brought here from France against their will?"

A tight expression clamped down on his face and he

straightened up from the desk. "They were brought here to follow their own profession and, since they refuse to do that, they must be put to tasks of a different kind."

"I feel so sorry for them. Why not send them back to France? That would be the humane thing to do. Surely you could arrange it, Klaus?" Her urgent appeal melted his expression and he smiled.

"You're investing more authority in me than I possess. Rebellion in any form against the Third Reich must be punished. One of the officers, whom I've just reprimanded, informed me that our commanding officer has already sent the Frenchwomen to the females' section of a place of confinement."

"Grini?"

He hesitated. "Yes." Then seeing her look of dismay, he hastened to reassure her. "I know there are rumours about the camps, but you must not believe all you hear. People are simply taught to understand what it means to reject Nazism."

"I'd hoped you might be able to help the Frenchwomen."

He put his head slightly on one side as he regarded her almost with amusement, as if her plea had been that of a child innocently requesting the impossible. "You have a tender heart, my dear. That's very admirable in the right circumstances." If he had been able to reach her hands over the desk he would have taken hold of them, but she was keeping her distance. "I have to say it, Anna. You're more beautiful every time I see you. It makes me all the more thankful that you weren't here to witness that unpleasant scene. You would have been even more upset. Young women like you should be cherished and protected. I don't even care to see you working here."

Anna knew what was passing through this Nazi's mind.

128

He was like so many others of his kind, believing Hitler's dictate that women were fit only for the kitchen and bed. "I've been told there were two male clerks here before the war," she said, "but both were shot after attempting to get away to England."

He shrugged his broad shoulders, unmoved. "Then, unfortunately, they were among those who couldn't accept that we had come as friends to save Norway from the British."

She wanted to demand if that was why he and the rest of the *Wehrmacht* had invaded Poland and Belgium and France and Holland and Luxemburg and Denmark, all before destroying the peace of Norway. Yet she dared not give way to showing her loathing of him and all he represented. Too much was at stake in every way. "If you hadn't come to Norway, I wouldn't have such a important date tomorrow evening."

He was delighted with her and smiled widely. "It is for me too, Anna."

The telephone rang at this point and she picked it up. "Hotel Ryan. How may I help you?" When the reply came, she put her hand over the mouthpiece. "I'm afraid this will be a long call, Klaus."

He raised a hand in acknowledgement. "I'll see you tomorrow," he said, drawing away.

The caller was one of Margot's friends, named Alf Ottersen. Anna recalled having a long and interesting talk with him at the party where Margot had taken her. They had also danced together three or four times.

"How are you, Anna?" he wanted to know.

"Fine. I had a break this week to visit someone, otherwise I'm busy all the time."

"Not too busy, I hope, to come and watch the ski contest with me on Sunday?"

She was taken aback, never expecting any of Margot's

friends to support an enemy-sponsored sports event. "I'll be working."

He must have caught how her voice chilled and yet he became persistent. "Can't you switch duties? Naturally none of our best men are taking part. God knows whereabouts they are now. But the Germans are entering two good skiers from their own ranks and some of their ski-troops are taking part. We've only four entrants and only one of those can hold his own. Maybe you'll know his name. When he was younger, he was in the Norwegian team that went to the last Winter Olympics held in Germany before the war and won a Gold Medal."

Suddenly suspense made her nerves tingle. "I was a bit young myself at the time. What's his name?"

"Nils Olsen."

She gripped the telephone tightly, not daring to hope. "Have you seen his name on a poster?"

"No, more than that. I saw him in training today. He's a late entrant, but he only arrived in Alesund last night."

She sank down on to the chair by the desk. Now she knew why Alf had phoned. He was as much into Resistance work as she. Nils must have asked him to get a message to her.

"Anna? Are you still there?"

"Yes, Alf," she replied. "Forgive me. I was distracted momentarily."

"I can see what you mean when you talk about being busy at the hotel. I suppose there's always a coming and going of those staying there."

He was covering up for her involuntary lapse of silence. Collaborators' ears listened into many telephone conversations as everybody knew, and she became more guarded. "You're right. No, I can't come with you, Alf, but thank you for asking me."

"I doubt if I'll go on my own."

130

She knew he wouldn't. He had carried out what he had been entrusted to do. "Maybe we could meet another time when I'm free," she suggested.

"That's a great idea. I'll ring you again. Goodbye for now."

Anna replaced the receiver and remained seated, her hands lying palm uppermost in her lap. Nils was safe! The thought rang through her head like a jubilant bell. She wished she could tell Karl, although he was likely to hear soon from some other source. It had been hard not to accept Alf's invitation, but for safety's sake it was best to stay away. She must be content that Karl's hopeful prediction had come true and that once again Nils had pulled strings and lulled the Germans into trusting him once more.

What a clever move it was to go straight into the public eye, appearing to give open support to the Nazi regime, no matter what his inward feelings. Then it crossed her mind that there was even a chance that he might be at the party. After all, as he had re-entrenched himself in the Germans' favour, he might be invited with the other civilian guests, especially if they knew that he had once been an Olympic contestant at Hitler's Garmisch-Partenkirchen. She began to hope that Saturday evening would prove to be better than she had first expected.

Chapter Twelve

When Saturday evening came, Anna took the borrowed gown she was to wear from its hanger. After she had accepted Klaus's invitation to the party, Margot had told her she would have to dress up.

"The German officers expect it of their civilian guests. They like to look smart themselves and – damn them! – they always do in any case. So it will be evening dress for all the invited women and the collaborators. I've plenty of evening gowns I haven't worn since before the Occupation. Take your choice."

So the selection had been made. Anna had decided on an oyster silk, quite plain, and Greta had offered her the loan of gold earrings and a necklace, which she had accepted.

Checking her appearance in her bedroom mirror, Anna knew she had chosen well. The pale sheen of the gown set off the sun-tint of her arms as well as her face, the result of skiing in the heat of the midday sun with her jacket and jersey tied by the sleeves around her waist.

Her thoughts drifted to another evening gown, one of shaded peach chiffon that Aunt Rosa had generously ordered from Paris for her seventeenth birthday. She'd had only one chance to wear it and she supposed it was still hanging up in her bedroom in Oslo. Her aunt was a great hoarder in any case and would still be keeping it for her. Anna felt a wave of child-like devotion go out to the woman who had been like another mother to her.

It was time to go downstairs. Anna picked up an evening purse and threw a velvet wrap, both borrowed, over her arm. She was buoyed up by the hope of seeing Nils and went cheerfully out of the room.

Klaus was waiting in the lobby and he looked up sharply as she appeared, a slow smile of immense appreciation spreading across his face. He desired her intensely, this lovely young woman coming down the flight to him now, pale silk shimmering over her slender, well-formed figure. Gold glinted at her ears and around her throat, her fair hair swinging softly and full of those same lights. He clicked his heels and bowed in tribute to her beauty before coming to the foot of the stairs as she reached it.

"Every man this evening will envy me," he said with satisfaction, taking the wrap from her to place it around her shoulders.

Anna thought with amusement that he, conscious of his own exceptionally good looks, would probably expect every woman to be jealous of her!

At the reception desk, Margot bade them an enjoyable evening. Her irony was lost on Klaus, who barely acknowledged her. She observed that he had eyes only for Anna and hoped that it would not prove to be a problem.

A military car was waiting outside and the army-driver saluted before whipping open the door. Taking a seat, Anna wondered what unfortunate owner in Alesund had had this splendid car commandeered from him. One of the first things the *Wehrmacht* had done was to take all the best cars everywhere with no compensation for the owners.

"Whom do you expect to be at the party this evening?" she asked as they were driven through the blacked-out

133

streets, the faint glow from the car's shielded headlamps barely showing the way. Klaus listed his commanding officer and some others to whom he would introduce her, but there was no mention of Nils.

Arriving at their venue, they went from the darkness into warmth and brightness. When Anna returned from leaving her wrap, Klaus offered her his arm and she had no choice but to place her hand in the crook of his elbow.

"This makes me feel as if the war has been won," he said with pleasure as he led her into the room where the party was already in full swing, "and we are at one of Berlin's many nightclubs."

She could not tell him that on Greta's hidden radio she had heard the BBC give the news that Berlin had been bombed again by the RAF, which boded ill for those nightclubs.

The music of a military dance band greeted them, the saxophones and trumpets catching the light with a silvery gleam. Couples were dancing on the circular floor surrounded by tables, each with a lighted candle. At one side of the room, doors were drawn back to reveal a buffet supper laid out.

As Anna and Klaus were shown to their table, she glanced towards the civilian guests seated with their German hosts. She recognised several known collaborators and most had brought their wives and even their grown-up daughters with them. Anna guessed that those girls were in great demand as dancing partners, for although every table was taken the officers more than outnumbered the women. She was aware of the sharply interested gaze of many of the officers as she went by with Klaus.

Their table was in a prime position on the edge of the dance floor and not too near the lively band. No sooner were they seated, when one of the resident officers at the Hotel Ryan came to speak to them. His rank was that of *hauptman*, and he was a red-faced, self-satisfied man with a loud voice, who would shout even louder in contempt when some of the domestic staff failed to understand his rapid German. So far he had not learnt a word of Norwegian beyond *skal*.

"*Guten abend, Fraulein Larsen*. And to you too, Major."

Before he could say another word, Klaus stopped him with a raised hand. "Listen to me, my good fellow, I'm having the first and last dance with my charming companion and all the rest in between."

Hauptman Bauer looked displeased. "You can't blame me for trying."

As he left, Klaus looked triumphantly across the table at Anna. "I'm pulling rank this evening. I want to keep you all to myself."

It was not what she wanted. It was only if there was conversation with others that she might pick up a snippet of something useful, because even a few casual words could be pieced together with other scraps of information.

"No, Klaus," she said with a little laugh, "that won't be the right thing to do. Of course the first and last dances are yours as well as most of the others, but, as a Norwegian, I'm very conscious of being entertained here this evening. What chance is there of furthering good relations between our two peoples if I seem to spurn dancing with any of lower rank than yours? It would appear very discourteous."

Klaus was slightly put out, but he could see that she would not want anyone to feel snubbed. "Very well, I agree, Anna. But don't escape from me too often."

He had expected reassurance from her, but a waiter had come to take his order for wine and the moment passed. When that was done, he took Anna onto the floor just as the band struck up *Lili Marlene*.

He was an excellent dancer, which was what she had expected. Such a man as he, proud and self-assured, would want to excel at anything he did. He was holding her very close, his clean-shaven chin smelling faintly of aftershave lotion, which was so pleasing that she thought it must be French. Anything good had flowed out of the occupied countries into Germany from the start, including cattle and corn from Norway.

Klaus drew back his head to smile down into her eyes. "You're looking serious, Anna. Those Frenchwomen aren't still on your mind, are they?"

"I wasn't thinking of them."

"Then why so thoughtful?"

As he had spoken, a woman vocalist in a red evening gown had stepped in front of the microphone to sing. It gave Anna an outlet to his questioning. "Perhaps it's this song of separated lovers that had a momentary effect on me," she declared, smiling again. "But I do like it."

They both listened to the song as they danced, he holding her still closer as if the poignancy of the words might have some significance for them. As it came to an end, people all over the room began taking it up again and the band played on. Soon the whole gathering was singing lustily, the vocalist encouraging them. To Anna it made a refreshing change from the constant dosage of *We March Against England* that still echoed daily down the streets.

The band-leader announced that the next dance, a foxtrot, would be an 'Excuse me' dance for the gentlemen. As a result, Klaus was tapped on the shoulder within half a minute and Anna was whirled away from him by a young *oberleutnant*.

"I saw you as soon as you came in," he said eagerly, knowing his time with her would be short. "Where do you live? I'd like to see you again. My name is Wolfgang. What is yours?"

That was the end of the conversation, for she had no time to answer as he in turn lost her to another partner. The pattern continued, but at the end of the dance she had gained a grain of information. One of her partners had expressed the wish that he had met her months ago.

"It's my bad luck that we are moving out the day after tomorrow all the way up to Tromsö," he had said.

The new posting of his company was nothing in itself, but there could be a special reason why a district was being strengthened.

By now much of the company was noisy, the singing of *Lili Marlene* having led the way for louder voices, some of the officers unsteady on the dance floor. Only the presence of the Commanding Officer kept a curb on an evening that might otherwise have become a drunken bout. Klaus introduced Anna to him when they came from the buffet room.

"Sir. Please allow me to present Fröken Larsen."

Oberst Weiss was grey-haired with chiselled features and a fine military bearing. A row of medal ribbons adorned his broad chest, including the Iron Cross. His whole attitude towards her was extremely courteous. "I'm honoured, *Fröken*."

Anna judged him to be of the old school of the German Army, privately having little regard for Hitler while holding a great love for his own Fatherland. He invited Klaus and her to join his table.

Klaus had to accept. Anna could tell it was something he had not expected and he was far from pleased. There were several other high-ranking officers at the table and he had to take a seat away from her. It also put an end to his having priority as her partner.

"It's a pleasure to have a charming young lady at my

137

side," Oberst Weiss was saying. She was seated next to him, somebody else having moved down, and wine was poured for her in a fresh glass. He and those nearest chatted with her, but all waited for him to take her on to the floor first.

To Anna it was like dancing with a grandfather. There was no attempt to hold her too close, her fingers were lightly clasped, and the conversation kept to the music of Grieg and the beauty of Norway. She liked him. The others at the table danced in turn with her afterwards. Anna saw how exasperated Klaus looked every time.

Yet they were dancing together when out of the corner of her eye Anna saw Nils arrive, dressed in what she guessed were borrowed evening clothes. She did not allow herself to look again in his direction until the dance brought him once more into view and she saw he was shaking hands with Oberst Weiss. The next time she glimpsed him, he was seated at the same table, but Klaus kept her for another quickstep before they returned there. She and Nils acted as if they were total strangers when introduced.

"We are fortunate to have an Olympic Gold Medallist with us this evening," Oberst Weiss explained to Anna. "My son won a Bronze in running at the Summer Games in Germany that year."

"Is he in Norway too?" Anna asked. Nils was seated on the other side of the Oberst, which had moved Klaus still farther away from her.

"No, he's on the Eastern Front and I'm proud to say he is serving the Fatherland well."

It was almost the end of the evening when Nils finally allowed himself to ask Anna to dance. The band was playing *The Blue Danube* and, with other dancers rotating around them with speed, they were able to talk closely together without being overheard.

"We must look as if we're chatting about unimportant things," she said at once, "because I know I'm being watched."

"By all the men in the room, do you mean?" he teased.

"No! By one man in particular."

"I know whom you mean. That Major hardly takes his eyes from you."

"Alf rang me. I was so thankful to know you were safe. How did you get away?"

"I'll tell you, but first there is something I want you to do for me. I'm involved here for the next two days in getting orders for supplies and I've an important message for you to deliver. Don't trust it to anybody else."

"I'll do as you say."

"Just inform the right quarters that an important delivery is to be made early Wednesday evening."

Anna guessed immediately that sections of the great gun would be arriving. "I'll do that tomorrow."

"Good." He smiled approvingly. "Now that's settled I'll tell you how lucky I was. As you know yourself, it was so quiet in the church that I heard when a truck drew up in the road. Then came the crash of boots as soldiers jumped out and I knew I'd been found. I threw on my coat and as they came rushing up the path, I started thumping on the door with my fists, yelling to be let out." He laughed quietly. "It must have surprised them, because when they threw open the door to seize me, I expressed my relief and thanked them for rescuing me."

"That was brilliant! Did they believe you?"

"Not at first. Their officer questioned me and I said I'd been at the wedding, but as there was no reception through the German ban on any gathering of people, I had stayed to look round the church. That's when I had been

139

accidently locked in. Your travel pass saved me, showing that I'd had permission to travel."

"Thank God for that! Did you know one of your fellow saboteurs was taken?"

He nodded, guarding his expression. "He and I came face to face as he was taken away, but neither of us showed any sign of recognition. Nobody does in those circumstances."

Anna felt heartsick at what that man's fate would be, but somehow kept an empty smile on her lips. She listened intently as Nils went on to tell her how he was taken to the wedding couple's home to be identified as someone known to them and to their families.

"I was certain that was the end, because they wouldn't know my name, but by sheer chance, the bridegroom's father remembered me from the district ski events before the war. 'That's Nils Olsen,' he said. 'I saw him at the wedding.' Then, because he could see I was in serious trouble, he added, 'He was there by invitation.'"

"Oh, Nils! That was luck indeed!"

"I still wasn't released. They kept me in custody overnight and took me to Molde next day for further identification from a German officer with whom I've done business. It was only then that they released me."

Anna knew that the waltz would soon be coming to an end and there was still much more to say. "I won't be at the jump tomorrow to cheer you on, but make sure you win."

"I will," he promised confidently. "I would have liked more time to get into my stride, although I had some practice runs today. I enjoy a challenge, as you know. The tougher the better."

"You always were spurred on by stiff competition, especially where girls were concerned," she agreed with a laugh.

"True," he admitted with amusement. "But don't rake

up my past, Anna. That was all before our summer together."

It gave her an opportunity. "That was only July and August. Two months, Nils. A fleeting, happy time."

"But not forgotten by either of us. I had competition then, I recall."

"Not really. I just couldn't believe you'd changed your attitude towards me at last. That's why at first I continued to keep dates with somebody else."

"But not for long." His clasp on her tightened lovingly. "I wasn't going to lose you then and I feel the same since finding you again."

The dance ended and they came to a halt so near Klaus, who was waiting on the edge of the floor, that she was startled at seeing him there.

"We were coming back to the table," she said.

Klaus smiled. "I wasn't going to risk it. This is the last dance of the evening."

Nils bowed slightly to them both as formal Scandinavian manners demanded and bade them both good night. "I'll be leaving now as I have a big day ahead of me tomorrow. It's been a pleasure to meet you, *Fröken* Larsen. And you, Major."

Anna did not see him leave, making sure she did not glance once towards the glass doors.

It was not until they were being driven back to the hotel that Klaus asked her what Nils had been saying to hold her interest so intently.

"We were discussing skiing," she replied.

He had taken hold of her hand. "What else? Was he trying to make a date with you?"

She laughed softly. "No. He's about the only one who didn't."

"But surely he asked if you would be at the contest tomorrow?"

"Yes, but I told him I couldn't be there."

"He looked particularly serious at one point. Was it when you told him that? Or was there some other reason? I'd like to know."

Anna's patience was running out. "Is this an interrogation, Klaus?"

"Why should you think of that?" he gave back keenly. "Some association of ideas perhaps?"

Anna knew herself to be on slippery ground. "No. I'm just not used to being cross-questioned."

Klaus brought his mouth close to her ear and lowered his voice in order not to be overheard by the driver. "It's only that I want to know everything about you and to see you look at me as you did at Olsen when you were in his arms. You didn't even blink in any other direction."

Anna did not find that surprising. She and Nils had been discussing a life and death situation. Yet maybe Klaus, watching closely, had seen something in her face of what would always be in her as far as Nils was concerned. "You must remember that one doesn't meet an Olympic Gold Medallist every day. He was kind enough to tell me what it's like to take part in the Games." That was true, but his account had been given to her and others seven years before. "At the time I followed it all on the newsreels at the cinema."

"I was an *oberleutnant* then, but I was lucky enough to be present when the Führer opened the Games."

There flashed into Anna's mind the newsreel image of thousands of arms raised in the Nazi salute and she almost shuddered.

At the hotel the entrance was locked, but Klaus had a key. On the first floor where his room was located, Anna stopped to say a brief good night, but he shook his head.

"There's no need for the evening to end yet. I thought we'd have a glass of wine together."

"No, it's late and I couldn't drink anything more."

"Then I'll see you to your door." He was carrying his hat and stuck it on the newel post before throwing his greatcoat over the bannister rail. He caught her up on the next flight. Again she would have parted from him, but he put a proprietary arm about her waist, ignoring her insistence that guests were not expected to go up to the fourth floor.

"Fru Sande doesn't sleep up here, does she?" he said, more as a statement than a question.

"No, she has her own small apartment adjoining the office, but Margot is my neighbour."

On the fourth floor Klaus looked around in surprise. "It's larger up here than I expected. What are all these doors?"

"Two lead into storage rooms, one to the bathroom and the other two are the bedrooms."

Having satisfied himself that there was no one in range likely to intrude, Klaus turned back to Anna. With a smile he set the flat of his hands either side of her on the door. "You intrigue me, Anna. There's something elusive about you I can't understand. I find everything about you fascinating – your looks, your voice, the way you laugh. Yet however close we are physically, as when we danced and how we are now, you keep your innermost self distant from me." His eyes were searching hers. "Tell me how I can get through to you, Anna."

She decided to use the truth to her advantage. "If I seemed more at ease this evening when I danced with Nils Olsen, it was because I was with a fellow countryman. You must remember that you wear the uniform of a conqueror."

He grinned widely and began to unbutton his jacket. "That's easily remedied."

"No, don't!" she exclaimed angrily, grabbing his hands

143

in an attempt to stop him. It was her mistake. Instantly
he seized her wrists and she thumped back against her
door as he held her pinioned, his mouth clamping down
on hers, his tongue probing. She was helpless, his whole
body pressed hard against hers. Her only weapon was a
total lack of response. As he became aware of it, he drew
his mouth away from hers, meeting her cold stare.

"I couldn't help myself, Anna," he said thickly. "You're
so lovely. Unlock your door. Let's talk this over." He
stroked his hands down her arms and she shook him off.

"Please go."

"*Liebling*, you must know how much I have come to
care for you! I could make a difference to your whole
life if you would only meet me half-way. Surely there
should be a time for loving in the midst of war? I care for
you and we need each other, Anna." He put his fingertips
lightly against the side of her face, looking deeply at her,
tenderness vibrating in his voice. "I can make you happier
than you ever dreamed possible."

She remained totally still. "I want you to leave, Klaus.
The evening is over."

He stepped back from her, angry colour rising up
his neck, and he threw out his hands in exasperation.
"You're impossible! I don't understand you. I know
you're attracted to me as I am to you. We're fellow
Aryans. There is nothing to keep us apart." He brought
his face close to hers again, his damaged ego spurring
him to mockery. "Don't tell me you're still a virgin with
your looks and in this house of men." Seizing her breast,
he squeezed as with his other arm he pulled her to him.

Instantly Anna shot up her hand and caught him under
the chin with the ball of her palm, making his jaw
crack and jerking his head back with all her strength.
His arm fell away and he drew back, staring at her
with narrowed eyes, his face congested with temper,

his nostrils dilated. "Where did you learn that trick?" he demanded heatedly.

Too late she realised that a slap across the face was what he might have expected, not a trained act of self-defence.

"A boyfriend taught me years ago. It's not the first time I've used it."

"But you dared to use it on me!" His furious outrage threatened to choke him. "*Me!*"

She stood her ground, her cheeks flushed, not knowing yet if he would attempt to strike her, but she was prepared to defend herself. Her training had taught her never to show fear and she could see her apparent calmness was exacerbating his humiliation at her rejection. She took a chance.

"Go!" she ordered crisply. "For your sake and mine. Now!"

He hesitated only briefly, scarcely able to grasp why the evening should have ended in this disastrous manner. Then, swinging away, his open jacket flapping, he went off down the stairs. Anna remained where she was until his door slammed two floors below, vibrating through the hotel. A moment later Margot looked sleepily out of her room, pushing back her hair.

"Something woke me up, Anna. How did the evening go?"

"I'll tell you about it in the morning."

"OK. Good night." Margot closed her door again.

Anna opened her own door, which she had never bothered to lock, but, after entering, this time she turned the key.

In the morning Anna sought out Emil and said she had to make contact, having an important message to deliver. He nodded and she knew it would be done on her behalf. Going on duty at the reception desk, her first task was to

145

sort the mail for the officers, which was brought by an army delivery. Almost all of it was in a personal category from Germany. As always, each had been opened and resealed by a German censor before leaving the country. Her guess was that not all the news of the Allied bombing of the country was allowed to get through to servicemen away from home.

Anna looked up as Klaus came through the lobby. He was on his way out and did not glance in her direction.

"One moment, Major Schultz!" she said quickly.

He stopped, impatiently flicking his gloves against his great-coat. "What is it? I'm in a hurry."

"There are two letters for you." She held them out.

He came across to the desk and took them from her. Turning them over he noted the addresses on the back. Then he raised his head and looked coolly at her. "There was no need for that little contretemps between us last night, Anna. I wasn't expecting a commitment from you, only my dues as a conqueror."

He turned away from the desk and went out. Anna supposed he thought she was left smarting from his sarcasm, but it had had no effect. She understood far better than he realised that his male ego had been cut to the quick and he was still furious with her. Probably no other woman had refused him before.

It was a relief to know she was free of him and he would not be asking her out again.

Anna was in the kitchen helping Cook prepare dinner when Emil signalled to her. She made an excuse and met him in the staff hallway.

"Your contact is waiting for you. He'll be looking in the bookshop along the street. The code word is 'Ibsen'."

A few minutes later, Anna was walking without haste towards the bookshop. There was nobody there when she arrived, but a man was looking in the neighbouring shop.

146

As she stood seemingly interested in the display of books on show, he came and stood beside her.

"Excuse me," she said, pointing in the window. "Can you see the title on that red book? I think it's one of Ibsen's plays."

There was no such book on display, but he gave her the answer she wanted. "Yes, it's Ibsen's *Ghosts*."

"There will be a delivery early Wednesday evening," she said.

"That's what we've been waiting for," he answered.

He strolled on as if their exchange had never taken place. Anna waited, watching in the reflection of the window, as two soldiers on duty with rifles came along on the opposite side of the street. The man had moved on just in time.

Leaving the bookshop behind her, she went back to the hotel. She met one of the young officers on his way there too.

"Good evening, *oberleutnant*," she said in reply to his greeting. He was easy-going and pleasant, by no means a dyed-in-the-wool Nazi. Greta had told her that he had been reprimanded more than once by Major Schultz for being too willing to turn a blind eye to some minor act of defiance.

"May I walk with you?" he said, falling into step beside her. "I was at the ski-contest this afternoon. Olsen won the jumping, but two of the ski-troops came second and third."

She was pleased with this result, but no patriot would applaud Nils's victory.

Chapter Thirteen

When Anna went out to collect the bread ration the following morning, it was another glorious day. She walked with a feeling of exhilaration that spring was letting its arrival be known. As Karl had predicted, the good weather seemed set to last for a considerable time, the days already lengthening towards the everlasting light of the summer nights. The snow had vanished quickly, although it would be at its best on the ski slopes. The mellow colours of the buildings glowed in the clear light. Resting at the wharves, the fishing boats had already unloaded their morning catch, but the shrieking seagulls continued to swirl overhead in thick fluttering clouds.

At the bakery Anna waited in the long line, turning her face to the sun, with others missing the ski-expeditions at this time of year in the past. Nobody chatted to her any more. Klaus had finished that for her when he had gained her priority treatment in getting apples that day.

On her way back to the hotel again she had to wait to cross a street. Two helmeted outriders, rifles slung across their backs, were approaching at the head of a convoy of army trucks coming from the direction of the harbour. Other pairs of outriders were keeping pace in escort on either side of each vehicle. As the first one passed her, Anna saw with a deep sense of shock the plight of those on board. These were the Russian prisoners-of-war being moved in to work on the site of the great gun about which she had informed the Resistance. Skeletal in appearance with their heads shaved, they did not have room to sit, but stood jammed together, listless and hollow-eyed, looking more fit for a hospital ward than heavy manual labour.

Pity overwhelmed her. As the second truck reached her, she sprang forward and hurled a loaf from her basket to the men. They uttered a strange kind of strangled shout as it reached them. She had to spring back quickly to avoid an outrider bearing down on her. He yelled at her, gesticulating with one black-gauntleted fist for her to get off the street, but she took no notice, waiting to take aim when the next truck drew level.

This time a forest of scrawny arms and claw-like hands reached for the loaf that flew through the air. Narrowly escaping motor-cycle wheels again and receiving similar abuse, Anna was ready to throw the third loaf when her arm was grabbed and she was spun round with a force that made her stagger to face Klaus, his eyes grim, his eyes blazing.

"What the hell do you think you're doing, Anna Larsen?" he demanded, snatching the loaf from her hand and tossing it away.

It landed on the street cobbles, causing her to cry out as she saw truck wheels trundle over it. "How could you do that! Those poor men are starving!"

He twisted her arm just enough to force her closer to him. "Poor men!" he echoed contemptuously. "They're *Russians!*"

"Human beings!" She was aghast that he should have spoken of the prisoners as if they were less than cattle.

"Look!" He pointed in the direction of the disappearing truck. "They're fighting among themselves over that bread. Is that what you wanted?"

"No." She was determined not to be browbeaten. "But it shows how desperate they are for food. You weren't

149

able to do anything for the Frenchwomen, but you could get adequate rations for those men!" It was on the tip of her tongue to add 'since you are in charge', but she checked herself in time. His being in command of the gun emplacement was not yet public knowledge.

He ignored her request. "I could have you arrested for what you've just done, but I'm letting you off with a warning." The last thing he wanted was to have her behind bars. The manner in which she had defended herself on Saturday night had made him wonder about her. He intended to look more closely into her absences. Neither did he want her out of his sight for more personal reasons that he could not dismiss.

"I'll heed the warning."

He released her. "Very well. But never interfere in military matters again."

As Klaus strode away, she rubbed her arm where he had gripped it, for it throbbed painfully. There would be more trouble when she faced Cook with the diminished rations.

Surprisingly Cook accepted the situation philosophically. "I don't know how I'll eke out what's left, but those prisoners needed the bread more than any of us." Then she gave Anna a sharp look as she added: "But if anyone has to go without altogether, it'll have to be you."

"That's what I want."

By the end of the week and without saying a word, Cook shared the loss by going without too. She told herself that at least she did not feel as if there were lead in her stomach, a common occurrence with the wartime bread.

It did not take Klaus long to get the information he wanted. He was relieved to read that an old woman of the name Anna had given had lived in Tresfjord, but she had died early in 1939. It bore out Anna's story and, for the time being at least, he allowed his suspicions to be lulled.

The great gun did not arrive at Alesund on the date of delivery after all. Anna had another meeting with Rolf, who told her jubilantly that the information she had passed on from Major Schultz's file and the additional message from Nils had been relayed to London. As a result, a British submarine in the North Sea had torpedoed the ship carrying the gun only a few miles from its destination.

Anna was with Margot, having visited a friend living at walking distance outside Alesund on the mainland, when they saw the trucks moving the Russian and Yugoslav prisoners. They were being taken to join other prisoners of the same nationalities already engaged in clearing heavy rocks for the Luftwaffe's new airfield. Two of the Russians must have recognised her as the one who had thrown the bread, for both gave a feeble little wave, their hands barely raised in case of being seen. She waved back vigorously and Margot followed suit. An outrider spat at them as he went past.

Margot was subdued by the starved state of the prisoners, not having seen any before. Anna understood her feelings and they walked in silence for a while.

"If that's how the Nazis treat their captives," Margot said at last, "what must it be like for those in Grini and in the Arctic concentration camps?"

Anna guessed she was thinking of friends and others known to her. "I've no idea," she answered wearily.

Margot's eyes were uncharacteristically filled with tears.

"I try not to show it, but I get so depressed at times. If the Occupation had never come, Johan and I would have been married. I might even have had a child now. Instead, not knowing whether he's alive or dead nearly drives me

151

mad when I can't keep my fears at bay. I miss him every moment of each day."

Anna linked a comforting arm through hers. "I know. I've seen how you are sometimes. You have spasms of not sleeping well then too. I've heard you moving about in the night."

"I'm sorry. Do I disturb you?"

"No, I have a wakeful night now and again."

"Would you come in and talk for a while next time if you hear me about?"

"I'll do that."

"I'm afraid it was the sight of those sad prisoners even cut off from all news of their families that triggered me into gloom."

"That was to be expected. I'm glad we've talked."

"You're a good friend, Anna. Now I mustn't go home in this mood." Margot let her shoulders rise and fall as if physically shaking off her depression. "Come on! We have to be cheerful for our conquerors."

Anna was amused, seeing that Klaus had unwittingly created a joke for Margot and herself to share. "That's what the Nazis *think* they are!"

With a laugh that they both needed, they went into the hotel.

Chapter Fourteen

As the days slipped by, the forests were spread with pale carpets of wood anemones in the sudden spectacular burst of the Northern spring. Almost overnight, the trees budded forth new green and a variety of birds returned to join the colourful little tits that remained steadfastly resident throughout the winters. Anna knew the waterfall at Tresfjord would have melted and amid veils of spray would be cascading down to the salmon river below. She yearned to see it and to wander along that peaceful valley. Sometimes the strain of her underground work and the busy routine of the hotel made her long for a brief respite just to be on her own.

When Emil had injured his back and had to rest for a couple of weeks, she had taken over the delivery of the transcripts that Margot took down from the BBC. The press that printed the underground news-sheet, entitled *Freedom*, was hidden in the cellar of a stationer's shop, which also printed posters and notices for the Germans. What the enemy did not know was that there were two presses, one that could be inspected and another that they never saw. Sometimes, instead of going to the shop, Anna would meet Solveig, the wife of the editor, with Inga, her baby, and the transcript would be tucked behind the pram pillow.

Anna had no idea who delivered the printed news-sheets locally, and she doubted if Emil knew it either. These true reports of what was happening everywhere were published under various headings all over the country and were avidly read and passed on again. News of enemy atrocities and reprisals were also included, some of them horrific, and yet the smouldering defiance of the people did not falter, no matter how bad the home news.

At the hotel Anna had twice narrowly escaped discovery when an occupant had returned unexpectedly to his room, but the risk had been worth it. She had been able to pass on three valuable pieces of information that Rolf had been glad to receive. By now she had met two other members of the local cell and once Alf was her contact. As he knew her socially, he was chosen to ask her if she would resume an unpleasant task.

They met at the seagull's rock and, because German rules forbade them from standing to talk, they had to walk on together. At first they kept their conversation to normal topics until they could be sure nobody was within earshot. It meant waiting until after they had passed a little scene that was not uncommon these days. Two civilians, one a middle-aged businessman and the other a fisherman, had been stopped at random in the street by two soldiers and ordered to scrub off a large patriotic cypher that had been painted on a wall.

"Get on with it!" one of the Germans barked when the businessman paused briefly to rest his arm before dipping his scrubbing-brush into the water again. The royal cypher was that of the King, the letter *H* interlaced with a 7 for Haakon VII. It was forever appearing all over Norway and seemed to infuriate the Germans even more than the wearing of paper clips or scarlet woolly caps, the colour of the Norwegian flag, which was the latest demonstration of unity.

"What did you want to see me about, Alf?" Anna asked

154

as they came to a play area where children were throwing a ball to one another.

"We'd like you to take up your relationship again with Major Schultz. There's something in the wind and we don't know what it is."

She frowned sharply. "I wish you'd asked me anything but that."

"You're on speaking terms with him, aren't you?"

"Only when necessary at the hotel, but nothing more. As I told Rolf at the time, I learned nothing of any value at that party and Schultz expected his dues, as he called it, afterwards. No thanks! I've had enough of him. I thought once I'd like to be a Mata Hari, but I've changed my mind. I came here to be a courier or a radio-operator, not to fawn on a Nazi."

"You're a radio-operator, are you?" Alf was interested. "I don't think Rolf knows that. You'd find it a nomadic existence, because the Germans can soon trace a signal in town. Sometimes it means living in the mountains for months. You'd always be on the move."

"It would be preferable to what you're asking me to do now!"

"Maybe you'll get a transmitter later on, but in the meantime try to find out what Schultz is planning."

She glanced at him in exasperation, but he returned her look steadily in a silent reminder that she was in the Resistance to work for the country's liberation, however unpleasant the task. With a heavy sigh she capitulated.

"I'll do what I can. But it will have to be gradual, because I'm uncertain about Schultz. It's just a hunch, but I've a feeling he has his reservations now about me too."

"You're an intelligent girl. It shouldn't be too difficult for you to talk him out of his doubts. And don't make the healing process too gradual. Time may be running out for us."

Anna gave a mock groan. "Anything more?"

"Only something that may or may not be important to you. A verbal message from Karl."

She held her breath. "Have you spoken to him?"

Alf shook his head. "The message was relayed to me by someone passing through."

"What is it?" she demanded eagerly.

"Only that the mountain flowers are still in bloom."

Anna tilted her head back with a soft laugh, diving her hands deep into her pockets as if to restrain the upsurge of happiness that swept through her. Alf probably thought it was a message in code and in a way it was. Karl, having to contain all he wanted to say in a single mundane message, had chosen to remind her of the past and to promise for the future in an oblique reference to their parting in the mountain snows.

That evening Anna made a start on the task allotted to her. She gave Klaus a slight smile as she passed him and sensed that he paused to look back at her. It made her wonder if intense hatred created an acute awareness of another person almost as much as love.

When Anna took the opportunity to repeat her smile, wider this time, Klaus acknowledged it with an interested nod. In his own mind he regretted having rushed his fences with her. It was why he had been very civil to her since after the morning when his temper still had the better of him. In spite of her firework anger that night, she was probably still attracted to him as he was to her.

There was also another reason why he wanted her company again. If Anna was dabbling in some underground treachery, however slight, he needed to know. Several times recently he had mulled over her behaviour when he had found her in his room. A check was made in the rooms every evening for fresh towels or anything else that was needed, and so there was nothing suspicious in that, but she had been in no hurry to leave, her attitude very friendly. She had been quick to take his coat and hang it up before returning, almost provocatively, to the bedside. She had even sat on the bed, which had struck him as something very close to an invitation. But when he had taken her up on that after the party, she had caught him entirely off guard with her deft act of self-defence.

Yet that wasn't all. Anna had been in Tresfjord when a saboteur was caught, and the young woman with him had eluded capture with another man. At first it was believed that they had lost themselves and perished in the snow, but since then it had become known that there was a mountain cabin they might have reached. On her own admission, Anna had acquired her tan by skiing on the slopes in that area.

As yet he had kept his suspicions to himself, not wanting the Gestapo to interrogate her. He knew what they would do to her beautiful face and body if they thought she had anything to tell. It was far better for him to handle the matter himself and, if she was innocent, there should be no hindrance to a satisfying relationship with her.

Within a few days Anna accustomed herself to Klaus pausing to chat with her whenever they met. It was a beginning, although she did not foresee achieving anything worthwhile from this growing truce between them. She had found nothing in his room to give her a clue as to what next he would take under his command. If her hunch was right about his being unsure of her, he would take care that nothing important was left for prying eyes. In case he had hidden relevant papers elsewhere than in his files, she had searched diligently, running her hand along the back of drawers, checking for any loose floorboards that could be raised, and tracing her fingers under shelves where his helmet and caps were kept. Nothing had come to light, except a tiny charred triangular-shaped scrap of paper that was blank, but might have been the corner of a letter. Although the waste-paper bin had been emptied by the cleaning-woman, it had caught in the decorative trim and a few black ashes had remained inside. For some reason Klaus had chosen to burn this letter and let it drop into the bin.

Anna could not put the scrap of paper out of her thoughts. She had brought it away to her room and it was presently housed in a small wooden box carved with a view of the local mountains. She was convinced it could provide a clue to what she had been entrusted to find out, if only some will-'o-the-wisp connection could be brought to the forefront of her mind. But so far it was eluding her.

It was raining hard when the officers returned to the hotel one evening early in May. Emil took their greatcoats from them in turn to dry in the laundry room. Klaus was the last to come in and, after Emil had taken his greatcoat, he came across the deserted lobby to where Anna was alone at the reception desk.

"Good evening, Anna," he said, putting his rain-damp cap and gloves on the desk. "I prefer snow to these downpours. We've had days of it now."

"Surely you've been here long enough to know how unpredictable the weather is on the west coast?"

"I have, and I would not mind another posting, but the coastline needs a strong defence."

She guessed he did not want a repeat of the Anglo-Norwegian commando raids that had ripped into two places further south. "Dinner is well under way," she said, indicating the direction of the dining-room.

"Never mind that." He lifted the flap at the end of the desk and entered to stand facing her.

She stiffened at his presence, but did not draw back. "What do you want, Major Schultz?"

He sat down on a tall stool that was there, resting the heel of his boot on the low rung. "I want to apologise for what happened between us that unfortunate night. I regret what I said and how I acted towards you." He spread his hands appeasingly, determined not to admit to the jealousy he had felt when she had danced with others, the Norwegian in particular. It was an emotion he had not experienced previously over any woman since his first youthful love affair. "My only excuse is that I'd drunk too much, but that was because I had to pass the time somehow while you had a variety of different partners for most of the evening."

She had no patience with him and was glad he did not know it. "I'd told you early on I wouldn't refuse to dance with anybody else."

"At least say that's all in the past." His jaw clenched involuntarily, for he was unused to apologising for anything he did, but he had to break the deadlock between them. "The amount of alcohol in me had a bad effect upon my behaviour."

"As it did on those officers that night the Frenchwomen were here."

"All right!" he snapped, dark colour rising in his face. "I admit I behaved no better and with less excuse. Does that satisfy you?"

She had met jealousy before, Nils having been almost beside himself when she had chosen to spend time with other people that long-ago summer, and she could see that Klaus had been equally tormented. Unlike Nils, who was of a different temperament, he stirred fear in her. "Why are you saying all this to me?"

"Because I want us to begin all over again! Can we make a fresh start?"

She drew in her breath, steeling herself. "It's not in my nature to harbour a grudge."

159

"Then forgive and forget," he urged, certain now that he was gaining the upper hand.

"Very well, Major Schultz."

"Call me Klaus as you did before."

She nodded and conjured up a smile. "Now you'd better go to the dining-room, Klaus, or there'll be nothing left."

His mood lifted. He was highly pleased with himself and convinced now that she had wanted to mend the rift all along. "I'll do that, Anna."

This encounter led Anna back to open the carved box and study once more the scrap of charred paper lying in it. What was it that continued to elude her? She asked Margot if she had any helpful ideas about it, but nothing was forthcoming.

Klaus did not let his advantage rest. He went to Greta's office the next day with a bottle of French champagne.

"I'd like you and Margot to share this with me, Fru Sande. Perhaps you'd allow Anna to join us too."

It was an awkward moment for Greta. She had come through from her bedroom, having been listening with Anna to the BBC news bulletin while her daughter took it down in shorthand.

"They're both with me as it happens. We'll need champagne glasses. I have some very fine ones in my sitting-room." She played for time, giving the girls the chance to get right away from the radio, which had been turned off at his tap on the office door. "What are we celebrating, Major?"

He could not reveal the main reason, but he gave her another. "My winning this bottle at cards last night. One of the players was getting low in funds, but as he wanted to stay in the game, he put up this bottle that he'd been hoarding. I scooped the jackpot and the champagne!"

160

"It was your lucky night." Greta led the way to her sitting-room. To her relief, Anna sat with a newspaper and Margot was knitting as if they had been there all the evening. Both looked up as she and Klaus entered. "Major Schultz has invited us to have a glass of champagne with him."

Anna helped her to take the glasses from a display cabinet. They had belonged to Greta's grandmother and Anna saw they were the same as some that Aunt Rosa had kept for special occasions. It gave her particular pleasure to see the bubbles rise in her glass as it was filled. In her thoughts she disassociated Klaus from the champagne as she sipped it.

He was very amiable and smiling, full of buoyant good humour. Sitting deep in the cushioned sofa as if he had installed himself for several hours, he had one long leg crossed over the other, his high, polished boots gleaming in the light. Margot was fuming inwardly that she had missed taking down all the news, but Klaus was totally unaware how unwelcome he was and did most of the talking. He did not single Anna out in the conversation, but every time she looked in his direction, his eyes were waiting for hers.

It was his suggestion that they listen to some classical music, for he knew Greta had a large collection of gramophone records. Margot made the selection and placed the records in turn on Greta's radiogram, which was an elegant piece of furniture that she had bought not long before the war. The radio itself was missing, having been surrendered when the Germans had confiscated all radios. They had not known she had hidden another.

The evening ended at last. Margot came into Anna's bedroom for a final chat.

"What a tedious three hours!" she complained bitterly.

"I felt more like breaking those records over his self-satisfied head instead of playing them. I wasn't interested in anything he talked about."

Anna had washed her hair and was drying it with a threadbare towel, replacement household goods having vanished from the shops. "I always listen as a matter of course just in case anything of slightest importance comes up, but as usual with him, there was nothing. I'd like to know why he was in such good humour."

"That's obvious. As you told me, he thinks he's back in your good books."

Anna lowered the towel and flicked back her hair. "I don't know. It seems to me he would take that as a matter of course."

"My grandmother would have been afraid you'd wear your brain out," Margot said teasingly with a grin. "You're always turning something over in your mind. I'm glad I haven't got your job. You're getting like Sherlock Holmes with your suppositions and clues. I wonder you didn't examine that half-burnt paper with a magnifying glass!"

Anna slept well that night. Afterwards she did not remember dreaming at all, but subconsciously her mind must have remained active, because when she awoke it was with a start that made her sit upright in bed. Her thoughts were entirely clear and she knew where the charred paper had come from. It was the corner of an underground news-sheet.

She sprang out of bed and rushed to the carved box. Rubbing the scrap of paper between her finger and thumb, she realised that it had been the particular quality of it that had haunted her. How could she not have thought of that before? Klaus had had a news-sheet in his room, but had wanted none of the domestic staff to know it, otherwise he would simply have crumpled it up and tossed it into the wastepaper-bin, for it was nobody's business what he

162

read. Why did he take the trouble to burn it? She was still no nearer the solution.

At mid-morning Anna was in the kitchen helping Cook, which she did at least two or three times a week, when Emil returned from an errand. He looked as grey as his hair as he opened the door from the staff hallway and stood there without entering.

"The Germans have located the *Freedom* press!"

Cook gave an unhappy moan, for she and all the rest of the staff read the news-sheet avidly whenever a copy came into their hands. One of the cleaners, a mop and bucket in her hand, shook her head in dismay. Anna was rigid with shock. She should have guessed! That was what Klaus had been planning! It was why he had been so cock-a-hoop yesterday evening. He had known the net was drawing tight around his quarry. And she had sat in the same room with him, drinking his looted champagne, while all the time he was gloating over his achievement.

"Are you sure, Emil?" she demanded harshly, feeling terribly responsible for failing to decipher the clue that had been in her possession.

"I saw the soldiers pouring into a house. A crowd soon gathered and, although we were kept back, the Germans wanted us to watch. They brought out bundles of tied up *Freedom* news-sheets and made a bonfire with broken up shelves, chairs, tables and a desk that they threw from an upper window. Even a baby's high-chair was thrown into the flames. Major Schultz is in charge."

"What of the people living there?"

"I thought at first they had been warned in time and fled, but after a while, they were all brought out – Martin, the editor, Solveig, his wife, their two teenage sons and his brother-in-law, all of whom work there."

"The baby? Little Inga! What of her?"

163

"I didn't see her. The mother was sobbing."

"Oh, my God! Was she left inside? I must go there!" Anna threw off her apron and darted past him into the staff hallway. As she opened the street door, he caught and held it, not letting her out.

"No, *fröken*! You mustn't get involved!"

His gaze was piercing, reminding her that she could be asking for her own death sentence if she allowed suspicion of any kind to fall on her, but she pulled free of him. "I have to make sure little Inga is safe!"

She wrenched the door open and ran out. He let his arms flap once at his sides in exasperation and then he followed her. Both Cook and the cleaner went outside in their wake to watch them go, but Anna and Emil had had to stop only a few yards away. In silence, the two women joined them to watch as the little group Emil had already listed was driven past, seated in an open army truck under armed guard, together with ten more people, who, Anna guessed, were distributors of the news-sheet and had been rounded up. She recognised several of them, including the owner of the shop where she had twice met Rolf in the storeroom.

As soon as they had gone past, watched by silent people all the way, Anna set off in the direction of the printer's building where she had sometimes made a delivery of Margot's transcripts. She saw it was in the process of being boarded up, Klaus still in charge of what was going on. He saluted her with a smile as she approached him.

"I'm busy, Anna, but I'll see you later."

"I can see there's plenty going on," she remarked easily, looking towards the building where the shop front was already half covered, hammering going on there and elsewhere. "The people you've arrested lived above the shop. Do you think their baby is still sleeping up there somewhere in spite of the noise?"

"I don't know anything about a baby."

"It's a little girl. She is nine months old."

"You know the family?"

"Only because printing was done here for the hotel, just as posters and leaflets were done for your Command. The baby wasn't with her mother in the army truck when it went past the hotel, and a bystander told me what had happened here."

"Is that why you came?"

"I'd be concerned for any child. May I go indoors and make sure she isn't sleeping somewhere in spite of the noise?"

"That's unlikely." Klaus smiled again. "You can go in if that will satisfy you, but don't be long." He turned to a sergeant. "Send a man in with *Fröken* Larsen."

The soldier, helmeted and with a rifle, clumped in after her. She passed the open door leading to the cellar where the secret press had been kept, but showed no interest. Upstairs there was devastation, drawers pulled out, contents scattered, the living-room almost devoid of furniture and the windows still open where it had been thrown out.

"Bit of a mess, isn't it?" the soldier remarked cheerfully. He had enjoyed looking at her legs all the way up the stairs. "What did you want to come in here for?"

"A baby might have been left behind."

"There's no baby here. It would be bawling its head off after all the commotion. Anyway, I think someone must have taken care of it. The wife here was in a real state. We had to drag her out, but just as she and the rest were being driven off, she shrieked out something to a woman with a baby. She wouldn't have been allowed to keep it with her in any case, not where she's going."

He did not elaborate, but Anna could guess the destination. Although she was relieved the baby appeared to be in safe hands, she still looked in every room on both the upper floors until they returned to the living-room again.

"You'd better close those windows," she advised.

"You're right," he agreed with a grin. "I'll only be sent back in again to do it."

As his back was turned, she picked up a family photo-graph that had slipped free of its frame and broken glass when it had fallen to the floor. She slid it into the pocket of her skirt and continued downstairs. Sooner or later she would hear who was taking care of Inga. The child might never be reunited with her parents, but at least she should have a family photograph to keep.

Chapter Fifteen

After the arrests Anna felt herself to be in an intolerable position. She could not show where her loyalties lay by hostility towards Klaus and yet the sight of him sickened her. He was in a triumphant mood, making no secret of his satisfaction with himself and what he had achieved. In addition he seemed to think that his benevolence in allowing her into the printer's house to look for the baby had further cemented his relationship with her.

"I have to go away tomorrow for a couple of days, Anna," he said on the fourth morning after the arrests. "So would you come to the cinema with me this evening?" Then, noticing that she appeared to hesitate, he added, "Remember, we are beginning again."

It was still daylight when they came out of the cinema and quite a lot of people were about, for the curfew had been extended with the long, bright days and short dusky nights that were the forerunners of the midnight sun in the far north.

Back at the hotel Klaus suggested that they sit and talk for a while. "I'll order coffee," he said.

"There's nobody in the kitchen now," Anna answered.

"Then you show me where the coffee is kept and I'll make it." Playfully he caught her hand again to set off in the direction of the kitchen, but Anna held back. There would be trouble from both Greta and Cook if she allowed him to cross the threshold of that last sanctum of the hotel.

"No, wait! Put a couple of logs on the embers in the *peisestue* and I'll bring the coffee to you."

To her relief he did as she said. When she brought the tray of coffee into the room, flames were dancing along the birch logs in the high-canopied corner fireplace. Only one shaded lamp had been switched on, creating a seductive atmosphere. He took the tray from her and set it on a low table.

"That's most welcome," he said appreciatively.

They drank the coffee sitting side by side in comfortable chairs. Klaus talked of his home in Berlin where he grew up, his parents and his sisters, all three of whom were married, his admiration for Hitler and his hopes for the future, which included marriage and children. In between he attempted to bring her out about her family and early life.

Although Anna appeared relaxed, she was keenly alert, convinced he was trying to spot any flaw in whatever she said. Fortunately she had been so steeped in her fictional background during her training that nothing he asked caused her any worry. It was after midnight when they left the room together and he saw her to the foot of the stairs. There he rested his hand on the newel post and made no attempt to touch her as they said good night.

"You know Anna," he said, "I never thought I'd need a second chance in my life, but you've given it to me when I needed it most."

He watched her go up the stairs, absorbing the sight of her unconsciously sensuous grace.

In the morning, after Klaus had departed and the rest of the officers had gone on duty, Greta came in search of Anna, who was sorting the hotel chits for reimbursement from the army office.

"There you are, Anna!" Greta exclaimed. "Bring those

chits to the office if they're ready. There's something I want to discuss with you."

"I've just finished them," Anna said when she put the chits down on the office desk. "That's everything up to date."

Greta nodded and waited until Anna was seated before she spoke. "This may seem an odd question, but did you have a snack in the kitchen before you went to bed last night?"

"No. Major Schultz wanted coffee and I made just enough for two cups for him and one for myself. Did I use too much coffee?"

"The amount you took was missed, because Edith has started marking the level of it, but that's not important. What about the three previous nights?"

Anna frowned very seriously. "I have never taken any food other than what I've been given."

"I was sure of it and I hated having to ask you," Greta said on a sigh, sitting back in her chair, "but I've had to question all the staff, including the part-timers. Edith has got it into her head that food is being pilfered. Do you think Major Schultz might have helped himself?"

"No, because after I went upstairs, he followed almost immediately and I heard his door shut after him. What is missing?"

"According to Edith, bread and cheese each time, two slices of beef left from the dining-room, some cold cooked potatoes, and also the dried apple rings in a jar have dwindled. It's so little in all, but not in times like these."

"When has this food been disappearing?"

"Edith isn't sure what time it happens. She doesn't always notice something is missing until she goes to use it. Her fear is that larger amounts might be taken next time and I share her anxiety, because, if the officers thought they weren't getting their full rations, I could be forced out of here and a German catering staff moved in to take over." Greta shook her head gravely. "I'm well aware that I'm hanging on here by the skin of my teeth and any kind of trouble on the domestic side would finish me."

"Yet you take the risks that you do. Having me here, for example."

"That's little enough, in my opinion. I wouldn't be able to survive this Nazi presence under my roof if I didn't exorcise it by helping the Resistance in the only way open to me. Margot feels the same."

That night, Anna sat on the bed in Margot's room as they discussed the mystery.

"I've been thinking," Anna said. "Do you suppose that someone on the staff is pregnant and can't resist taking a bite to eat when nobody is around?"

Margot, brushing her hair before the mirror, paused to look across at her. "Well, it's not you and it's definitely not me. Who does that leave?"

They counted up. There were five possible and two unlikely.

"That doesn't help much, does it?" Anna concluded, rising to her feet. "We can't solve anything tonight. It's my morning as trainee assistant to Edith again tomorrow and so I hope nothing has been pilfered in the meantime."

"Good luck!" Margot said with a laugh. "She was like a lioness deprived of her young today."

Fortunately, when Anna went into the kitchen to take up her work, Edith was in an amiable mood.

"Nothing more has gone," she announced cheerfully. "Whoever had a few moments of weakness has now overcome them. We all know what it means to be hungry."

It was typical of her charitable nature that the matter was closed as far as she was concerned. But by early evening she was in a fury again. The rifling of a bag

170

of oats had escaped her notice earlier, but it had come to light when she noticed a few oats scattered on one of her spotless shelves. Margot, who was in the kitchen at the time, put the pregnancy theory to her. The woman's reaction was to look hurt.

"I hope anyone pregnant on the staff would feel able to ask me for a little extra. I'd have found something. It's the thieving I can't abide. Anyway," she added firmly, "women in that state don't usually knock back brandy. I had a bottle in the cupboard I've always saved for a medical emergency, such as an air raid, and that's been swigged too. I have it well hidden now."

When Margot repeated the conversation to Anna, she added, "If anyone had a taste for brandy, you'd think Edith's bottle would have been sampled long ago."

Anna agreed. "You said once I was like Sherlock Holmes, but this is a problem someone else will have to solve."

More pilfering was reported the next day at noon. Margot was on her way to tell Anna, who was taking a turn at mending the linen, when a visitor called in at the hotel.

"There's somebody waiting to see you, Anna," she said. "I showed him into the *peisestue*."

"Who is it?" Anna asked, puzzled that anyone should come to see her.

"It's Nils Olsen, the collaborator who won the ski-jumping contest a few weeks ago. How do you know him?"

Anna was alarmed. Something very important must have come up for Nils to seek her out here. Neither Margot nor her mother knew anything about him, for she had always kept to her false background as she had been instructed. "I had one dance with him at that party I went to with Klaus." She stuck her needle back

171

into a pin-cushion. "I never expected him to turn up here."

"You are having trouble," Margot commented with amusement, having seen how bewildered Anna was by this unexpected call. "German officers fancying you like mad and now, worst of all, a Quisling too."

"You shouldn't jump to conclusions!" Anna gave back sharply before she could stop herself.

"Oh, sorry," Margot said quickly. "Is he really a patriot?"

"I've no idea," Anna bluffed, trying to cover her slip of the tongue. It had sprung from a deep-rooted loyalty always to defend Nils against criticism, but it was a sharp lesson on how easy it was to be caught off guard. "Your telling me I had a visitor made me nervous."

"It was my fault. I should have said he's tall and dishy without a whiff of the Gestapo about him." Margot tilted her head with a smile. "Anyway, if he is a patriot, enjoy the visit."

Anna closed the door of the *peisestue* behind her as soon as she entered. Nils was standing by the window and his pleasure at seeing her suffused his face as he crossed the room.

"What are you doing here?" she demanded anxiously.

"Seeing you." He swept her into his arms and kissed her hard, but her eyes remained open and she stepped back as soon as he released her.

"Do you mean this is purely a social call?" she demanded incredulously.

He laughed at her concern, catching her hands in his and pulling her towards him. "Don't look so worried! It's all above board with the Germans. Aren't we lucky?"

"No!" She was angry. "You were mad to do this! You could be jeopardising your rôle and mine."

"If either of us should be arrested, do you mean? Forget

172

it! You and I are coming through this war together with a whole new future waiting for us."

"But the war isn't won yet. I've enough on my hands with Klaus Schultz breathing down my neck. He won't be pleased if he hears that you were here."

"It's all right. I told *Hauptman* Bauer and another officer staying here that I had a spare programme of the 1936 Olympics that I thought would interest you." His eyes danced. "I added that you wanted to see the name of an old friend in it who had taken part. Fortunately they didn't ask to see it, because even my own was lost when my home was burnt down in the Molde air raid."

"And what if either of those two men ask me to show it to them?"

He looked surprised that she was making an issue of it. "Tell them that you felt you couldn't accept it. What's the matter? It's not like you to get upset and I can see you are."

She put her hand to her forehead as if to thrust away her anger. "I didn't mean to fly off the handle. I'm glad to see you. I always am, but life is so complicated at the moment."

"Can you tell me about it?" he asked sympathetically.

She looked into his eyes. "I want to tell you, Nils. You won't like what I'm going to say."

"As long as you don't say you're walking out on me, I can cope with anything else." The joking tone he had adopted faded away as he saw the anguish on her face. "What's happened?"

"Let's sit down," she said.

He sat opposite her, leaning forward with his arms across his knees. "So tell me," he said uncompromisingly, his gaze fixed on her.

He listened without a word as she told him how she had first met Karl in London, and that subsequent meetings had drawn them together without their realising it, until the time they knew themselves to be in love with each other. "If it hadn't been for Karl getting me away in the mountains as he did," she concluded, "I'd be in a concentration camp or, at worst, dead."

"I should never have let you go off alone in that valley!" Nils clenched his hands in self-reproach.

"You had no choice."

"But to think you might have been killed in that forest! You're grateful to Karl for getting you through it and that's understandable, but what you feel for him is no more than that."

"But it is."

"No, I don't believe that," he declared stubbornly.

With despair, she saw that he was unable to come to terms with what he had been told. "Please listen to me, Nils," she implored. "I love Karl. He's everything to me."

Her words finally seemed to sink in and he looked down, shaking his head. "You don't know what you're saying," he said very quietly.

"I tried to make you see that nothing was the same when we talked in the church."

Still he did not look up. "But you told me there was nobody else."

"I didn't know it myself then." Anna reached out and put a hand on his arm. "Please look at me, Nils."

He raised his haggard face and her hand fell away at the starkness of passion blended with sadness in his expression. "Nobody can do this to us, Anna."

"That's what I used to think, but I was wrong."

"You're forgetting something. I know you better than anyone else. No matter how confused you are now, you'll come back to me. Our lives are intertwined and always will be."

"In one way, but not another."

His jaw set. "I'll wait for you to get over this."

"No!" she protested vehemently. "That would be useless. If I should lose Karl through this war, I'd go on alone."

He had risen to his feet, ready to leave, and he shook his head again. "You're mistaken, my love. You'll need me more than ever."

Anna made no attempt to follow him out of the room. She was close to tears. There had been so many times in the past when she had run to Nils, firstly as a child full of hero-worship and then as a girl in love. Now she had done what he had never done to her. She had turned away from him.

Chapter Sixteen

Although Anna tried to sleep that night, thoughts of Nils were heavy on her mind. When finally she dozed, it was only to be disturbed by a creaking board and instantly she was wide awake again. Another board creaked as somebody moved about and she guessed that Margot was having one of her sleepless nights too.

Throwing back the downy *dyne*, Anna put her feet into slippers and reached for her dressing-gown. She went to Margot's room and tapped lightly on the door before opening it. To her surprise, her friend lay fast asleep.

Puzzled, Anna shut the door again and was about to return to her own room when she heard creaking boards somewhere on the stairs below. Only Emil slept on the premises and his room was on the ground floor beyond the kitchen, where his room had a view over the water. If it was the food thief going down the stairs, it had to be one of the officers.

Her first thought was to investigate on her own, but it would be wiser to be accompanied by a witness. She returned to Margot's room and woke her up.

"Is it an air raid?" Margot asked sleepily. When Anna had explained, she was alert at once and soon they were both going down the stairs as quietly as possible. Outside each door that they passed a pair of jackboots stood awaiting Emil's collection and polishing in the early morning. Every time a board creaked underfoot, they froze before continuing on again. Apart from themselves and the unknown person they were stalking, the whole hotel appeared to be fast asleep.

The emergency light in the blacked-out lobby gave just enough glow to show that the doors to the dining-room and *peisestue* stood open and all was silent within. Anna led the way to the kitchen where a sliver of light, streaking out from under the door, showed that whoever was in there did not expect to be discovered. They listened against the door and heard the bread drawer open.

"Now!" Anna whispered.

They flung open the door and entered, only to halt in total astonishment. A strangled gasp had met them, followed by the clatter of a bread knife falling on to the floor and the thump of the loaf that followed it. Both had been dropped by a terrified boy of about ten years old, brown-haired and dishevelled, a stranger to them both. He stood as if rooted to the floor.

"Who are you?" Margot demanded as Anna swiftly closed the door in case he made a sudden bolt to escape. "How did you get in here? Have you been breaking into the hotel every night?"

"Don't give me away!" he begged, his face white. "I'll be killed if the Germans get me!"

"I might do that before I finish with you," Margot threatened angrily. "You're a thief! Aren't you fed enough at home?"

"I haven't a home. Not any more. The Germans took it."

"They've taken over mine too. What's new about that?" Without giving the boy a chance to reply, she wagged an angry finger at him. "You've been swigging brandy too, you little thief! You're a bit young for that, aren't you?"

The boy made an unconsciously comical grimace. "I didn't like it!" he protested vehemently. "It's worse

177

than medicine. But my uncle always slept after he had brandy, and I wanted to sleep in the daytime to be awake at night."

"So you could break in and steal!" Margot was outraged.

Anna, who had picked up the knife and loaf, setting both aside, could see that the boy was almost paralytic with terror, with none of the defiance and bravado that might have been expected of a young thief caught in the act. She had drawn her own conclusion as to the reason and frowned slightly at Margot. "I think we should start all over again." Drawing a chair out from the table, she sat down facing the boy. "I'm Anna and this is Margot. So what's your name?"

Her calm attitude had some effect.

"Magnus Jacobsen."

"Are you Jewish?" She pulled out another chair for him.

He nodded. "The Nazis took my father and mother away as well as my older brothers and my grandparents too."

Margot, immediately overwhelmed by pity and bitterly regretting her sharp words, sat down too and rested her arms on the table. "Where was your home, Magnus?" she asked gently.

He was wary of answering her, uncertain whether she would explode into rage again, but Anna reassured him. "There's no need to be afraid now that we know your circumstances. Please tell us where you lived."

"Trondheim."

"It's quite a long way from here. How did you get this far?"

It came out that after a bout of diphtheria he had been sent to convalesce on a mountain farm, his parents visiting him at weekends. When he was packed and ready to go home again, word came that they and his family had been

178

taken away in the mass arrest of seven hundred-odd Norwegian Jews throughout the country. Magnus had remained in the care of the farmer and his wife until it became too dangerous for him when the Germans moved into the locality to build a lookout fortification. He had been taken down the mountainside, hidden in a load of hay. Since then, he had been sheltered by different people in various places until it had become necessary for him to be moved on again.

"So where have you been staying in Alesund?" Anna prompted.

"With Herr and Fru Halstad, the printer and his wife. There was a delay in getting me to them, or else I would have gone to England on the Shetland Bus. But with the light nights there are no more sailings until the autumn and they were going to keep me until then. But the Germans came for them too."

"You were in the house at the time?" Margot exclaimed. "How did you get away?"

"As soon as the Germans started hammering on the front door and smashing in the windows, Fru Halstad kissed the baby and pushed her into my arms, telling me to run to the neighbour. I gave Inga to the lady, who'd never seen me before, and she rushed indoors and left me on the doorstep. So I just kept on running."

"You poor kid!" Margot exclaimed. "What happened then?"

"I didn't know my way, 'cos I'd never been out of the house since I arrived. After a bit, I came into this street as Herr and Fru Halstad went by in the army truck. They didn't see me in the crowd. Neither did you, *fröken*," he added to Anna, "when you were standing outside with Margot and two other people. The door out there was open." He indicated the direction of the staff hall. "I darted indoors and, as there was nobody about, I

179

kept going until I reached the top floor. I hid in the storeroom there."

"Have you been there ever since?" Anna asked incredulously.

He shrugged. "It was all right. There's a big cupboard across a corner and I hid behind that whenever somebody came in, which wasn't often. I slept in one of the sleeping-bags stored on a shelf there. Being hungry was the worst part." His gaze went yearningly towards the loaf Anna had left on the kitchen bench. "At night I came downstairs to find something to eat in the kitchen." He looked anxiously at her again. "I tried not to choose anything that would be missed. I didn't take much."

"We know you didn't. How long did you think you could go on like that?"

"I hoped to hang on until the autumn and then get away on a boat." He looked at Anna hopefully. "Could I still do that?"

"That's something that has to be discussed," Anna said, exchanging a look with Margot, "but in the meantime I think we should find you a meal more substantial than what you've been having up till now."

Margot grinned and replied in a sing-song voice, "Edith isn't going to like this." Then in a normal tone she added, "I'll look in the pantry and see what I can find."

Away from the kitchen in the dimly-lit lobby, Klaus had let himself into the hotel. He was tired and irritable, having had an uncomfortable journey over mountain roads. He had intended to stay overnight at the comfortable Grotli Hotel, which had been requisitioned early on in the Occupation, but a message had come through from headquarters that had necessitated his more immediate return to Alesund. He had missed dinner, for there had been nowhere to eat on the way.

He had already decided to wake Emil. The fellow could

make him a coffee and produce a snack as on a previous occasion when the rest of the staff had gone off duty. It meant going through the kitchen regions, but he knew where Emil slept, having been shown his room during a routine inspection some while ago.

Dropping his hat and gloves on to the hall table, he strode off in the direction of the kitchen. Seeing light coming from under the door, he was pleasantly surprised that somebody was already on the spot. As he reached the door, he heard Anna's voice and paused with a smile that she should be there at this unlikely hour to wait on him. Perhaps one of his fellow officers was also being given some late refreshment. Even as he would have reached for the door-handle, he caught some of her words.

". . . sure that we won't let the enemy get you, Magnus . . ."

For an incredulous moment Klaus thought he must have misheard, but as she continued he knew there had been no mistake.

"You may not be able to stay on in hiding here," she was saying, "but there are a number of safe houses in Alesund where you wouldn't be found. Somehow we'll find a way to get you to one of them . . ."

Klaus was consumed by a gush of fury that corded his face and made his fists shake. The bitch! She'd led him by the nose with her tricks and lies. In an instant all he had felt for her was replaced by an unremitting hatred. So she knew of safe houses, did she? The Gestapo should get a list of those from her!

He drew his revolver from its holster. The Resistance member with her would be armed, but unprepared. Taking a deep breath, his nostrils already dilated by temper, he pressed down the handle and flung the door wide.

To his total astonishment Anna sat at the table with an unknown boy. Although the colour drained from her cheeks, her only move was to clamp her hand over the boy's wrist to keep him seated beside her. But in panic the child tore himself free, terror in his eyes, and sprang to his feet, knocking his chair over with a clatter. Before Anna could reach out to stop him, he had snatched up the bread-knife from the kitchen bench and held it defensively.

"I won't go with you!" he shrieked wildly.

"What's going on here?" Klaus demanded contemptuously, advancing into the kitchen.

Anna, thankful that Margot was out of sight in the pantry and hoping she would have the good sense to stay there out of trouble, answered him with a sharpness that came from her own strained nerves. "I could ask you the same question! What a fright you've given us. Bursting in here for no reason with a revolver in your hand. No wonder my nephew thought you'd come to arrest us." She twisted in her chair to speak to Magnus. "Come and sit down again. Major Schultz has been away. He didn't know that you were coming to stay with me."

Magnus did not move, although Anna had set his chair upright again. Terror seemed to have dulled his hearing and his wits as he continued to clutch the knife defensively.

"So he's come to stay here out of the blue just as you did, Anna," Klaus remarked with angry sarcasm. "Until you can find a way to move him to a safe house? That's the plan, I believe."

Wretchedly, Anna wondered how much he had overheard outside the door, but still she bluffed. "Did I say that? I meant a home away from the military. This is no place for children."

"Stop lying, Anna!" Klaus exploded. "There's only one reason why you'd want to hide this boy." His flinty gaze went to Magnus. "You're a Jew!"

182

Anna stood up quickly and moved in front of Magnus. "Don't bully him!"

She thought for a moment that Klaus was about to strike her. She had never seen such hatred in another's eyes, his features congested with temper, but he kept himself under control and only thrust her aside to glare furiously at Magnus.

"Put down that knife!"

Anna was afraid Magnus might lunge at him in panic. She addressed the terrified boy quietly. "Give me the knife, Magnus. You're in my charge and nobody is going to hurt you. Please." She unlocked his fingers from the handle and, as she took it from him, he burst into tears, clinging to her. After putting the knife down on the table, her arms went around him protectively as she looked at Klaus in appeal. "Couldn't you forget you've seen him? He's only a child."

"You amaze me, Anna," Klaus sneered sarcastically. "You must have inflated ideas about your attraction for me to suppose I'd let him escape the net! How many others have you smuggled through? I think I'm beginning to see what's been going on in this hotel. What better place to hide somebody wanted by us than under our very noses! How long have you and the others in this hotel been deceiving the German Command?"

"You're wrong! Nobody else is involved!" she cried, bluffing desperately. "I had arranged it all secretly."

He did not believe her. "You couldn't possibly house such a young enemy of the Third Reich in this hotel without the co-operation of others!"

"But I did! You've no idea how long he's been here, being fed at night and sleeping by day in the storeroom opposite my room. I thought the time had come for him to move on. That's what he and I were discussing."

Her persistence was exacerbating his anger to a pitch

that made his finger quiver against the trigger of his gun. "You're both under arrest as Greta Sande and her daughter and the staff will be! Now I'm going to wake the whole hotel." He indicated sharply that she and the whimpering boy, clinging to her like a limpet, should go ahead of him out of the kitchen. "Go on! Move! Into the lobby!"

He did not see or hear the iron saucepan that Margot crashed down on his head. His knees sagged and he reeled, all expression wiped from his face, the revolver dropping from his hand. Even as he fell, he caught the back of his neck with a thud against the black rim of the stove and tumbled into a sprawling position full-length on the tiled floor.

Anna thrust Magnus away from her and darted across to kneel beside him. She felt his pulse, put her ear to his chest, and then checked again. She looked up at Margot, who still stood holding the saucepan by its handle, her face ashen. "He's dead!"

"Good!" Margot exclaimed on a shrill note.

Anna rose quickly to her feet. She could see that both Margot and Magnus were in shock and she felt shaky in the legs herself, but she had to keep a clear head and decide what to do. When Margot had loomed out of the pantry, holding the heavy saucepan high above her head, it had all happened so swiftly, and the situation must be solved with the same speed.

"Wash that saucepan, Margot!" she instructed as a first practical move. "Make sure there's no blood or hairs left on it."

Margot stared at her in horror. "I can't."

Anna snatched it from her by the handle. "Then hunt for Edith's bottle of brandy. It's hidden somewhere."

"I saw it yesterday tucked behind some blocks of green soap in the laundry room."

"Then get it." Anna turned in time to see Magnus about

to pick up the revolver. "Don't touch that! Put some wood on the stove. I want a fire going."

After placing the saucepan in the sink under a running tap, she took a clean cloth to pick up the revolver itself, having seen enough Hollywood films to know about incriminating fingerprints. Still keeping the weapon wrapped, she knelt once again beside the dead man and slid it back into its holster, which she fastened afterwards through the cloth, giving it a wipe for good measure. Then she examined the back of his head, seeing some blood, and cleaned the back of his broken neck in case a tell-tale mark remained from the stove.

As she lowered his head again, she was overcome by nausea and remained bowed over, struggling against it. Margot thrust a glass with a little brandy into her hand.

"Drink this! I've had some and I feel better now. What are we going to do?"

Anna gulped the brandy down and it helped. "I'm trying to work that out."

She looked at the kitchen clock. It was almost three o'clock and far too light outside to deposit the body in the street as if Klaus had been attacked there. In any case, that would bring reprisals down on innocent townspeople, which must be avoided at all costs.

Magnus crouched down to bring his worried face on a level with hers. "The fire is going well."

"Well done."

"I am hungry," he said wistfully, suddenly unable to think of anything else but the hollow aching in his stomach.

Anna could see that with the German dead his fear had diminished and his trust in Margot and her to protect him would be absolute. "Help yourself to bread and cheese as you did before. Later today I'll find you something more substantial."

Wearily she rose to her feet. How incongruous it was to talk of food at such a time! Especially as an idea was forming in her mind as to how to cover up what was virtually a murder, even though Klaus might not have died if he had not fallen against the rim of the stove. It was fortunate it was not alight at the time, for nothing could have disguised a burn on his neck.

"The saucepan will be clean now, Margot. Take a fresh cloth from the drawer, dry it and put it back where it was. After that we must drag Klaus to the foot of the stairs. It has to look as if he fell backwards down the flight."

"That's crazy!" Margot exclaimed in dismay. "Nobody would be taken in by that."

"Have you a better idea?" Anna countered angrily. "Or do you want him left here on the kitchen floor?"

Margot looked shame-faced. "No. It's whatever you say."

While she dried the saucepan, Anna threw the cloth she had used into the flames of the stove. Leaving the kitchen, she went to the lobby to look up the steep flight and down again to decide exactly how Klaus might have fallen and where he should lie. Returning to the gruesome task awaiting her, she found Margot waiting to take one of his arms while she took the other. After she had placed a kitchen chair cushion under the heels of his jackboots to avoid any scrape marks they proceeded to drag him away to the lobby. They left Magnus staring fearfully after them as he tucked into bread and cheese.

"We ought to have woken Emil to help us," Margot whispered breathlessly, for Klaus was heavy to pull.

"No," Anna whispered back. "I wouldn't want him or anybody else to be involved."

Nervous of making the slightest sound, they arranged Klaus's body at the foot of the stairs. Anna dismissed Margot's idea that they sprinkle the rest of the brandy

186

over him as if he had been drinking, for if there was an inquest it might come to light that he was sober when he fell. Finally Anna took his hat and gloves from the lobby table and stooped to skim them across the floor as if they had flown from his hand.

They were careful to erase all trace of his having been in the kitchen, wiping the rim of the stove and cleaning the floor tiles where his head had lain. The cloths they used all ended in the flames. Last of all the remains of Magnus's meal were cleared away. Margot noted that he seemed to think their presence had given him *carte blanche* to eat as much as he liked. Tomorrow there would be no hiding from Edith a missing half a loaf or the disappearance of a large amount of cheese. Magnus had even drunk a full glass of milk.

Upstairs, after seeing Magnus back into his secure hiding-place, Anna and Margot embraced each other in silent commiseration at what they had been through together. As they went to their own rooms, both wondered what they might have to face in the days ahead.

Chapter Seventeen

Anna was dressed and ready, as she knew Margot would be, when the commotion started as Klaus's body was discovered. There were shouts as well as footsteps running up and down. She went out on to the landing, Margot doing the same, and saw Greta half-way up the flight to them. Her face was stricken.

"A terrible thing has happened! Major Schultz fell down the stairs last night! He's dead! Someone has phoned the medical officer and he's coming at once. Wait where you are for a few minutes. The Major is being carried to his room and we don't want to get in the way."

Margot turned pale. It was a sight she did not want to see. She exchanged a look with Anna when Greta signalled that they could follow her. All the officers in the hotel were out of their rooms, some still in pyjamas, others partly dressed, their faces grave. When they saw Anna their gaze followed her, believing that she would be particularly distressed as she and Klaus had formed a relationship. One detached himself from a group outside the dead man's room.

"I'm so sorry, *Fröken*. I can guess how you're feeling."

She made the most suitable answer possible in the circumstances. "Major Schultz died in the cause of the Third Reich even if he was not on a battlefield."

"Most aptly said!" he endorsed fervently.

Greta and Margot had gone ahead. Anna was alone on the stairs leading down to the lobby when the medical officer arrived. She had to wait while Hauptman Bauer, fully dressed, explained how the body had been found.

"Why was it moved?" the medical officer demanded testily. "I should have made a preliminary examination of it first."

"It was a natural reaction not to leave him lying there. He was carried up most carefully."

"So I should hope! Any blood?"

"Just a small patch where his head was lying."

Both men peered down at the dried stain. The medical officer gave a grunt of satisfaction. "That's not enough for an attacker's blow with a sharp instrument."

Hauptman Bauer looked surprised. "We've never experienced any aggression in this hotel. There are only three women here at night and an old man."

"I was thinking more along the lines of the Major being set upon outside and staggering in, but that seems unlikely. Who found the body?"

"The hotel's handyman, whom I've just mentioned."

"I'll want to question him later. Now I'll go upstairs."

Hauptman Bauer led the way up past Anna, enabling her to continue on her way. She guessed Greta and Margot were in the office together, but she did not join them. It had been agreed the previous night that Greta should be given all the facts, but Margot was the one to do it.

On the way to the kitchen she met Emil with a bucket of water and a cloth. "Is it all right to clean up the floor now, do you think?"

She nodded. "Did you hear Major Schultz fall down the stairs in the night?"

"No, I can't hear anything where I sleep, I'm pleased to say. Only the bell if one of the officers has forgotten

189

his key. I found the Major when I came through to draw back the black-out curtains."

"I need to see Rolf about what happened here and something else. It's urgent. Could you make contact today?"

"Leave it to me."

It was not yet half-past six, but Edith was already making porridge, for there were always officers wanting breakfast before early duties. Two part-time waitresses were tying on aprons and discussing the Major's death, but not with any regret. Next to *Hauptman* Bauer he had been the one the staff had most disliked. All three women looked askance at Anna, never having been entirely sure about her association with him, even though they knew Fru Sande would never employ a traitor.

"There's one Nazi less for breakfast, Edith," Anna said as if his absence was due to some mundane reason.

Her words were enough to reassure them. The two waitresses suppressed a giggle and Edith looked relieved, but she had something else on her mind, far more important than the demise of an enemy. Even as she opened her mouth, Anna went across to press her arm meaningfully.

"Did you want to discuss the bread? It's my day for collecting the ration. I'd like to talk about it later and anything else in the pantry that you want replenished."

Edith could tell by Anna's tense expression that at last she was to be given an explanation for the missing food, including the fresh loss discovered this morning. She just had to wait until the two of them were on their own. She gave a nod, unable to resist a surreptitious glance at Anna's flat stomach. It didn't show, but that Major Schultz with his brutish good looks wouldn't have been above rape if it had suited him.

Other part-time workers were arriving. Edith delivered dramatically the news of the fatal accident in the night to every one of them. Anna did not stay for the exclamations and comments, but went to the office. It was deserted, but Margot called to her from the sitting-room.

"Mother and I are in here."

As soon as Anna saw Greta, she could tell that Margot had related everything. The woman had just lit another cigarette and there were three stubs already in the ashtray by which she sat. For the first time she looked her age and more, her skin so devoid of colour that her rouge stood out sharply across her cheekbones, her lips unusually vivid. Yet, in spite of the additional shock her daughter had given her about the uninvited presence of a young refugee on the top floor, she remained her usual sensible and practical self.

"Have you seen the boy today, Anna?" she inquired crisply.

"No, I told Magnus he wasn't to move from the storeroom. I'm going to take him some porridge as soon as I can."

"It will mean confiding in Edith. She's to be trusted, but such a secret is an unfair burden on her."

"I will try to ease that."

"From now on Magnus must be properly fed. He will have to bath and his clothes be washed. It will mean doing that at night."

"I'll see to it."

"How has the poor child passed the time?"

"He told me he has watched the fishing boats from the window, and on one of his nocturnal forays he found a spare chess set and has been playing against himself. Apparently his grandfather taught him. Magnus is a very intelligent child."

"You realise he can't stay on here indefinitely? Not only is it far too dangerous, but it's wrong for him to remain cooped up. But, whatever happens, I want nothing done in haste that could add to the peril he's already in. He's come through far too much already for any child of his age."

"I agree," Anna said. "You're taking this very well, considering that so much has happened in such a short while."

Greta gave a wry smile. "Don't think I'm not scared as hell at what might come out of it all, but I've matched my wits with the enemy before and you and Margot are the best people I could have with me." Abruptly she stubbed out her half-finished cigarette. "I must stop smoking these German hand-outs! I feel ashamed of myself for accepting them. I'll not light up another!"

Breakfast was over by the time Anna had a chance to speak to Edith on her own. "I know you're a patriot as I am," she began. "For that reason I'm going to trust you with some information that you must never repeat."

Edith put a maternal arm about Anna's shoulders and sat her down at the table. Pulling out a chair for herself, she leaned forward sympathetically. "When is your baby due?"

Anna looked at her in astonishment. "Have you been thinking that? Oh no, that's not the case at all. It's a matter of life and death."

Edith could tell by the gravity of Anna's expression that she was speaking the truth. "I know I like to gossip, but I can keep my mouth shut when it's important." She clamped her lips together to emphasise her vow. "How can I help?"

"There's a young Jewish boy who has to be fed. Don't ask me where he is or anything about him."

Edith took what she had heard to heart. "What do you need?"

When Anna had gone up the little-used back stairs with the porridge, Edith put on her coat and went home. It was only a ten-minute walk. When she returned, there were some of her sons' childhood books in her pockets, together with crayons and a half-used sketchpad. She also carried a package of underwear and a couple of shirts that her boys had grown out of, but which she hoped would prove useful. Anna received the clothes gratefully and Magnus was overjoyed with the rest.

Klaus's body left the hotel at midday, the coffin covered by a swastika flag. The medical officer had concluded that it was an accidental death with no suspicious circumstances. The bruise on the back of the neck had troubled him, but he had come to the conclusion that the edge of a tread had caught it in the fall. One of the officers thought he had heard a noise of some kind in the night, but although he had not looked at his watch he knew it had been in the small hours, which tied up with the time of death. The matter was all but closed.

Later in the day Anna met Rolf at a friend's house. When he had heard everything, he gave a low whistle at the seriousness of the situation.

"We must get the boy to safety as quickly as we can. Not only from the hotel, which is far too dangerous, but from Alesund as well. There are too many German spot-checks and house-searches in this port for him to stay until the Shetland Bus starts up again. Have you any ideas, Anna?"

"I haven't stopped thinking about it. Suppose I travelled with him? Magnus could be a child entrusted to my care and too sick to be questioned. I could take him to wherever you say. You'd be able to get a doctor's certificate and a travel pass."

"That wouldn't present any problem. All the doctors in this town are patriots with us. Is Magnus a sturdy child?"

"Yes, he is. Until he came to the Halstads' home he was at places where he could climb in the mountains and have limited freedom. What were you thinking of?"

"It's going to be difficult, but we could get him through the forests into Sweden. It's a far more dangerous escape route at this time of the year than on skis during the winter, but I know somebody who'll be going soon and he would take the boy. Of course, you know him. It's Karl."

Anna felt a little glow within her at hearing Karl's name so unexpectedly. "Where would Magnus and I meet up with him?"

"It means going all the way to Oslo. You'd be in danger every minute, but if you get the boy there I think I can say that his life will be saved."

"I'll get him there."

"We'll have to think of some way to get the boy out of the hotel in the first place. There'll have to be some diversion to make sure he's not noticed as we get him away. What reason can you yourself give for leaving your present employment?"

"That's no problem. From the start the Germans were told I was only there temporarily for part of my training. Fru Sande knows a safe hotel in Oslo where I can go."

"Then I'll start making arrangements. I'll let you know when the plan has been fully worked out. Don't contact me in the meantime unless there's an emergency."

The days of waiting that followed seemed endless. Greta wrote to her friend in Oslo, knowing he would read between the lines and understand why she wanted Anna to go to his establishment. As she had expected, a reply came quickly in which he wrote he would be glad to have extra help as getting reliable staff was a problem.

"By 'reliable'," Greta said after reading the letter aloud to Anna, "he means a fellow Resistance member. You'll be in good company." She gave one of her broad smiles. "If ever you want a position of trust in a hotel when this war is finally over, come back here. You'll be welcome. We're going to miss you."

Margot said much the same when Anna was playing Chinese Chequers with Magnus in her room. "I'll have to write and tell you all the news."

"You do that! And I'll let you know what it's like in Oslo these days."

"Have you any friends living there?"

Anna's thoughts flew to Aunt Rosa. "Nobody whom I wouldn't endanger by a visit."

"That's a pity. At least here you've come to know quite a few people."

Magnus, studying the game, interrupted with a triumphant shout. "I've won!"

Anna clapped a hand over his mouth. "Do you want to be heard all over the hotel, silly boy!"

"Sorry," he apologised automatically, his mind still on his triumph. "Let's play Ludo now. You too, Margot. I want to beat you both."

"I expect you will," Margot said wearily, drawing a chair up to the little table. She had never liked board games, not even as a child, which was why the sets she had turned out were in remarkably good condition. But if this was a way of letting Magnus get rid of some of his surplus energy, she had to join in. On his improved diet and reduced boredom, he was full of life and fun. He made them both laugh many times, for he was a likeable, friendly child. Fortunately the night of Schultz's death, which she could not think of without a shudder, seemed wiped from his mind. Perhaps his terror at the time had kept it from registering.

When they had put him to bed, Margot spoke of it to Anna, who shook her head.

"I don't think it's that. So many traumatic things have happened to him that I believe he's developed the ability to close shutters on what he doesn't want to remember. Haven't you noticed? Whenever he speaks of his parents it's always as if they're still in his old home with all the rest of the family around them. One day when he's older he'll come to terms with it all, but as yet he doesn't know how."

It was Nils who ended the waiting for the go-ahead to the escape plan. He came to the hotel as he had done before. This time he was talking to two of the officers in the lobby when Anna saw him. He looked across at her and smiled.

"Excuse me, gentlemen," he said, "but I can see *Fröken* Larsen is here. I want to have a word with her."

They continued on their way out and he went with her into the room where they had talked previously.

"I hadn't expected to see you again," she admitted warily as they sat down.

"Whyever not?" he queried. "Our friendship is still intact, isn't it? Even though other things might have changed?"

"Yes!" she exclaimed on a rush of relief that took her by surprise, making her realise how much she had been inwardly brooding over the rift between them. "I wouldn't want it to be any other way."

He grinned. "That's it then. Friends."

"Always were and always will be," she said, smiling.

His gaze lingered fondly on her for a matter of seconds before he gave the reason for his visit. "I'm here to help you get the boy away."

With a slight sense of shock she thought how fate had contrived to bring them together once again as had happened so often in the past. Nils had been woven like a thread through almost her entire life. "How is it to be done?" she questioned.

In a businesslike manner he told her the escape plan for Magnus. She was intrigued by the ingenuity and careful thought that Rolf and others had given to the

196

timing and every other tiny detail. Nothing had been overlooked.

"Just follow everything as Rolf has directed," Nils concluded, "and all should go well. I'll soon be off to Sweden myself and would have taken the boy with me if it had been possible. But I have to travel officially on the Germans' behalf in an attempt to gain food imports from the Swedish government." He chuckled quietly. "There's not a chance of it, of course. The Swedes willingly send powered soup and milk for our schoolchildren, but they'll not supply the troops."

"So why are you making a journey you know to be pointless?"

Nils grinned widely. "It suits me to go along with it. I've a little trip of my own to make at the same time."

She took a calculated guess. "Is it to London by that route to which the Swedes turn a blind eye?"

He was surprised. "How did you know about that? Even in the Resistance it's not generally known."

"Karl told me when I was in Bergen. There was an air raid warning and when nothing happened he thought one of those planes might have been slightly off course."

"Well, I wasn't at the controls that time, because I've never met anti-aircraft fire or a German plane yet, but then I've only made a couple of flights to London."

"But you only flew small civilian planes before the war."

"It was arranged in London by the SOE that I should have a short, intensive flying course with the RAF as I had a licence already. It was in case of any emergency. Karl has taken the same course. He takes over the controls whenever he flies to England."

"I didn't know."

"Perhaps we shall meet in Oslo next time, Anna. I've an office there for my food supply business. Was there anything you wanted to ask me about the escape plan for Magnus?"

He left soon afterwards, having answered a couple of questions she had put to him about it all. But before going he had hugged her to him and kissed her on the brow before releasing her with a cheerful farewell. Yet there had been enough possessive tenderness in that brief contact, even if he had not intended to show it, that had told her he still considered her to be his own.

If he hadn't, she thought more wisely than before, it would have been entirely out of character. She knew him of old and should have remembered that he was the type of man who would go on fighting for what he believed in even when the cause was lost. Only time would settle everything.

When Anna explained the plan to Magnus, his reaction was that of any healthy child. "Why does it mean going to hospital? I'm not ill!"

"Of course you're not, but ultimately it's the best way to get you out of Alesund. Now I've been over the first stage of it all again, and you must remember it. You've got crayons and drawing paper in the storeroom. Make yourself a Norwegian flag and I'll find a stick for it. Then you'll be ready for the great day tomorrow."

"It won't be like it used to be," he said wistfully. "On one Seventeenth of May I walked in the procession of children past the King at the Palace. There were hundreds of us. And races and entertainment afterwards. I won a prize."

Anna could see it all in her mind's eye. Until the invasion and the banning of the country's Constitutional Day by the Germans, Oslo had been a sea of flags and children and youthful brass bands, a pattern repeated all over the country, even in the smallest hamlet.

Yet every year of the Occupation, either privately or with a little burst of open defiance against the Germans, a few children all over the country had celebrated with a procession of their own, remembering the fun and excitement of the day in the past. If they were seen, the Germans always dispersed them, but never with any violence and often with good humour if the soldiers had children of their own. Tomorrow in a boldly orchestrated step Magnus was to take part.

In the morning when all the Germans had gone from the hotel, Greta and Margot were on the alert to make sure none of the staff ventured anywhere near the staff hall where Anna waited tensely with Magnus. He was pleased with his flag, which had been fastened with drawing-pins to the stick, and waved it now and again. Edith was keeping to the kitchen for her own sake as Anna had requested and Emil was on an errand.

At the stroke of eleven o'clock Anna opened the door. She could see the children pouring out of a house at the end of the street. As they set off, waving their flags, the young boy in the lead blowing a toy trumpet, several other children darted out of their homes or from walking past to run and join in. Passers-by were stopping to clap the little procession, several little girls at the end no more than four or five years old, too young at the last pre-war celebration to remember it.

As the head of the procession drew level, Anna held Magnus back for a matter of seconds and then gave him a little push. "Now!"

He darted forward and blended in with the rest of the children. Anna watched him go. He was wild with excitement to be out of doors and with some boys of his own age. Nils would have seen him come out of the staff doorway and know which of them he had to take by the hand and lead away at the right moment.

Anna watched anxiously. For once there did not seem to be any Germans about and she did not want to lose sight of Magnus before he was in Nils's safe care. Parents were following their children, giving their support and ready to protect their offspring if the need arose. Anna was filled with admiration for them. This was one small act of resistance that would never be recorded, but it was no less courageous for that.

She hurried to catch them up, for already Magnus had disappeared from view as the head of the procession turned into the next street. The children were being applauded every step of the way, the discordant trumpet meeting approving laughter.

Suddenly a large open army car screeched to a halt, two high-ranking officers seated in the back. One of them, a *generalleutnant*, sprang to his feet. "Stop those children!" he roared.

The children, not understanding German, were paying no attention, continuing happily on their way. A *leutnant*, sitting beside the driver, had sprung out and he ran across the street to throw out his arms in front of the children.

"Halt!" he yelled in Norwegian. "Throw down your flags!"

The trumpet wailed into silence as the procession came to a stumbling halt. Parents rushed forward to get their children, but the officer bellowed again. "Stay where you are!"

Some of the younger ones had burst into tears, frightened by being shouted at, and rushed to their mothers. The older children remained at a standstill. Having been taught to respect their national flag, none of them wanted to throw it to the ground. Although Magnus had been warned that the procession was likely to be checked and there was no need for fear, his expression was one of sheer terror and he was keeping the same paralysed grip on his flag as he had on the kitchen bread-knife. Anna bit deep into her lip in her anxiety that he might shriek out in spite of all her assurance.

People watched in contemptuous silence as the officer went along the line of children, snatching the flags and ribboned favours from them. The trumpet-player and two others in scarlet caps had those snatched off as well. Magnus's flag had to be jerked twice to release it and then with a force that must have left splinters in his hand, but to Anna's intense relief the officer paid him no attention and Magnus remained silent.

By now soldiers had come running up, rifles ready in their hands, having been attracted by the sight of people gathered together. The officer handed his spoils to one of them. "Destroy these!"

As people were dispersed and parents reclaimed their children, he returned to salute his superior officers and take his seat in the car again. He was uncomfortably aware that those stubborn Norwegians had been mocking him in their silence that the Third Reich should be brought down to crushing the play of children. Damn them and their paperclips and scarlet caps! And their thousand ways from small irritations to devastating sabotage that showed, even after four punishing years of occupation, they still refused to accept that their nation was conquered!

Anna took her time strolling back to the hotel. It helped to ebb the tension that had been high in her until she had seen Nils take Magnus into his charge as if he were the boy's father and lead him off down the street. It had been a splendid way to transfer Magnus out of the hotel and all under the noses of the Germans. Yet it was no time for being satisfied. There would be far more dangerous moments ahead.

Chapter Eighteen

Anna applied for a travel pass at the local German department. Her leaving Alesund was above board as far as they were concerned, several officers at the hotel believing that grief over Klaus Schultz had accelerated her move.

She was putting the pass into her handbag as she came away from the building when Alf caught her up and fell into step at her side.

"Great news!" he said, keeping his voice low. "We've just had a special communiqué. Allied forces made a landing on the beaches of Normandy early this morning! And Free Royal Norwegian fighter squadrons are taking part!"

"It's come at last!" Her face was radiant.

He parted from her and she hurried back to the hotel to pass on the news to Greta and Margot.

That evening it was easy to see that there was plenty of discussion going on between the officers, but their attitude was confident, showing that they believed the attack would be driven back into the sea.

While they were talking the next stage of the escape plan for Magnus took place. Greta's doctor, a pleasant, grey-haired man, came into the hotel, carrying his medical bag, and spoke to Anna at the reception desk.

"Hello, Anna," he said in his deep, booming voice, which could be overheard by everyone. He had known her from the day she had helped him when one of the part-time cleaners had been taken ill on the premises.

"Good-evening, Doctor Svensen," she replied, sounding surprised for the benefit of those able to overhear everything. "Is Fru Sande expecting you?"

"No, it's you I've come to see. Don't ask me to sit down anywhere, because I'm on my way to a house-call and, although it isn't a life or death matter, I don't want to delay too long. I've heard that you're leaving soon for Oslo."

"That's right. At the end of the week."

"I've a great favour to ask."

"What is it?"

"I've a young patient whom I'm concerned about. He's only ten and physically fit, but he lost his parents in tragic circumstances. His reaction in shock was to stop talking. Nobody can get a word out of him, and yet in every other respect he's a perfectly normal child."

"Isn't that very unusual?" Anna asked, playing along with the doctor's imaginative tale in which some truth had been woven.

"It is in an over-prolonged silence. I've done what I could and now I want to send him to a specialist at Oslo Hospital. I can't take him myself, or spare my nurse, and the child has no relatives. Could I prevail on you to do this for me? I know it's a great deal to ask, but I'd be most grateful."

"I'll be glad to help out."

"That's most kind of you. I have all the necessary papers and he can leave whenever it suits you. When could you come along to meet him? He's been staying at my house, because I'd hoped family life might have some effect, and my wife is good with children, but it's been to no avail."

"I'm free for a couple of hours tomorrow afternoon."

"Splendid. I'll be at my surgery, but my wife will be at home, and you can make the boy's acquaintance."

As the doctor moved away from the desk, an officer, who had been waiting, moved into the vacated place and regarded her with smiling sympathy. "I couldn't help overhearing. You've landed yourself with quite a task. It's a long journey to Oslo and you could have trouble all the way."

"I hope not, Major," she replied cheerfully, taking a message from one of the pigeon-holes and handing it to him. "But I'll be prepared for any emergency, you can be sure of that."

She was certain that her greatest difficulty would be keeping Magnus silent. A seemingly sudden return to speech on the way could undermine the whole escape plan.

This was confirmed by the doctor's wife when Anna arrived at the house as arranged. "Our teenage daughters have been playing games with him in which he must not answer any questions, but whether that will help, or not, I don't know. He was subdued when he came to us, being nervous with strangers, so although that soon wore off here it might keep him quiet on the journey."

Magnus was glad to see her and she gave him a hug. He had lots to tell her and was excited at the prospect of going on a fjord steamer and a train.

On the morning of Anna's departure, Edith and all the staff wished her well. Earlier, quite a few of the officers had done the same before they left for morning duties. Lastly, both Greta and Margot embraced her in turn.

"Don't forget what I said about your coming back here when we're liberated again," Greta urged.

Margot interrupted teasingly. "Don't expect that, Mother. Anna will probably end up reigning over the Grand Hotel in Oslo."

Anna laughed, thankful for a little humour to ease these final moments. "Whatever happens, Margot, I'll be back on your wedding day when Johan comes home again!"

On a deliberately light-hearted promise to be a bridesmaid, Anna left the hotel. Emil carried her suitcase to the harbour where she took it from him.

"Thanks for all you've done, Emil," she said as they shook hands.

"I'm saying the same to you, *Fröken*." He gave her a wave as he left.

It was a small steamer tied up at the quayside. Anna waited, her suitcase on the ground beside her, and watched anxiously for Magnus to appear with Doctor Svensen. A lot of soldiers in full kit were filing up the gangway. As it was a mild sunny day, many of them took up places at the ship's rails, relaxed and watching the shipping and the coming and going on the quayside, while others settled themselves on the deck.

As Anna scanned the scene herself, she saw Nils come out of the harbour-master's office and stand studying a paper in his hand. He would know she was there, but he was keeping far enough away to keep an eye on everything and make sure there was no hitch to her departure with the boy.

There was Magnus! He was trotting along at the doctor's side, looking down, with a book under his arm and wearing a blue ski-cap, its peak pulled low over his eyes. They had come safely through the check-point, but he looked cowed, keeping very close to the doctor's side and clutching his hand. Anna could tell that the sight of so many German uniforms everywhere had reduced him once more to his terror.

Doctor Svensen looked relieved to see Anna waiting. "Here's your young charge," he said with a smile. "He's been looking forward to seeing you again."

Magnus had already transferred his hold to Anna's hand, but still did not look up.

"He'll be fine," she said. "Thank you, doctor."

He stayed to watch her go on board, not permitted by a guard to help with her suitcase and a little one his wife had found for Magnus's few clothes. From another part of the quayside, Nils was also watching and saw her give the doctor a final little wave before taking the boy down below where they would be less conspicuous.

The saloon was a bleak place in which to sit with dark leather-upholstered bench seats fitted against the walls, port-holes letting in circles of sunshine. Two soldiers, their kit on the floor beside them, were already stretched out to sleep for most of the voyage, a third writing a letter. The only civilians there were two farmers, both in best suits, who looked as if they might be travelling to a funeral, their talk of crops and sheep.

Magnus sat in a corner seat, Anna between him and the other passengers in the saloon. Although he clutched his book, he did not open it, and the trembling of his whole body passed through their linked hands. Anna guessed that under the peak of his cap he was watching the Germans with his eyes full of fear. She talked quietly to him, but he scarcely seemed to hear. Soon the throbbing engine took on new life and the steamer moved away from the quayside.

Taking the book from Magnus, Anna read to him in a quiet voice and after a while he began to pay attention. The steamer did not stop anywhere along the great fjord, which was why it had been chosen. Yet when it drew near Molde Anna was unable to resist kneeling up on the seat to look out of a porthole. Magnus scrambled up to look out with her, their heads together.

With a sharp intake of breath, she saw Aunt Rosa's country house come into view, large and white and mellowed by time, its windows open to the sun as they had been in the past. She felt that if she could step ashore and run to it, her aunt would be there to welcome her. It was only a momentary illusion, instantly dispelled when a military car drew up and an officer got out and disappeared indoors.

She caught a glimpse of Molde, but Karl had warned her that the bombing had changed it greatly and she was prepared. After that neither she nor Magnus looked out again and it seemed a long time before the steamer arrived at its destination of Andalsnes.

It was exactly as she remembered it, the little town dominated by the high mountains. There would be a wait for the night train, but Rolf had given her the address of a safe house. When they reached it, the door opened before she had time to knock. It was Karl who swept her indoors and jubilantly swung her around in the spacious hall, his mouth on hers in a long and loving kiss.

"I thought we weren't meeting until Oslo," she gasped happily as he set her on her feet again.

"That was the original arrangement," he said, reaching out through the door to bring in the luggage and close it again, "but I decided to come here and travel back with you on the train." Setting his hands on his hips, his elbows jutting, he looked down at Magnus. "So you're going to be my travelling companion when we go into Sweden. You'll like it there. The shops have candy to sell and in the winter there's no black-out and the lights are on all the time. I'm Karl."

Under the peak of his cap Magnus saw that Karl had stooped to hold out a hand to shake his. Cautiously he looked up into a friendly, handsome face with twinkling grey eyes and a wide smile that encouraged confidence. Slowly he put out his own hand.

"I'm Magnus Jacobsen," he said. "Why isn't there a black-out in Sweden? And isn't there rationing?"

"Sweden is neutral. That means not being at war with anyone. Yes, there is rationing, but nothing like it is here. Everybody has enough to eat. You'll be able to go to school again and play football and ski and have friends, just as you used to here."

"Aren't there any Nazis in Sweden?"

"None to harm you. Mostly they're diplomats at the German Consulate. They have to behave themselves or else the Swedes would kick them out, just as we're going to do in Norway one day."

Unexpectedly Magnus laughed. He had not imagined that anyone could do that to Nazis. "Shall I be able to come home then?"

"Yes, nobody will ever deny you that right again."

It was a reassuring promise. Magnus took off his cap and went with his new friend and Anna to meet the two elderly sisters who lived in the house.

Shortly before it was time to go to the railway station Anna had a few minutes alone with Karl. "Are you able to tell me your route into Sweden?" she asked.

"No, but I promise you I'll get Magnus to safety."

"I know you will! Can you make sure he gets a good foster home with a Jewish family where he'll receive kindness and affection? I think it's the only way he's going to grow out of his present terrors."

"I'll explain his circumstances. The Swedish Red Cross will take care of him at first, and you can be sure that he'll be treated with compassion and understanding. They'll want Magnus to have the right home as much as you, Anna."

She nodded, satisfied. "It's a relief to know that. Are you flying to London afterwards? Was that why you were going to Sweden in the first place?"

"I am, but what made you guess that?"

"I might not have thought about it, if Nils hadn't mentioned that he would be going there soon and thought you never missed the chance to fly an aircraft yourself."

"I admit that's true." His arms enfolded her closely. "One day when the war is over and liberation comes, there'll be no more partings like this one. We'll have the rest of our lives together." He kissed her, gently at first, savouring the sweetness of her mouth, and then with increasing passion. She pressed her hands against the back of his head, not wanting their kiss to end or to let him go without fulfilling the yearning for each other that burned in them.

He continued to hold her close for as long as time allowed after their kiss was over, his cheek resting against hers. He had loved deeply once before and that had given him memories he would never forget. But he had fallen in love with this woman in the midst of war, which heightened every emotion, and no moment together was ever taken for granted. It would be the same in the future if they both survived, for it would be impossible for either of them ever to forget that once partings might have meant never seeing each other again. It was why Anna did not ask him how and where they would meet next. It was a matter of always hoping.

It was dark when Anna and Magnus waited for the train with other passengers. Karl was just behind them, but no look or word was exchanged and they appeared not to know each other. As the great locomotive hissed to a standstill, they had to hurry to the only two carriages for civilians at the rear of the train, the rest occupied by troops. As soon as Anna was on board, she saw there were no seats left, people already standing. It was going to be a long and uncomfortable journey of several hours before Oslo was reached.

She and Magnus sat on her suitcase in the aisle. Karl, who had a rucksack, used it as a back-rest as he sat on the floor beside her. Magnus had withdrawn into deep fear again as soon as he had seen that the platform was full of soldiers, and had clung limpet-like to her hand as their travelling passes were checked. He did not dare look up as the train left the station, although the blinds were down and nobody on the platform could have seen him. Tiny blue lights gave the only illumination.

Anna found the journey interminable. The train stopped at many stations, mostly for the disembarking of troops and for more to get on. Magnus slept with his head on her lap and she dozed now and again. Karl closed his eyes for a while, but awoke with everyone else as a German voice boomed down the length of the carriage.

"Inspection of papers! Put those blinds up!"

People stirred, some yawning, and a baby began crying as the blinds went up in turn, letting the early sunshine in. Two soldiers, one on either side, jostled those in the aisle as they thrust their way along. Karl's papers were checked and handed back to him.

Then it was Anna's turn. Fortunately Magnus was in a deep sleep and she had taken the precaution of drawing him on to her lap with his face resting against her neck. To her increasing concern, the soldier took his time reading every word of her and Magnus's papers, twice flicking back to the doctor's certificate. Finally he looked at her with a doubtful frown.

"It says that this child has to have special treatment in Oslo."

"That's right. As you have read, I volunteered to bring him with me."

"Is he dumb or something?"

"It's hoped that he will be cured."

"Sounds odd to me. Let me have a look at him."

"Please don't disturb him," she appealed. "He's tired out from the journey."

"Do as I say! Stand him on his feet!"

Anna gave Magnus a little shake to wake him and whispered in his ear. "A soldier just wants to speak to you, but don't say anything, even if he asks you a question." She was reiterating the warning that had been instilled in him, but did not know how he would react when sleepy. But there was no need for that warning. The boy's whole body had stiffened with terror and stopped his voice in his throat.

She guided him to his feet and he stood with his head bowed, his chin on his chest, staring with horror at the soldier's jackboots. He winced as his ski-cap was pulled from his head, his silky brown hair flopping forward over his forehead.

"What's your name, boy? Answer up, or it'll be the worse for you! Do you want a beating? Because that's what you'll get for defiance!"

Anna's fear for Magnus was akin to his own. "He can't answer you!" she cried out. "The doctor's certificate told you that!"

"It didn't say he was deaf too. Look up at me, boy!"

One of the men standing in the aisle, almost on top of Anna in the crush, had watched the whole incident sympathetically, as had others within view. "The child is ill. Anyone can see that."

Instantly the German swung up his arm and struck the man across the face, cutting his lip and making him reel back. "I want no interference here!"

At that moment there came a commotion just beyond the injured man and the other passengers pressed close to him.

"What's happening?" the German shouted, unable to

see what was taking place. People in seats were standing up and there was a lot of talk and activity going on. "Let me through!"

Impatiently he thrust the papers he had been holding back at Anna, before slinging off his rifle and using the butt of it to make a way for himself. Karl pushed Magnus back into Anna's arms and she was almost choked by the boy's arms clasping her tightly round her neck. The other soldier, who had caught up with his comrade in the inspection, followed in his wake as with shouts of pain and indignation people gave way to his rifle butt too.

"Whatever can it be, Karl?" Anna whispered after she had loosened Magnus's arms and told him to try to sleep again. Nobody was paying attention to them any more.

"A woman has fainted."

"How do you know that? You couldn't see?"

A smile touched the corners of his mouth as he turned his head to meet her eyes, his own amused. "No, but I knew ahead that might happen."

She released a long, slow breath, smiling to herself. So, nothing had been left to chance by the Resistance. One of their women had been primed to cause a diversion at any dangerous moment. A signal must have been passed. It had not been Karl and therefore, one of the men standing close by must have done it. Perhaps it was the man who had been struck across the face. It was unlikely she would ever know.

Although the Germans continued their inspection after the woman had allowed herself to recover consciousness, neither returned to question Magnus again.

As the train steamed into Oslo station, Karl stood behind her as they waited with the other passengers to get off. He took her hand and caressed it lovingly. Just for a matter of seconds, she leaned back against him in fond acknowledgement.

Anna and Magnus left the station together, but by the

time they reached the nearest tram-stop Karl caught them up. On the tram he took at quick look round, but although there were some Germans on board he could see nobody from the train. This time, when they took seats, he sat with Magnus in the window seat beside him, and Anna took a place next to one of the Germans. Other passengers on the tram were following the usual routine of preferring to stand instead of sitting beside the enemy.

At the next stop Anna got out and walked away. There had been no goodbyes said, no final hug for Magnus, but that was how it had been arranged. She could not even look back as the tram rattled on its way.

Chapter Nineteen

At the next stop Anna caught a tram going in the opposite direction to that which Karl and Magnus had taken. It was a relief to put down her suitcase, which had been getting heavier with every step, and she took a window seat. As the tram-driver clanged his bell, she settled back to gaze out at the passing streets that she had known since childhood and to look away when she passed Rosa's home on the faint chance of being seen and recognised.

It seemed to her that the blight of Nazism was particularly noticeable in this once bright and lively city. Scarlet banners with the swastika hung down on either side of the entrance to the *Storting*, where previously the now-exiled Government had conducted Norway's peaceful affairs. The enemy was patronising the open-air cafés and, passing the Grand Hotel, Anna caught a glimpse of the black uniforms of the dreaded SS, seated at the window corner table where Ibsen had once sipped his daily apertif.

At the head of the wide street the Royal Palace, now occupied by Quisling himself, stood on a rise at the heart of the city. In its simple, neo-classical style it was also a palace without encompassing walls to isolate it from everyday life in the city, for the King had always been a man of the people. His broadcasts from London continued to encourage and showed that he was still in close touch.

Anna alighted near the palace and set off down a

214

tree-lined street, looking out for the hotel that was her destination. Then she slowed her pace as she saw some military activity ahead. After another few steps she halted abruptly, seeing with dismay that people were being dragged out of the address that she had been seeking and were being pushed into a waiting army truck. Behind her there came a sudden rush of hurrying footsteps, and she looked round quickly to see a slim, attractive woman of about forty hurrying to catch her up.

"Don't go any farther, Anna!" the woman gasped urgently. "Come away now! Walk back with me."

"Who are you?" Anna asked cautiously. "How do you know my name?"

"I was the one who fainted on the train. For God's sake, do as I say! The hotelier is being arrested now!"

Anna looked back over her shoulder as she hurried away with the woman. A large man with his hands up was being shoved by rifles towards the truck. Then she did not dare watch any more, being powerless to to do anything to help.

"My name is Christina Jensen," the woman continued as they kept pace together. "I've followed you from the railway station."

"Thank you for what you did on the train," Anna said. "I hadn't known an emergency plan had been arranged."

"The boy's life was at stake. Yours, too, if the truth had come out. I'd intended meeting you at the hotel to avoid any risk."

Anna studied the woman out of the corner of her eye. Christina was tallish and in appearance she had the looks and air of a successful Oslo businesswoman in her neat, dark suit, green hat with a feather and her pre-war handbag, gloves and shoes of good leather. Her hair was chestnut and drawn smoothly back into a coil at the nape of her neck, her features very fine and, under arched brows, her eyes were greenish-grey. Although quite slim, she seemed strong and full of energy as if, when young, she had been a top athlete. It was difficult to imagine that she had ever fainted in her life. Yet her performance on the train must have been convincing.

"Where are we going?" Anna asked. "Apart from getting away from here?"

"I'm taking you to my gown shop on Storgaten."

"How long have you been in business?"

"Since my divorce some years ago. I started in a small way, but with good clothes. I built up a clientele until I was able to move into my present, more prestigious premises. After that I did my buying in Paris. Such lovely gowns! I employed a French *vendeuse*, who'd had experience in *haute couture*. She liked Oslo and lived in the apartment above the shop until she went back to France just before Germany invaded Poland. It wasn't that she thought the Germans would come here any more than the rest of us in Norway, but if there was to be a war she wanted to be home, and I would have felt the same. Now I employ only one seamstress and a part-time milliner, who will help out with the sewing." She broke off as they came to a tram-stop. "We'll wait here."

"What stock do you have? I thought it was virtually impossible to get fabrics or clothes of any kind."

"So it is. I never have anything new to sell these days. The work at the moment consists of repairing and remodelling women's own clothes, making a garment out of anything else they manage to get hold of. Sometimes it's cutting up something to make a coat for a child. Quite often in straitened circumstances my former customers – all so prosperous before the Occupation – bring their pre-war garments to sell back to me. That helps to keep trade ticking over, because otherwise I'd have nothing in the shop for sale."

216

Anna listened with interest. Aunt Rosa had often shopped at Christina's and would be remembered there. It was frustrating not to be able to ask for any news of her. Perhaps at some time she could get Christina talking about her customers and gather a grain or two of information.

"I remember your shop from when I lived in Oslo for a while."

"Do you? So you know Oslo well?"

"Like the back of my hand."

"That's good. Have you any idea what you should do now that you can no longer work at that hotel?"

Anna shook her head. "Everything has changed so quickly. In any other hotel, I'd be hampered by hours of duty in carrying out any sortie for the Resistance. Yet I must get employment soon. I can't risk the Germans pushing me into a factory for making uniforms or some such work. I must also find somewhere to live."

"I can help you with that now. You can have the *vendeuse*'s apartment for as long as you like. Here comes the tram!"

The shop in Storgaten was exactly as Anna remembered it, for she had never gone past without looking in. The elegant frontage consisted of one window and an inset entrance with a gilded cypher on the glass door. Having started out as being expensive and exclusive, there was still only one garment displayed for the view of passers-by, artistically draped even though it had been re-trimmed and was secondhand. Beside it was a stylish hat, which Christina told her had been steamed and re-blocked from one of her own.

Inside the shop the décor was pink and gold. There were a dozen newly furbished hats on stands and some men's ties arranged in a fan on a table.

"These ties are made from scraps of any suitable left-over material. We try to have a good stock for

217

Christmas, because then they're snapped up. I've even had Germans in buying them to send home."

As they were early at the shop, neither the seamstress nor the milliner had arrived. Anna saw the room where they worked, large windows giving plenty of light. Upstairs was the salon, the mirrors gilt-framed, its colours in harmony with the shop below. On the floor above was the apartment and Christina led the way up the stairs.

Anna could see that although the rooms were small there was everything she would need and it was pleasantly furnished. "Why haven't you a tenant here?" she asked. "The door in the hall could be locked against access to the shop and its other door has a flight down to a rear entrance."

"I'll show you why." Christina went to a cupboard in the narrow hallway. Opening it, she stooped down and raised the floor of it up on concealed hinges to reveal a ladder going down into the darkness.

"Wait until I've switched on the light and then follow me," Christina said as she sat down and swung her shapely legs into the aperture.

As the light went on, Anna descended the ladder to find herself in what had been one of the changing rooms for customers on the floor below. The walls were still lined with mirrors. A divan and a comfortable chair had been added, together with a shelf of books.

"What a perfect hiding place!" she exclaimed.

"It was easy to seal it off and it's quite impossible to detect from the salon itself. To date, ten people have remained hidden here when all the buildings in the street were being searched. Once there were three of them here together."

"It's an ideal apartment for me and I'm grateful to you for it."

"There's no need to be. The arrangement will suit me

as well. Whenever the enemy has made a house-search of these Storgaten buildings I've always been afraid the apartment would be commandeered by an officer to install his mistress in it. By the way, how are you at sewing?"

"Not good enough to join your seamstress," Anna replied regretfully.

"How about helping in the shop? It would give both of us a chance to get away on Home Front matters, leaving the other in charge. At the present time I have to rely on my milliner, who thinks I go off to play bridge or whatever else I tell her."

Anna hesitated. Aunt Rosa had so many clothes that it was unlikely she ever came into the shop these days. Any acquaintance from the past would be easy to dodge, for the shop bell would always alert her. "I'll work for you, Christina. Just for as long as the Resistance wants me to be in Oslo and that could be anything from a from a month to a year."

"Yes, of course. I'm so pleased you're going to be here. At the present time the local cell won't know where you are. I'll make sure that somebody is told today. Go and unpack now and make yourself at home. Tomorrow is Sunday, so come and spend the day with me."

As Anna had expected Christina had an elegant home. In the middle of the afternoon when they sat talking the door-bell rang. Christina went to answer it and returned with a healthy-looking young man with ruddy cheeks. Cheerfully, Christina introduced him to Anna.

"Meet your contact, Andreas Nordheim," she said before leaving them on their own together.

"Welcome to Oslo," Andreas said, shaking Anna's hand and then sitting down. "I hear that you had quite an adventurous time getting here. It was a relief to all of us that you escaped arrest with the hotelier and the others. He was one of our best men."

"Where were they taken?"

He looked grave and shook his head. "To the Gestapo headquarters in Mollegaten."

She shivered. "Have you lost many people?"

"I'm afraid so. Tell me, were you given any special instructions before you came?"

"No, it was expected that I'd receive them from the hotelier."

"Right. Then you'll be ready whenever we call on you. It might not be for a few weeks. We have a lot of tasks in hand, but people have already been allotted to them."

"Isn't there anything I can do in the meantime?"

"Only that which has become second nature to all of us in the Resistance. Keep your eyes and ears open for anything that's unusual or might be of interest to our cause."

It was not very satisfactory, but Anna had to accept it.

Chapter Twenty

Anna had been ten days at the shop before she wrote her first letter to Margot. She had waited until she could be sure that Greta had been informed personally through the Resistance of her friend's arrest. It was impossible to give any details of it in a letter, for it could be opened by the German censor, a spot check being made on mail as on almost everything else.

It made her guard her words and she made no mention of Christina's help or of seeing the arrests. She wrote that when she had found the hotel shut by the German authorities, she'd had to look for other work immediately and was helping in a shop. Next morning she took the letter downstairs to take it later to the nearest postbox. She was dusting the display stands when Christina arrived. One look at the woman's face was enough to tell her that something terrible had happened.

"Is it Karl?" she burst out frantically, all her colour draining away.

Christina shook her head quickly. "There's no news of him yet." She took Anna by the arms. "I have to tell you that your friends at the Alesund hotel, Greta and Margot Sande, have been arrested, as well as several of the local Resistance group there."

Anna uttered a desolate cry. "No!"

Christina led Anna into her office. "Sit down in here. The two sewing-room women will be arriving at any minute and you don't want them to see you in this shocked state."

Anna sank down into a chair. "How did it happen? And why?" she stammered.

Christina perched her weight on the edge of her desk. "I don't know that either," she said sympathetically. "I'm afraid it looks as if the somebody must have talked under Gestapo pressure."

"Don't you mean torture?" Anna said bitterly.

"Yes, I do," Christina admitted. "It must have been bad, because Andreas told me the hotelier was the last man ever expected to give way, no matter what was done to him."

Anna groaned despairingly. "Aren't those Nazis ever going to halt their barbarism!"

"No, they're not," Christina answered wearily on a sigh. Getting up, she patted Anna on the shoulder as she went past to answer the outside bell and admit her two employees. After giving Anna some time to recover in private, Christina returned to find her on her feet and tearing up a letter that had been put ready to post.

"I hope the Resistance won't be distrustful of me after what has happened," Anna said in a drained voice.

"But you've had nothing to do with it. They know how you saved Magnus. Surely that's proof enough of your integrity."

Anna's eyes were dark blue depths of unhappiness. "But we know that sometimes an infiltrator is allowed to get away with something by the Germans to give false assurance to the Resistance. Perhaps that is what the Oslo group are thinking about me already."

"Why on earth should they be suspicious in your case? There's no reason."

"But doesn't it strike you as odd that hotel arrests should take place after I've left Alesund and then again just before

I arrive at the next one? It's as if I were being protected from involvement!"

"It was chance and nothing more. Stop tormenting yourself! You've received dreadful news about your friends and you're still in shock. Later you'll think more logically. Take the day off. Go for a walk or rest for a while. Anything you like. After all, you're only here to have cover against German questioning. and you're a free agent, able to come and go as you like. I'm not even paying you a wage."

"Neither are you charging me rent. That makes us even." The tinkling of the shop-bell just then announced the arrival of a customer. "I'll go, Christina."

Anna left the office and Christina heard her greet the new arrival. There was a slight quiver to her voice, but a complete stranger would not notice it.

The days went by, warm and full of sunshine for many hours every day and remaining light at night. Anna concentrated on her shop work and it was quite a busy time. Women brought in winter coats that showed signs of wear and these were turned whenever possible, making them look new. Wider pads in the shoulders in military style followed fashion, which seemed to pass along an invisible grapevine even in wartime, taking no heed of international barriers. Anna often thought to herself that the style was about the same as that followed by women in Britain before she left and probably anywhere else where it was possible.

Sometimes a woman brought in one of her husband's suits to be made into a jacket and skirt for herself, the more elegant resulting from dinner wear or tails. Anna was reminded of Scarlet O'Hara many times when curtains were turned into skirts and blouses. Once a blue and white checked tablecloth made a smart summer jacket.

Anna never went down Karl Johan Gate if she could

avoid it, not wanting to risk being seen by her aunt from a window, and she kept a sharp look-out wherever she was in the city. Rosa had always been one for getting out and about, meeting friends, taking walks in the park and sipping coffee at one of the outdoor cafés. There was no reason to suppose that even a war would have changed the pattern of her ways, even though her enjoyment of shopping would have been curtailed by circumstances.

Yet it was in Karl Johan Gate when Anna had been making an important delivery on Christina's behalf, unable to reach the address by any other route, when a woman's voice called out shrilly to her. It was just after she had passed her aunt's home without looking in its direction.

"*Fröken* Marlow! Stop!"

In horror at being addressed by her own name within earshot of everybody going by, a German or two among them, she spun round in alarm to see her aunt's house-keeper running breathlessly towards her.

Anna reacted swiftly. "Frida!" she exclaimed with pleasure, throwing her arms around the woman. "How good to see you! I'm just back in town."

Frida thrust herself away. "Don't try to softsoap me! Why haven't you called on Fru Johansen? She's very upset!" Her voice was high-pitched in her outrage, the bright spots of colour in her cheeks as much from anger as from the exertion of hurrying.

"Just give me a chance to explain." Anna was aware that several people were glancing curiously in their direction. "I've wanted to visit her."

"You've chosen a very strange way to show it," Frida snapped back angrily. "Never a look or wave whenever you went by."

"Please keep your voice down," Anna implored in a whisper. "Do you want the whole street to hear what you're saying? I'm here in Oslo secretly. Surely you can understand why?"

"I understand all right." Frida wagged her head knowingly from side to side. "You didn't want your aunt to find out that you couldn't stay away from that young man."

Incredulously Anna grasped what might be forthcoming, but they could not stand talking. "Come along, Frida. We must keep on the move or else some German will shove us on. We'll go as far as the National Theatre and then we'll go our separate ways. I'll take your arm." She took it before there could be any argument about it, but Frida hung back.

"You're going in the wrong direction away from the apartment. Aren't you coming back there with me?"

"I can't. We have to talk about it. Now tell me which young man you mean."

"Don't pretend that you don't know," Frida declared, allowing herself to walk on and subduing her tones, although she was no less angry. "Nils, of course. He was the only one you ever had eyes for! He knew how your aunt opposed a marriage between you, and so he persuaded you to return to Norway without her knowledge. After all, you'd lost your father – my sincere condolences there, of course – and there was nobody to stop you doing anything you wanted. Although Great Britain was already at war, you must have come back to Norway on a neutral country's ship just before the invasion."

"You really have been putting two and two together, haven't you?"

"That's not all. I know it's Nils, who's keeping you away from your aunt. He's told you not to visit her and you've taken notice of him, which has hurt her deeply. I know your move to Oslo must be recent, or else Fru Johansen or myself would have spotted you long ago.

225

Your aunt said that one day you were even wearing the *kofte* I knitted you. Sooner or later, I'd have picked that out in any crowd."

"So I've been found out," Anna said with apparent guilelessness, taking advantage of Frida's assumption as to why she had returned to Norway.

"I'll remind you that your aunt is no fool and neither am I." This time Frida nodded in a self-congratulatory manner. "How you thought you could get away with it, I don't know. Where is the young man? Are you meeting him somewhere?" She looked about sharply as they walked along, like a hen ready to peck an enemy.

"No, I'm not."

"It's just as well. I'd have given him a piece of my mind. I remember him as a boy, always ordering the other children about and they obeyed like sheep. You were one of them. Then every time he walked into your aunt's country house, even when he was young, and later when he came to the Oslo apartment, he always made himself at home as if he owned the place, airing his political views that your aunt opposed, and knowing better than anybody else."

"Frida! Stop it! You're being spiteful and vindictive! All because you and Rosa had somebody else in mind for me. I liked him, but I'd always loved Nils."

"So you're still doting on him! Then I'll say no more, except to ask you straight out if you're going to continue to slight your aunt, or are you coming back with me?" They had reached the National Theatre and slowed their pace to a standstill.

"I can't see her yet. You'd do her and me the greatest favour possible if you'd forget you have seen me. Let my aunt think she was mistaken and you followed a stranger who looked a little like me. I'll not use this street again, whatever the circumstances, and arrange to leave Oslo as quickly as possible."

"I'll do no such thing!" Frida expostulated angrily. "What's happened to you, Anna? Has Nils changed you so much?"

"I'm just the same. He's got nothing to do with my staying away."

"You always did defend him. I'm not telling your aunt anything but the truth."

Anna knew from past experience that Frida never made idle threats. "Then I'll ask you to give her a message. Tell her I can't visit her in the foreseeable future, but one day I'll explain everything. Say also that I still love her as I always did. Will you do that?"

"No, I won't. If she draws her own conclusions that you no longer care what happens to her, that's up to you."

"Why should anything happen to her?" Anna demanded anxiously. "Isn't she well?"

"She's not as you remember her and rarely goes out these days. The doctor comes to see her now and again. Then there's the danger of arrest too. When the Jewish family in the top apartment feared imminent transportation, they entrusted her with their valuables, some of religious significance. She has it all hidden in the apartment under the heavy bookcase. In the meantime we get enemy house-searches from time to time and if those possessions were discovered the Nazis would know the origin immediately. Surely you want to call on your aunt while you still have the chance? You wouldn't want to add to her misery in some dreadful camp by letting her believe that she no longer matters to you?"

"Stop it! This is emotional blackmail, Frida!"

"So now will you come and see her?"

Anna gave a reluctant nod. "I'll come."

There was a triumphant bounce in Frida's walk as they retraced their steps. She had missed Anna almost as much as her employer, and it would breathe new life into the home to have the girl around once again. At her side Anna was full of misgivings, uncertain of how her aunt would receive her. There had never been anything but harmony between them, but it sounded from Frida as if Rosa were deeply and irrevocably hurt. It was understandable in the light of the misinterpretation both women had put upon her staying away.

As the lift ascended to the floor of her aunt's apartment, Anna began to dread the meeting, for she could give no explanation to clear the air between them.

"We're here," Frida said when the lift stopped, as if hinting that Anna had probably forgotten everything in her supposed infatuation with Nils.

They entered the apartment and Frida went into the kitchen, letting Anna go alone into the drawing-room where her aunt awaited her. Rosa was standing with her back to the windows, making it difficult to see her expression, but she came forward at once and threw out her arms in welcome before Anna could speak.

"My dear child!" she cried joyfully. "You've come!"

They clung to each other and both shed tears, unable to speak at first. In spite of the high emotion of the moment, Anna was aware of the same lovely fragrance wafting about her aunt's bosomy embrace as it always had in the past. Releasing each other, they both laughed in shared relief, knowing that nothing had changed between them.

"How on earth can you get your favourite French perfume in these days?" Anna joked, wiping her wet eyes.

Rosa gave a little chuckle. "I still have a few drops left in the last bottle I bought before the Occupation and I save it for special occasions. So I dabbed on some to be at my best when I saw you crossing the street with Frida. I'll use the rest of it on the day the King comes home again!" Rosa was drying her eyes with a fine handkerchief trimmed with wide lace, and she waved it to demonstrate how she would welcome the royal return. They both giggled a little foolishly, which amused them all the more, and felt extraordinarily optimistic as if that day of rejoicing were not far distant, even though the odds were against it.

"You're as elegant as ever, Aunt," Anna said admiringly, standing back to look her aunt up and down. Rosa was a little thinner and she had aged, but her skin had not lost its bloom in spite of her sixty-odd years. Her make-up, although scant, emphasised her well-bred features, the arrogance of the nose with its delicate nostrils countered by the generosity of the mouth. Her china-blue eyes were as quick to sparkle with amusement as to swim with tears if she were touched to the heart as today. Ever a little larger than life, always dressing with flair to suit her exuberant personality, she was the same on this June afternoon as she had been all her life. Her pre-war Molyneux dress was coral georgette and flowed about her like a cloud, pearls in her ears and around her neck.

"I had to give up tinting my hair," Rosa said regretfully, patting it with a graceful hand. "My hairdresser couldn't get the gold colour any longer."

"I think the platinum look of it suits you wonderfully. In fact, you look marvellous altogether, as if you've come straight from Paris."

Having been used to compliments all her life, Rosa knew how to accept them graciously. "Thank you, my dear. All I do know about myself today is that I feel twenty years younger just because you're here again."

"I have worried about you," Anna said as they sat down on one of the silk damask sofas. "Are you managing financially?"

"It's not easy," Rosa admitted, "because, as you know, so many of my investments are overseas and nothing can come from there, and I've had to sell some jewellery, but all pieces that I never wore. But Frida and I manage very well. We live simply as everybody else does and, so far, no German officer has wanted to move in here, which I hope will last." She shook her head impatiently. "But I don't want to talk about myself. I want to hear all about you."

"I'll tell you as much as I can, Aunt," Anna said, looking around, "but give me a few moments to savour being home again. Nothing has changed, has it? Everything is how I've been remembering it."

"I believe it is."

Anna stood up and began to wander about the large and graciously proportioned room that was spread with a vast Persian rug, a treasure that vied with a rare collection of ivory as well as jade that her aunt and late uncle had bought on their diplomatic travels. Art Nouveau silver gleamed and on the walls were the paintings she had always loved. Three of them were early Munchs, which her uncle had bought at his wife's insistence when the artist had been young and penniless, and on the opposite wall there were four striking paintings by Astrup purchased about the same time, together with a Monet, a Seurat and Degas.

In an alcove by itself was a twelfth-century ikon of remarkable beauty and rarity, depicting the Virgin with the Christ-child on her lap, her robes of sapphire edged with a braid of crimson and amber. Although the artist had elongated her face there was a look of extraordinary tenderness and tranquility with the faintest hint of a smile in the lips as she held the playful fingers of the baby reaching for a tendril of her hair. As he gazed up at her, the golden nimbi about their heads seemed to suffuse them both in a bonding heightened by the darker hues that backed them like deep, forest shadows.

At some distant time in the past it had been housed in a carved oaken case with doors that closed over it. On the few occasions in Anna's childhood when it had been shut she had waited, holding her breath, for it to be opened. Then, as the little doors swung wide the ikon shone forth, glowing and dominating magnificently all else in the richly adorned room.

As a teenager with her mind full of love, Anna had learned that the priceless ikon was one of several valuable keepsakes Rosa had received from her German lover in halcyon days before the Great War. Her husband, a dull, self-important man according to Rosa, had been too wrapped up in diplomatic matters to suspect anything, his wife no more than a vivacious and beautiful social appendage, who was liked by everybody and could unwittingly bewitch people who were important to him. When he had first visited the Kaiser's yacht in Norwegian waters he had not known that when his wife stepped on board at his side, her eyes met those of the man whom she was to love for the rest of her life.

Anna knew that the ikon was the most treasured of all Rosa's possessions for reasons she had never disclosed, but it must have been something exceptional. He had given her the parure of diamonds and emeralds after his first declaration of love, and other beautiful jewels had followed moments precious to them. He had bought the gilt and blue enamelled clock, which had belonged to Marie Antoinette, at an auction during one of their secret weekends together.

The clock tinkled its melodious chimes as Anna came to the grand piano on which stood a collection of silver-framed photographs. She picked up one of the handsome German lover, Hans von Werner, with his deliciously wicked eyes and passionate mouth. He was in yachting attire and leaning on the rails of the Kaiser's yacht during one of the many summers when his Imperial relative cruised the Norwegian fjords. Hans was always invited to join the party of guests on board and after meeting Rosa he never refused.

"If Hans had not been killed on a French battlefield in the last war," Anna mused aloud. "I wonder what he would have thought of all that Hitler has done to his country and the rest of us."

Rosa answered from the sofa where she sat. "He would have been horrified. Honour and integrity and respect for the rules of war had been instilled in him from his cadet days. I've thought of him every time the soldiers come rampaging through the building searching for goodness knows what and spilling out the contents of drawers and cupboards. No end of damage has been done at different times."

"Has nothing ever been stolen?"

"I have missed a few little things easily slipped into a pocket, but the soldiers are forbidden to loot. My parure is with the rest of my valuable jewellery in the concealed safe, which they have never found."

"Shouldn't your ikon be in there too?"

"Then I couldn't look at it and relive my memories every day. I close its doors quickly whenever the Germans come and then it looks like an ordinary carved plaque, too dark to catch the eye and be of interest. Luckily the soldiers usually start their searches on the floor below, which gives me plenty of time. Naturally it goes into the safe whenever I go out, just in case they should come then."

Still standing by the grand piano Anna replaced the photograph. "Where are the photos of you and Uncle with the King and the late Queen Maud?" she asked, glancing over the rest that were arranged there. "The American president has gone too and those of the British Royal Family. Have you hidden them with the Jewish valuables?"

232

"Yes, I had to do that, or else the Germans would have smashed them up. Frida had no business telling you about my storing those belongings, because you'll start worrying about me and that's the last thing I want. But at least now, if she and I are taken ill or have to leave this place for some reason, you'll be able to make sure that the Jewish treasures are returned to their rightful owners."

As Anna sat down again on the sofa, Rosa studied her thoughtfully. "You've grown up, my dear, haven't you? I don't just mean because you're twenty-two now. You've seen something of life. Death, too, in these terrible times, quite apart from the loss of your father. Yet your looks have taken on a rare beauty as I always believed they would. Love can do that."

Anna smiled at her aunt's romantic turn of mind. "If that's the case, you must have been extra stunning during your time with Hans."

"I was," Rosa replied without the least conceit. "So how is Nils?"

"He's still in my life, but not as you suppose."

"Are you sure?"

Anna nodded. "There's somebody else."

"Yet Nils remains in the picture. I knew you'd never be free of him. That's why I opposed the relationship when I did, you being too young to know your own mind and he much older and experienced with women. More than that, I could see that he was really in love with you and such a possessive man could have trapped you forever. Am I right?"

"I'll not deny it. He and I both know our lives are linked and always will be. I don't know why it is, but we both recognise it. Yet there's no need for you to be concerned any longer, because we've channelled our relationship into friendship."

Rosa decided not to express her doubt. "So who's this new man?"

"Someone with whom I want to spend the rest of my life. I can't tell you his name yet, but I will one day."

"Is he in the Resistance with you?"

The unexpectedness of Rosa's perceptive question made Anna turn pale. "Whatever made you ask that?"

Rosa smiled. "I never believed a word of Frida's supposition that you had come back on a neutral ship and all that nonsense. You have a British passport and, since you couldn't have returned to Norway as a Norwegian national, it would have been impossible for you to leave England in time of war, unless on some secret matter. I don't know how you got here, and I'm not intending to ask, but I knew that not even Nils could have kept you from visiting me. Neither do I believe he would ever have done such a thing. He and I didn't much like each other, but that wouldn't have come into it."

"You've been as busy as Frida in working out everything about me," Anna said, raising her eyebrows in mock-surprise while giving nothing away. "Just let her keep to her theory, but think whatever you like yourself. All I can tell you is that I'm working at Christina's in Storgaten and have a tiny apartment on the top floor."

"Is that where you are? I haven't been in that shop since early in the Occupation. Couldn't you come and live here instead?"

"No, that's impossible. I may have to leave Oslo at any time and you mustn't worry, or make any enquiries at the shop, if I don't come to see you for a time."

Rosa looked anxious, but she nodded. "If that will help you, I'll do whatever you say."

"Is my birthday evening gown still in my room?"

"Everything is as you left it when you were here last. Why not go and see for yourself?"

In the bedroom Anna went across to slide back the door of the wardrobe. The gown hung there, tissue paper looped over the hook and covering it completely. She slipped the straps off the hanger and held the filmy, shaded peach chiffon against her in front of the full-length mirror. It had always reminded her of a Twenties dress with its petal skirt, a pearl sewn to every pointed tip, and was as lovely now as on the one and only time she had worn it.

Nils had been at that birthday party, having been taking part in ski-jumping events at Holmenkollen. It was when he had first realised that the child-girl he'd always had under his wing had grown up overnight. He would have had every dance with her if it had been possible. The following summer he had swept her off her feet. It had all happened in what might prove to be the last romantic era in history, now that world peace had been snatched away in the greatest conflict ever known. Yet the most powerful love of her life had burst forth gloriously out of the horrors of war.

She hung away the gown again. There were other clothes in the wardrobe that she had forgotten. A winter coat and a couple of skirts, even a dress with a schoolgirl-type collar and little buttons down the front. Had she really dressed like that?

She explored the rest of the room, finding some of her pre-war satin lingerie packed away for her in hand-embroidered linen sachets. There were silk stockings too. In the make-up drawer was a box of Côty face powder with a design of powder-puffs all over the lid and one of the *Tangee* lipsticks, which had always looked orange, but came out red on the lips. She put some on, remembering that she had bought it for sixpence in Woolworth's before coming to Norway on holiday. It was like delving into history, everything belonging to a time that had slipped away for ever.

Anna returned to the drawing-room and exclaimed over all the discoveries she had made in her room.

"Aren't you taking anything with you?" Rosa asked.

"No, I can't. I have to travel as lightly as possible and at the present time I have all I need. Do you have a dress that needs alteration at the shop? I could take it with me and then bring it back. A perfect excuse to visit you whenever I can."

"Do you have such a need for secrecy in all things?" Rosa asked anxiously.

"I'm afraid so. Make sure that Frida doesn't talk about my visit now or at any other time."

"I will, but you needn't worry. She has never been one to gossip. I'll emphasise that your being half English could get you arrested and she would never want that to happen."

As Anna left the building, she would have liked to look back and wave, knowing that Rosa would be at the window, but it would not have fitted in with a saleswoman taking a customer's garment back to the shop for alteration. She carried it over her arm, together with a tape-measure she had borrowed from Rosa to give credence to her visit.

There were no customers in the shop when Anna returned, but Christina came out of the office.

"You have a visitor waiting upstairs to see you," she said with a smile. "And Magnus is safe now in Sweden!"

Anna thrust the garment into Christina's hands and ran up the stairs. When she reached the apartment, she hurled herself into Karl's arms.

Chapter Twenty-One

Their first kisses were frenzied in their joyous reunion, she with her arms wrapped about his neck, he holding her so tightly that her feet left the floor. When Karl did set her down again, it was only to keep her within his embrace while she cupped the back of his neck in her hands.

"Well, after all that, hello," he said with a grin as she leaned back in his arms.

She gave a soft laugh. "I've never been so thankful to see anyone before in my whole life! Did all go well? Christina said that Magnus is safe."

"That's right. We had quite an eventful journey, but he's a courageous kid and never complained, not even when I shoved him under the false floor of a truck. Neither did he whimper when we were hiding in thorny undergrowth within a few feet of a German patrol going past. Now he's in just the kind of good foster home that you wanted for him."

"What a relief it is to hear that!"

He twisted his wrist around to look at his watch. "I've been waiting over two hours for you. At least it gave me a chance to check your security here and Christina told me about the hide-out under the cupboard. But now there are only a few minutes left for me to be with you."

"Is that all?" she exclaimed in disappointment.

He nodded regretfully. "I shouldn't have stayed this long, but I was desperate to see you. I'm not sure when

I can get to Oslo again, my darling. I only arrived back in town this morning. The local Resistance group told me what had happened to you and why you were working from here."

"I can't bear to think that I've missed time with you." She pressed her cheek against his shoulder, her eyes closed tightly as she struggled to come to terms with having him snatched away from her again after so brief a reunion. "Can't you stay a little while?"

"No. I'm leaving for the west coast right away. Others are waiting to travel with me."

"At least tell me how you found London faring under these new rocket attacks."

His expression was grave. "They come without warning by day and night. When the engine cuts out and they drop, there is devastation. Great craters are left and they cause a terrible loss of life."

"Is it as bad as that?" She was dismayed. "Christina hasn't a radio and the daily newspapers are full of Nazi propaganda that their new weapon is breaking England down. Not that I ever believed anything could. The Blitz proved that once and for all."

"You're right, but it's a terrifying weapon and people are war-worn just as they are here."

"Sometimes it seems forever since the war started," she sighed. "How did you get back into Norway from England?"

"I dropped by parachute into the Jotunheimen mountains. I floated down with a shipment of containers holding German uniforms for our sorties and emergency rations for those having to hide out in the heights. All I could think about was that I'd soon see you again." His eyes went to her mouth and his voice throbbed with desire. "I'd hoped for so much more when we two were together again."

"I, too!" she whispered.

238

They kissed again, fiercely and hungrily, while he caressed her lovingly. She scarcely knew how to let him go when he drew away from her, his hands sliding down her arms to her fingers, keeping contact until the last possible moment. He gave her a final look of love that almost made her cry out in anguish at his going. Then he went down the stairs to leave by way of the shop. She darted to her sitting-room window and watched him walk away down the street until he turned a corner and was out of sight.

She remained by the window for several minutes, holding to the sound of his voice, his strength and warmth, her whole body re-awakened by his nearness and loving hands. There had been no time to tell him of her belief that the Resistance had lost faith in her, of meeting her aunt again, or even of Greta's and Margot's arrest.

Finally she forced herself to stir and went to explain to Christina about the skirt that had been thrust into her hands.

When Anna visited Rosa again she spent longer with her, Christina being generous in the matter of her being away from the shop. Frida had overcome her initial resentment and made as much fuss of Anna as in the past.

"Come back as soon as you can," Rosa said when Anna left again. This time Anna carried away an evening gown that Rosa wanted to sell and she made sure that part of it protruded from the carrier-bag. It was not that she thought anyone would be curious, but it had become second nature to be cautious in all that she did.

On one of these visits Anna noticed the little doors were closed over the ikon. "Why isn't the *Virgin of Smiles* on view, Aunt?" she asked, missing its rich glow.

Rosa went to it at once and opened it up. "There was a German raid next door this morning and I was nervous that they might come here too." She stood gazing at it. "I could lose all else I possess, but never this."

Anna moved across to put an arm about her aunt's waist as they looked at the ikon together. "I know it's precious to you for many reasons."

"That is true, my dear. Spritually it is of great importance to me. I find it both inspirational and a comfort. It strengthened me when I was on the brink of suicide."

"You've never mentioned that before," Anna said gently in surprise. It was hard to imagine this woman of forceful character ever giving way to despair.

"Maybe it's time I told you then, my dear, especially in these days of uncertainty. Hans had inherited it from his Russian grandmother and it was to be handed down through his children and their descendants."

Anna understood. "You were expecting his child."

"I miscarried when news of his being killed reached me. He was one of the first casualties of the Great War."

"Why didn't you get a divorce from Uncle long before?"

Rosa's lips twisted ruefully as she turned away from the ikon to face her niece. "Divorce wasn't easy in those days. In any case, Hans was married too. It was an arranged marriage and a tragedy, because his wife had become a housebound invalid. He couldn't leave her any more than I could have destroyed your uncle's career with scandal. That's how it was before the Great War."

"I'm so sorry."

"Life was bleak for a long time after that," Rosa admitted as they strolled across to chairs by one of the windows. "But then one day I received that letter from your father asking me to take care of you and I began to live again."

Anna smiled as they sat down opposite each other. "I caused a big upheaval in your life."

"It was exactly what I needed!" Rosa paused for a moment. "Would it surprise you if I said I would like the ikon to be returned to Russia one day?"

Anna considered. "No. It's where it belongs."

"If the Hermitage is still standing when this terrible war is over, I should like it to be there. I remember Leningrad as St. Petersburg and once I danced at a ball at the Winter Palace. The Tsar and Tsarina were present. All that has gone forever and poor Russia must have lost many wonderful treasures during the German onslaught, but at least the ikon will have been saved."

"I promise to do everything I can to carry out your wishes."

Rosa sighed with satisfaction. "I knew I could rely on you."

The summer rolled on. In the shop Anna took over whenever Christina went out on some secret business that she never disclosed. Daily Anna became more exasperated that no call was made on herself.

"Be patient," Christina advised. "I'm sure that, sooner or later, you'll be contacted. I've been questioned about you several times."

It was a particularly hot day in late August when Anna met Nils again. She had just left the shop when she came face to face with him. With his hair sun-bleached to a lighter shade and his features tanned, he looked much the same as he had done in summers long since gone. She was overwhelmingly happy to see him and guessed he had returned to Norway by the same means as Karl.

"I was on my way to find you!" he exclaimed, equally pleased. "I heard on the grapevine that you were working in a dress-shop here in Storgaten. Have you been given the afternoon off?"

"I can take time when things are slack." Automatically

they began walking along together in case they should be moved on. She had no hope that he would be in Oslo for any length of time. "This is a flying visit, I suppose."

He had taken hold of her hand. "No, I expect to be here for a while. My office is in Prinsens Gate. I'll show you it sometime. Where were you going now?"

"To see Aunt Rosa. We met up again."

He frowned and thrust out his lower lip doubtfully. "You know that it was a dangerous thing to do?"

"You don't have to tell me, but it came about quite accidently. The housekeeper came running after me in the street."

He shrugged. "Well, it couldn't be helped then. In a way it was to be expected. Oslo is too small a city not to meet anybody one knows here before long. Is it OK if I come with you to see Aunt Rosa again?"

Anna hesitated. "But you never really liked her."

"You're wrong. The boot was on the other foot. She was the one who never favoured me. But surely after all this time she won't be holding anything against me?" With his eyes twinkling mischievously, he held up one hand as if taking an oath. "I promise not to argue politics with her."

"How could you anyway?" Anna said bluntly, refusing to be amused on such a topic. "There's only one regime these days."

"I know," he agreed soberly, leaning his head towards her. "But one day things will be better than ever they were before this war started."

"Are you going to be instrumental in that?" She threw him a smile. "You were planning on standing at the next election when the war came."

They were strolling along where they could not be overheard, but they continued to keep their voices low as a precaution. His brow creased determinedly. "New blood will be needed. It's needed now! The present government in exile with the King will be totally out of touch with everything after the war is over. I believe I have a good future ahead of me. Quisling is a fool. The sooner he's kicked out, the better. He thought Hitler would make him master of Norway and he's still the underdog."

"You used to boast that you'd be a government leader one day," Anna reminded him.

He raised his eyebrows and laughed. "So I shall be! All wrongs will be put to rights. Don't ever doubt it, Anna! I remember how I used to enjoy saying I was a future prime minister to your aunt just to rattle her."

"She thought your views too extreme and, looking back now, I realise they were. No wonder she disapproved of you." Anna shook her head in mock reproof.

"Ah, I've sobered down now and know exactly the path our country should follow when peace comes."

"I'm relieved to hear it. So remember your promise and keep to ordinary conversation with Aunt Rosa. I won't have her upset. She has enough to put up with as it is."

They entered the apartment building and went up the wide marble stairs, the lift being stationary through an electricity cut.

Rosa herself opened the door. "Anna, dear! I wondered if you would come today." If she was disappointed to see Nils as well, she was too polite to show it. "This is a surprise, Nils. It's a long time since we last met. How are you?"

They shook hands. "Very well, Fru Johansen. It's a pleasure to see you again."

"Come in."

"Where's Frida?" Anna asked.

"She heard there were early apples on sale at the market. I'm sure they'll be small and sour, but she has gone to line up for some."

Nils made an offer. "I think I could get you a little sugar on the Black Market."

Rosa's face seemed to close up. "Thank you, Nils, but we'll manage," she said, even though they all knew sugar had vanished from the shops long ago.

Anna wished her aunt had not rebuffed Nils's goodwill gesture so quickly, for it had been well-intended. Yet it had always been the same between them.

Fortunately Nils had not taken offence and stood looking admiringly around the room. "I've never forgotten your lovely home here, Fru Johansen. But shouldn't you hide some of these splendid things away for safe-keeping?"

Rosa went to open the ikon's doors, which she had closed before going to see who was calling on her. "Anna said the same thing to me, but so far I've been lucky and I couldn't live without looking at my ikon every day."

As she set wide the little doors, it was like releasing a jewel's radiance into the room. Nils was gripped by the sight of it. "That's beautiful! It must be priceless! Was it always there?"

Rosa nodded. "It's not surprising that you don't remember it," she said drily. "As I recall, you only had eyes for Anna when you were here."

He agreed good-humouredly. "That's right. It's a wonder I noticed it now with Anna here in the room." He looked across at her with a grin.

"Sit down," Anna said with mock sternness. "The only sensible thing you've said so far was that Aunt Rosa should hide away some of her treasures."

Rosa intervened when she saw he was about to settle his rangy frame into one of her most delicate chairs. "Why not sit on the sofa, Nils? You'd be more comfortable."

He guessed the reason. She was still getting at him, but he was determined to keep the peace. Sitting down on the sofa next to Anna, he took up the subject of security again. "I've heard that Field-Marshal Goering is collecting valuable paintings from every occupied country. Suppose some German officer should come in here one day and realise what you have on your walls? Even your ikon would be at risk, and it could be on its way to Berlin in no time at all."

Anna added to his expression of concern. "I have to agree with Nils. It has been worrying me, because I know what its loss would mean to you."

Rosa had looked distressed at such a prospect, but she shook her head determinedly. Had Anna been on her own, she might have voiced her private conviction that the ikon was linked in some strange way to her own life's span. Perhaps Hans had foreseen his own demise when he had given it to her, for all the world had known that Europe was on the brink of war. In her own heart their love for each other had bridged death. She had no fear of it at all.

"Neither of you will change my mind. Let us talk of something else. Tell me about your parents, Nils. Are they still in Trondheim?"

After that the conversation flowed easily. When Frida returned she had managed to get six apples, which were exactly as Rosa had expected them to be, but she was triumphant, having obtained two pears at the same time, which she thought might help to sweeten the apples when cooked. She was very cool towards Nils and disappeared quickly into the kitchen. Nils and Anna left soon afterwards.

"I've an idea," Nils said thoughtfully as they strolled along. "I don't know if I'll be able to arrange it, but I'm seeing a high-ranking officer tomorrow, who has charge of your aunt's district and is responsible for inspection raids. He was a fellow competitor on the German ski-jumping team in the same Winter Olympics in which I took part. We get on well and often have a drink together. I suppose sportsmen always have a mutual respect for each other, whatever the political situation. I believe that if I asked him to make sure your aunt was left in peace, he would oblige me."

Anna came to a standstill, her expression incredulous. "Would he trust you that much?"

Nils's eyes danced. "I've dealt out enough false information with a fraction of truth in it to convince the Germans, wherever I go, that they need never doubt me. I'd say Fru Johansen was my aunt, which she wouldn't like, and that she and Frida are too old to be engaged in anything subversive. I know your aunt would resent being under any obligation to me, and in this case I think you should make the decision on her behalf."

"Yes! Please try! Frida told me that one day Aunt Rosa was pushed to the floor and kicked when she protested about something during a house-search, although she herself has never told me. I'd be so relieved to know that she would be left undisturbed."

"If I'm successful, I'll confess to her after the war. Do you think she might agree then to burying the hatchet?"

"I think there would be a good chance," Anna said jokingly, "but you'll have to prove yourself an exemplary government leader to finally convince her."

"Watch me!" he answered in the same tone.

They spent the rest of the day together. He had plenty of food coupons and took her out to a meal. When she asked him if he purchased them on the Black Market, he shook his head and said that in his work for the Germans plenty of coupons came his way. It always made her uncomfortable to eat food provided by an enemy source, but otherwise she enjoyed her day with him.

When he took her back to her apartment she did not

invite him in and he did not ask. He kissed her lightly and quickly.

"I'll see you in a couple of days."

She could tell he was hoping to mend matters between them until they were back on their previous footing, but would not risk rushing her. Neither did he have any intention of giving her up.

Before the two days were past Nils called in to see her. "It's all arranged. Your aunt shouldn't have any more inspection raids on her home."

Anna was full of gratitude. "It was so good of you to do that for her."

He looked at her seriously. "I didn't do it for her. It was to give you peace of mind." Then he grinned widely and held up the bottle he was carrying. "Find a couple of glasses and we'll celebrate."

It was German wine.

Chapter Twenty-Two

Christina passed on the message to Anna that the Oslo Resistance group wanted to see her at last. Two of them came into the shop on the pretext of buying ties and went with Anna up to her apartment. They were tallish men, nothing remarkable about them, except perhaps their sharply observant eyes. She could tell they were summing her up as they seated themselves in her little sitting-room.

"We know you've been wondering why you haven't been contacted before now," the slightly older one said, his name Edvin. "Christina told us why you thought it was, but nothing was being held against you. We've been keeping you on ice for the right assignment. You did some good work in Alesund."

"Do you know why my friends at the hotel were arrested?" she asked quickly.

Edvin glanced at his companion, who had called himself Arne. "I believe you know more about that than I."

"I'm afraid I do," Arne said, rubbing his chin in his reluctance to pass on bad news. "Apparently a watch was set on Emil's comings and goings. Then he was caught when he was delivering a message. The result was that Greta and Margot were rounded up with him as well as others and taken away."

Anna gave a nod and spoke grimly. "I hope you have

the right sortie for me now. I want to do something worthwhile on their behalf."

"You're getting the chance, Anna. We know from Karl that you're a trained saboteur." Without preamble, Edvin proceeded to outline a highly dangerous task. "The Germans have a large airfield at Gardermoen, just about sixty English miles north of Oslo. In ten days time an important armament train will be going through on its way north from Oslo with several wagons of bombs and ammunition for the *Luftwaffe* there. You will take an earlier train to Jessheim, which is the nearest railway station to the airfield." He produced a map from his pocket and held it forward for her to see. "You will meet Karl there—"

"Karl?" she interrupted. "But when I saw him last, he was off to the west coast."

"He didn't know that he'd complete his sortie there as soon as he did." He pointed to the map again. "As I was saying, Karl will be waiting for you in this café at the fork of two roads." His finger prodded an inked cross. "He'll use the name of Steffen Jansen. Your reason for being in Jessheim is that you've a date with him."

He proceeded to outline every detail of the task to be carried out and she listened intently. Finally he asked her if she had any questions to ask.

"Will Karl have the explosives?"

"Yes," he replied. "You have a gun?"

"No. Karl lent me his once when we were in a jam in Tresfjord. It's always been safer for me not to carry one in case of a body-search."

"Right, but this time you might need a weapon. I'll see that Karl brings it to you." He produced a travel pass for her and told her the time of the train she was to catch.

Although Edvin had made it all sound simple and straightforward, she knew as well as he and Arne that it was a highly dangerous sortie, for everything was to be done in daylight. If they were spotted at their sabotage, they would be shot on the spot. Yet she was exhilarated that she had been given such a task, for every bomb destroyed was one less for an Allied target.

"One last thing," Arne put in when all the details had been discussed. "Memorise the map, Anna. Don't take it with you."

After the two men had gone, Anna pored over the map. She and Karl were to have been together in a sabotage sortie when she had first arrived in Norway. Now nothing should prevent them carrying out the work together this time.

She hid the map away before leaving the apartment, for Nils was coming that evening, and she could not reveal the task she had been given to him or Christina.

When Anna next visited Rosa, she was more grateful than ever to Nils for ensuring her aunt's privacy. She had found her lying on the sofa, her face very white.

"Aren't you feeling well?" Anna asked anxiously. She had used her own key to enter when Frida had not answered the door. It was the first time.

"How did you get in?" Rosa demanded almost crossly. She felt at a disadvantage, not having wanted Anna to even suspect that there was anything wrong with her. She'd had a little heart trouble for years that only her doctor and Frida knew about. It was not right for Anna to have any extra worry when she must concentrate fully on whatever Resistance work she was undertaking.

"I still have the door key to the apartment that you gave me once, as well as one to the country house. I took them with me to England."

Rosa's expression softened. "So you were always determined to come back?"

Anna smiled widely. "Not even a war has kept me

250

away." She took hold of her aunt's hand. "Is there anything I can get you? Do you need a doctor?"

"Heavens, no!" Rosa waved away the suggestion and propped herself still higher against the cushion, which she would not have been able to do earlier when the pain was acute. "You had Nils with you last time you came. I'm glad to have you to myself today."

"At least you and he were more amiable towards each other than I ever remember."

"I admit that I should have been more tolerant of him in the past." Rosa only meant that less opposition might have caused the liaison to fizzle out, but Anna took the remark at its face value.

"But this is a new beginning for the two of you, Aunt. He's kinder than you could ever guess."

Rosa accepted resignedly that her days of interfering in the relationship were over, but she reserved her own judgement and hoped for the best. Yet it was on the cards that Nils and Anna would end up together. What chance did that other man in Anna's life have in these days, especially when the fact she wouldn't talk about him could only mean he was in the Resistance too. It was unlikely that their paths crossed very often, whereas Nils appeared to be established in some provision business that gave him freedom of movement and, more dubiously, easy access to the Black Market.

Anna was opening her purse. "I have some money for you. Those last two dresses sold well." The purchaser had been a young woman, excited that she was shortly to marry her German fiancé, and eager to gather some kind of trousseau together. When she stood in her slip between trying on the dresses, it was obvious that she was pregnant.

Anna, watching the seamstress pin the alterations on her, had wondered if she knew how swiftly she would be

251

shipped off to Germany and what might await her there if her fiancé's family home was in an Allied bombing zone. Marriages with Norwegian women were allowed, but the presence of wives was not.

"Please thank Christina for me," Rosa said. She did not mind that the woman took quite a high percentage. Everybody had to make a living.

"I will."

Before leaving, Anna resisted giving her aunt an extra kiss and a hug, not wanting to give any hint that she would soon be putting her life on the line. Their parting was as usual after Frida returned, because she had not wanted to leave Rosa on her own when unwell enough to have to rest.

The days crept on towards Anna's assignment. She saw Nils often, and there were times when it was almost as if they had never been apart, particularly when they laughed together over some remembered incident in the past. Yet there was a change in both of them, she with her love directed elsewhere and he in some indefinable way that she could not pinpoint. Knowing him as she did, she felt that he wanted to speak of what troubled him deeply. Instinct told her that it had nothing to do with the change in their relationship, for he had a blind spot as far as Karl was concerned, never referring to him, as if he were a mere figment of her imagination. Yet, whenever she gave him the chance to talk of what was on his mind, he became wary and made sure they talked of something else.

As Nils had access to a radio, he was able to tell her the latest war news. Anna knew from the German-controlled press that a terrible new rocket, the V2, was falling on London from sites in Germany and Holland in what was a second Blitz. But the good news was that the September advance of the Allies had liberated Paris and was through Belgium into Holland. On the Eastern Front there was a life-and-death struggle at Warsaw, but elsewhere the Russians were continuing to break through.

It had become noticeable that the German troops no longer sang 'We March Against England' as they stamped through the streets, because they knew that passers-by were laughing privately at them. As if to counteract the news of the Allied successes that were filtering through to the Norwegians, the Nazi rule was re-enforced all over the country with still more ruthless reprisals. Arrests were made on the slightest suspicion, and at Oslo's ancient fortress the condemned patriots, often with their bodies broken by torture, were shot in the executions carried out daily.

It was just before curfew when Anna's street doorbell rang. She went downstairs to call through the door. "Who's there?"

"Karl."

She flung open the door and he was in at once, taking her into his arms. They laughed and kissed and talked all the way up the flight until they reached the living-room. There he stopped to hold her back from him and look searchingly into her eyes.

"Are you clear about everything that has to be done on our sortie. Any doubts or queries?"

"None!" she answered firmly.

"That's settled then." He picked her up in his arms and his mouth covered hers as he carried her through to the bedroom.

It was the time they had both been yearning for since they had been together in the mountain cabin. Then they had made love after a brush with death, and now the same danger awaited them very shortly. But, in the meantime, they had the whole night ahead in which to rediscover each other completely.

As they lay down naked together in her bed, everything

else faded away and nothing existed for them beyond each other. His hands trembled with passion as he caressed her, she marvelling at the smoothness of his skin as she stroked him lovingly in return. The curtains at the window were open to the moon-glow and his stark love-face was as clear to her as her own joyous features were to him. She exulted in watching him make love to her, only closing her eyes when his touch became almost too delicious to be borne.

"You're so beautiful," he murmured, his lips travelling over her, his breath soft and warm against her body. Now and again he groaned with pleasure as she found her own ways to add to their enjoyment of each other. Their limbs, ivory-pale in the translucent light, made constantly-changing patterns as they interlaced and entwined on the white spread of the sheet.

When at last he was taking her with tender violence to the ultimate moments, she clung to him as if drowning in love and then reared ecstatically as all his wonderful strength vibrated within her.

Now and again throughout the night hours they dozed blissfully, her lips moist with his kisses, only to stir and make love again, until in the early morning they slept.

Anna awoke just seconds before the alarm of her clock was about to go off and she silenced it quickly. Karl was still asleep, his head on their shared pillow. She slid from the bed and padded across to draw the curtains closed across the window. Then she turned to look towards the bed. He lay handsomely sprawled, occupying most of the space with a knee bent and his other leg stretched out. He had been holding her within his arm and its position was unchanged as if waiting for her to return.

After slipping on a robe Anna went back to sit on the bed, knowing it was time to wake him, but he had already missed her.

"Where do you want to live after the war?" he muttered sleepily. "Would Oslo suit you?"

"Initially. Aunt Rosa will want me to stay a while."

His eyes shot open, clear-grey and brilliant, and he caught her wrist in a firm grip. "I didn't mean your aunt's place, and you know it." He sat up, pushing his hair back with spread fingers. "I asked you to marry me the day we met."

She raised her eyebrows with mock incredulity. "I don't remember."

His lips spread in a wide smile. "But you knew as I did in that London office there would never be anybody else for either of us."

"What conceit!" she exclaimed, shaking her head with amusement. "It didn't happen that way at all."

"You've just forgotten!" He pulled her across his chest and, laughing with her, made love to her again.

They talked little over breakfast, smiling at each other and holding hands whenever possible, their eyes full of the night they had shared. Yet he did tell her of the part she had played in taking a package to Tresfjord on the day they had fled together from the Germans. "It was London's directive that Hitler should be fooled into believing that the Allied invasion would come through Norway instead of France. The seeds were planted long before you came back, but you helped in the delivery of forged letters to add to the false trail." He grinned widely. "As a result Hitler has five hundred thousand troops tied up here that are badly needed on the Eastern Front."

She was surprised. "I'd no idea."

"Now he daren't move them in case the Allies make a second great landing on Norwegian shores!"

Then, because the war was ever with them, they talked softly of what they hoped for in a future together. Soon it was time for him to leave. She went with him down to her street door. They kissed again.

"I'll see you at Jessheim," he said, his gaze serious.

"I'll be there."

He cupped her face tenderly in his hand and then left.

Chapter Twenty-Three

Anna was in good time to catch the train that would stop at Jessheim and was early enough to get a window seat. The countryside out of Oslo was gently undulating with stretches of birch woods and pine forests that were the haunt of elk. She had dressed unobtrusively in a plain skirt and blouse with her knitted *kofte* as well as her leather lace-up shoes in case she had to run for her life in an emergency. Excitement and trepidation were high in her, intoxicating as alcohol, but outwardly she appeared quite relaxed, her gaze fixed on the passing view. The forest flirted with the railway line, closing in for miles, and then drawing back again as Jessheim came nearer.

There the platform was crowded with soldiers and airmen waiting to board the train, some lined up with sergeants barking orders and officers looking on. As the train drew to a halt, she saw that one of them was Leutnant von Heller, whom she knew from the hotel in Alesund. He was young and alert, very physical and virile, with the blue-eyed, fair-haired colouring and chiselled features that made him the Nazi stereotype of the pure Aryan soldier. Fortunately he was not looking in her direction and she jumped out quickly to thread her way to the barrier. But luck was not with her. He reached her side just as she had shown her papers and was about to pass through.

"This is an unexpected pleasure, Fröken Larsen!" he exclaimed truthfully, his salute accompanied by a sharp click of his jackbooted heels. "How are you? What are you doing here?"

"All's well with me," she answered brightly, "and I've come from Oslo for the day to visit a friend. Let me ask you the same questions."

"I'm fighting fit, as you can see," he declared, unashamedly proud of his looks and physique. "I'm stationed nearby at Gardermoen, but I get to Oslo quite often. Where are you working? I'd like to see you next time I'm there."

"I'm helping at Christina's dress shop on Storgaten."

"I thought you were going to continue your hotel training when you left Alesund."

"I was, but when I arrived, the hotel was closed. It's difficult to get in anywhere else at present, but I'm looking out all the time."

"I wish you success." He glanced back along the platform. "I would have liked to talk longer, but I can't just now. Do you have a telephone number?"

"The shop is in the book."

"Good. I'll ring you soon. *Auf wiedersehen.*"

As Anna walked away, she was both furious and anxious that such an unlucky twist of events should have caused her to be recognised when she least wanted it.

It did not take her long to reach the café where a freckle-faced girl stood waiting to serve behind the counter. Anna saw Karl at once. There were only half a dozen other customers in the café, two of them reading newspapers.

"You're on time," Karl said with a smile, coming to meet her. "I'll fetch some coffee now. Would you like anything to eat? There's fish sausage on the menu."

Anna made an amused little grimace of refusal, knowing he was teasing her, for she had told him once that she found fish sausage one of the most nauseating of wartime foods concocted through necessity. It eased her tension that they could share a little joke even at such a time.

As they sat down at a table, she noticed that his light canvas rucksack lay on the spare chair. She guessed it contained the explosives. Nobody was paying them any attention. At the next table a bored toddler was fractious and noisy, giving cover to their quiet conversation. She told him of meeting Fritz von Heller in the railway station.

"In that case," he said in the same low tones, "we'd better stage a parting. Ask the bus times. That should put you in the clear in case of any questioning later."

Anna knew that she had become a dangerous lead that could be followed up. Yet she hesitated to disassociate herself from him, whatever the reason. "We're in this together," she reminded him sternly.

"That's why I want to be sure that you live to fight another day if anything else unforeseen happens. Follow me out after five minutes."

She nodded reluctantly. At the next table the child had dropped a rag doll, unnoticed by the two women at the table, who were continuing their own conversation. Anna leaned down to pick it up.

"So you can't stay after all, Steffen," she said, using his assumed name just loud enough for the women to overhear, as she handed the doll back to the child.

"Thank you," the mother said.

Anna smiled absently as if concentrating on her conversation with her companion and turned back to him. After another minute he rose to leave, shouldering on his rucksack.

"I'll be seeing you sometime," he said casually. Then he left.

Anna waited for almost five minutes before going to the girl at the counter and asking about a bus to Oslo. In the original plan she and Karl would have simply faded from the scene, but circumstances had changed. Now she must cover her tracks completely. Since she would not be on any bus, she would have the answer ready that she had obtained a lift with a farm-lorry.

The girl looked at a timetable on the wall. "There's a bus leaving Jessheim for Oslo in three hours."

"That's a long wait. I think I'll walk for a while."

"It's a lovely day for it."

Outside Anna turned for the road that would take her to the forest, following it away from the little town. There were few people about. The sparse traffic was mostly connected with the *Luftwaffe*. She kept to the shade of trees, which at first were silver birches already turning russet, ochre and red. Soon the tall pines began to take over. When Jessheim was well behind her, she checked that there was nobody in sight before slipping into the forest. It was darkly shadowed with pockets of sunshine. Karl was watching for her.

"Over here!"

Anna ran to him. "I'm ready," she said, slinging the strap of her purse across her.

He led the way, keeping low, she following close behind as they went deep into the forest. It gave her pleasure to dart through the green and gold pattern of the trees. Briefly it was like being a child again. Then suddenly, cutting a clearing through the forest, was the railway track.

Karl set down his rucksack and unstrapped it, revealing the explosives within. There was also a gun for her, which he gave her. Neither spoke and both took what they needed. She dropped to a knee by one rail while he did the same at the other. A soft breeze played around them. But they had only just begun their task when Karl looked up sharply. A trace of smoke was showing in the distance.

"The train is coming! It's early! Get out now, Anna! I'll finish here!"

She shook her head, her fingers working swiftly. He yelled at her even as he worked. "For God's sake, go!"

Grimly she continued and set the last explosive into place. He finished an instant before her and was already on his feet, catching up his emptied rucksack at the same time. His iron grip hurtled her forward with such force that she fell sprawling, but he caught her up and they ran within a few feet of each other, plunging through undergrowth and slashed by low branches. They could hear the train now, for it was approaching at speed and its sound became louder every moment.

On and on they ran, making for the road and greater cover beyond. Pine cones flew up from under their feet, uneven ground made them stumble, and treacherous tufts of fern hid tiny streams that splashed icy water up their legs. Anna lost her shoe among the pebbles of one, which made her fall, and precious moments were lost as she retrieved it, not daring to leave any clues. Karl came rushing back to find her.

They had put some distance between themselves and the track, but they were not yet out of the danger zone. It was with intense relief that Anna saw the road lying ahead through the thinning trees, but when they would have emerged from the forest they both halted abruptly. They heard motor cycles and then saw a pair of outriders approaching in escort to an open staff car with two officers on their way to Jessheim. Anna dropped down into the undergrowth, Karl with her.

"Get under the overhang of that large boulder!" he hissed. "Be quick! I'll follow!"

She crawled and scrambled her way across to it and threw herself down in time to watch through the tall grass and wild flowers at the roadside as the outriders roared past and the car swept by. Then Karl, who had drawn his revolver where he had crouched, dashed forward to fling himself over Anna for her further protection as the world seemed to split apart.

Explosion after explosion followed, the deafening noise filling the forest like thunder, the ground lifting and vibrating as the locomotive and its wagons leapt and vanished in a searing spiral of red-gold fire, the blast wiping out a wide area of the forest and cleaving the earth into a hideous crater. The sky was darkened by smoke and flying debris. On the outskirts of the blast, trees were toppling, uprooting others as they pitched down.

A great pine came crashing down on the boulder in a shower of vast splinters, making it shake as if it must split asunder. More trees were tossed across the road and rocks, clumps of earth and branches rained down, even a wagon-wheel and a twisted length of rail, which clanged and leapt about before they settled.

"Are you all right, Anna?" Karl asked, throwing off some twigs and foliage that had fallen on his back. He helped her up with him.

"Yes," she said breathlessly. There was earth and grass in her hair and her face was scratched and bleeding from a whipping branch in the rush through the trees, her skirt torn. He held her to him for a few moments.

"We're literally not out of the woods yet. Are you ready to run again?"

She drew a deep breath and nodded, knowing it was time to have her gun in her hand.

They pounded on once more, keeping level with the road, but here trees were still standing and made a protective screen. They had to drop down every time an army vehicle went speeding by, troops being rushed from all directions to the scene. By the distant orders being shouted, Anna guessed that the soldiers were leaping

262

out of the trucks into the road some way beyond the boulder.

Just when she was wondering how much longer her legs would keep going, Karl branched away from the road along a cart track to where a military car was parked under the trees and covered by greenery to camouflage it. They pulled all that away.

It was a two-seater with what was known generally as a mother-in-law's seat at the back, which closed down like a luggage boot. It was the type of small car that young officers used when they could not get anything better, particularly the *Hird*, for the Germans commandeered all the best cars for themselves. Karl had driven it from Oslo that morning and proceeded to change back into the *Hird* uniform he had worn on the way.

"It's worse being togged up as a traitor than as a German," he said with distaste when he was ready, jamming on the peaked pill-box cap.

"It won't be for long," Anna said consolingly, having packed his own clothes into the rucksack as they were discarded.

"You're right." He opened the rear of the car where the seat had been removed. Cushions and a soft travelling rug lay in the space that had been made. As she was about to climb in with the rucksack, he took her by the shoulders and kissed her hard and quick. "I love you! I wish you could ride beside me, but I'll get you back to Oslo as soon as I can."

He closed her into the car. The cushions helped, but it was still an uncomfortable way to travel. She was bumped about considerably along the cart-track until the car swung out onto the Oslo road.

As Karl and Anna had expected, the Germans had set up road blocks and thrown out cordons in the hope of catching whoever was responsible for the destruction of the train. It was not long before Anna felt the car draw up. Then she heard Karl being questioned as to why he was on the Jessheim to Oslo road.

"I was on military matters in Jessheim when the explosion occurred and I'm on my way to report it to Prime Minister Quisling. One of the wagons carried *Hird* weapons."

There was a pause as his forged papers were examined, including a document signed by Quisling. Yet the German did not seem satisfied. She heard Karl get out of the car and there seemed to be some sort of argument in progress. She held her breath as she heard heavy boots coming round to the rear of the car and guessed the guards were awaiting orders to start searching it. Incredulously she heard one of them drumming his fingers on the lid as he waited.

There were agonising minutes before Karl threw himself back behind the wheel with permission to go through. She almost wept with relief as the car shot away, although the force of it threw her painfully against the side.

Karl called back to her. "That sergeant wanted to be difficult, but that was all. It's this uniform. The Germans have no more time for Norwegian traitors than we, even though they need their information."

He was stopped twice after that, but went through smoothly. Soon Anna heard the sounds of the city and, from what she had been told previously by Edvin, she knew Karl was making for an old district near the harbour. The bump of cobbles told her when they had entered a long, crooked alley that ran between the windowless backs of warehouses. At the moment when the car was out of sight from either end, Karl swung it through open doors at the rear of one of the warehouses. Men's footsteps came running and the doors closed after the car with a hollow slam.

Karl sprang from his seat and came to help Anna out. "Are you badly bruised?" he asked with concern.

"Not enough to matter."

He lifted out his rucksack and began changing back into his own clothes, while she flexed her arms and legs, thankful that she had escaped cramp on the journey. Then she turned as the car was started up again and saw that a man was driving it down a ramp into an underground area, which she guessed spread under the whole warehouse. A second man was hurrying down after it.

"What's going to happen to the car now?" She was combing her hair.

"It will be hidden down there until it's needed again." He was frowning. "You can't go back to Storgaten, Anna. I was thinking it over on the way here. It's highly likely, when check-ups are made about strangers in the area of Jessheim, that the Gestapo will want to question you."

"But I covered my tracks." It was her first chance to explain how she had done it, but although he heard her out he still shook his head.

"Every farm vehicle would have been turned inside out at the road blocks. They'd know you weren't on any of them or a bus. You've deep scratches on your cheek from the forest and a bruise on your forehead from the car."

"I fell down the stairs," she answered impatiently. "I have to return to the apartment. If I'm not there to answer for myself, Christina will fall under suspicion. I won't have that."

Karl could see there was no persuading her. He gave in reluctantly. "I'll even have to let you walk back to Storgaten on your own. You can't be seen with me."

Her expression softened. "I know," she said, moving into his arms. "Take care wherever you go. I hope we meet up again soon."

He kissed her hungrily, she responding with equal

fervour. Then he took her to a side door and she tore herself from him and left. He remained with his shoulder lodged against the door jamb and watched her out of sight. Partings were becoming harder for them both each time.

Chapter Twenty-Four

The shop was shut when Anna arrived back in Storgaten, for it was early evening. She let herself in through her own front door and took off her *kofte* as she went up the stairs. On the threshold of her living-room she halted, startled. Nils had leapt up from a chair.

"Where the hell have you been all day?" he demanded, his rage born of the anxiety he had endured. "What have you done to your face? It's scratched and your skirt is torn."

"How long have you been here?" she countered, being in no mood for a tirade.

"I've been coming and going through the shop until Christina wanted to go home. So then I stayed. I couldn't get out of her where you were—"

"She didn't know," Anna interrupted. "We lead independent lives."

"In working hours? I even called on your aunt in case you were there."

Anna's own anger burst forth. "You had no right to do that! You would have set her worrying about where I might be."

"She's on to your being in the Resistance, is she?"

"I didn't want her to know, but she's an intelligent woman and guessed."

"Then if she knows, at least you can tell me, a fellow underground fighter, where you were today."

267

"I set some explosives, that's all."

"For the armament train?" he exclaimed incredulously.

"Maybe."

"You did! When I nipped back to the office to see if there were any messages about an hour ago, I met Wolfgang, the sportsman I told you about. He had heard about the explosion on the army radio. You couldn't have been on your own in something that big."

Anna sighed. "Listen. I'm tired and I'm going to have a bath and get to bed early. I'll see you tomorrow. Let yourself out."

She would have turned for her bedroom, but Nils caught her by the arm and jerked her round to face him. "Who were you with? Was it Karl?"

She saw that intense jealousy lay behind his renewed fury. "Yes, I was."

"I would have gone with you! You'd have been safer with me!"

"My safety didn't come into it. Karl and I did what had to be done and we got away. That's the end of it. In any case, you're not linked to the Oslo group. You told me yourself that you prefer to work independently with your own Resistance contacts." Impatiently she drew his attention to the phone, which had begun ringing persistently throughout their argument. "I'll have to answer that!"

She went to the extension from the shop in the hall and lifted the receiver. "Christina's Gowns."

"This is Edvin! Christina has been arrested! Get out, Anna! Now!"

Ashen-faced, Anna ran to her bedroom, calling out as she went, "They've got Christina! I have to get away!"

She snatched up her suitcase before throwing in her few things. Nils scooped a couple of blouses and a skirt from hangers for her to add to everything else. She pulled off her torn skirt and threw on her other one. In all it had been only a few minutes before she was in her coat, a wad of stored money tucked into a secret pocket with her gun, and was making for the stairs with her suitcase.

"Thanks for your help, Nils," she said gratefully, as they hurried down the flight to her street door. "We'll part outside."

"I'm not leaving you."

"Don't be a fool!" she exclaimed desperately over her shoulder. "You know what would happen if we should be caught together!"

"They'll not get you if I can help it."

Then there came such a crashing on the street door that they both stopped abruptly and she almost fell back against him. "Dear God!" she breathed. "They're here!"

Even as she and Nils dashed back up the flight, there came the sound of glass being smashed in the shop door. Their only other escape route had been blocked.

"I'll help you through the hall fanlight onto the roof!" Nils was unable to think of anywhere else.

"No! Come with me!" Anna ran to raise the cupboard floor and toss in her suitcase. "Go down the ladder! I'll follow, because I know how to close everything."

He eased himself swiftly through the gap and she followed as soon as she could get her feet on a rung after him. The soldiers had broken through from the street and their heavy boots were charging up the stairs, more coming from the direction of the shop. The cupboard shut on the second that the door of her hall burst open.

In the inky darkness Anna let her forehead rest on the top rung, needing time to come to terms with what was happening. She wondered how many of the Resistance the Germans had expected to find with her, for as far as she could judge, an excessive number of men had been sent

269

to arrest one woman. Angrily she found that she could not stop trembling.

Nils, standing at the bottom of the ladder, took hold of her ankles. "Come down, Anna," he urged softly.

She descended slowly and he took her into his arms, holding her close as they listened to the thumping of feet and the creaking of floorboards above as the search for her went on.

"I wish you hadn't come here today," she whispered unhappily. "In fact, you should have stayed away from me altogether for your own good. You've only put yourself in unnecessary danger."

As he answered, she could hear the smile in his voice. "How could I ever not be with you when I had the chance?"

It was not the time to continue the argument they had begun upstairs and she remained silent, remembering that he would have risked his life still further for her if they had left the apartment in time to escape this search.

Overhead boards creaked and furniture was overturned with reverberating crashes. They both grew tense as the cupboard doors were flung open and everything on the shelves was tossed out in turn, but the floor-lid remained untouched. Yet they both knew that somebody might return to it.

Then they heard her kitchen table being set down and dragged into position under the skylight. It showed that she would not have been safe if she had crouched on the roof. When the soldier who had climbed up to look out jumped down from the table again with a thump, it seemed as if he must surely come through the ceiling of the hide-out.

Still the soldiers did not leave. It could only mean they were searching for evidence against her and anyone associated with her.

"What of Aunt Rosa?" she whispered fearfully.

"She won't be touched. There's nothing to link her with you. Remember that she's my aunt now."

Anna pressed her cheek against his in speechless gratitude. His arms closed tighter about her and he was further convinced that he had only to be patient and she would come back to him.

Neither Anna nor Nils knew how long they stood together before the heavy footsteps went away down the stairs again and finally left the building. There was only a pause before the boarding up of her street door and that of the shop began. Yet she knew that they had to be prepared for a trick. There had been times when somebody had deemed it safe to emerge from hiding only to find the enemy still waiting to pounce.

"We must wait a while longer," Nils warned as if reading her thoughts. "Is there any way out now other than the roof?"

"There's a high window in the office if it hasn't been boarded up."

"We'll look later."

"I don't think I'll risk switching on the light yet. Let's sit down. It's been quite a day."

She guided him across to the divan and took the chair herself. The darkness was therapeutic. She began to feel drowsy. Nils slept first and did not wake as she did whenever a board settled or there was the sudden tumble of something that had been precariously lodged.

When Anna awoke in the middle of the night, it was through the creaking of the shop stairs. She sprang up and shook Nils into wakefulness.

"There's somebody in the building!"

He was on his feet immediately, and together they listened intently. There was no mistake and he drew his gun from his shoulder-slung holster. Anna took hers from the secret pocket of her coat. Then the floor-lid was being lifted. The beam of a flashlight was directed down the ladder.

"Anna? Are you there?" Karl's voice demanded.

"Yes!" she cried out in relief. "And Nils is with me!"

"Thank God you're safe!"

He had already come through the aperture to descend the ladder, and his flashlight enabled her to cross to the light-switch. The shaded pink lamps illuminated the room.

"How did you know I was here?" she asked eagerly as he stepped off the last rung and gave her a quick kiss. Neither noticed that Nils put his gun away slowly as if he would still like to use it. He fiercely resented what he saw as an unnecessary intrusion.

"Edvin rang me after he's spoken to you, Anna," Karl explained, his arm still about her. "I was still at the warehouse. I came here straight away, but the Germans had arrived before me, so I waited and watched. When they didn't bring you out with them, I had to keep out of sight until after curfew when I could get into the building after dark and find out if you were trapped here." He turned to Nils. "How did you reach Anna?"

"I was here already when she arrived. Did you come through the office window?"

Karl gave a nod. "We can leave that way too."

They discussed as to where Anna should go to be safe in this emergency. Nils suggested that she go to her aunt's home for the time being. Anna argued furiously against it.

"You've really no choice," Nils said. "You mustn't be found, and that's the obvious place to hide as your aunt already knows you're in the Resistance." To Karl he added, "Through pulling some German strings, I've managed to stop any surprise raids being made on Fru Johansen's apartment."

"If that's the case, you should go there, Anna," Karl endorsed. "There'll be a watch kept day and night for you at the railway and bus stations. Civilian vehicles of all kinds will be turned inside out at check-points. As soon as the hunt cools down, the Resistance will get you away." He drew her to him. "If it's humanly possible, I'll meet you wherever you are."

"We'd better get going, Karl!" Nils snapped. With a sense of shock, it seemed to Anna that a wave of hatred emanated from him like a cold, invisible mist.

Anna delayed only long enough to take a couple of travel passes from the secret compartment of her suitcase and push her toilet-bag into her coat pocket. Toothbrushes were like gold these days. She left everything else and went up the ladder after the two men. Standing in her hall again, she caught a glimpse in the flashlight's beam of the destruction in her living-room. She turned away from the sight.

Downstairs in the shop the large display window was intact. Outside the rain was pelting down, the blacked-out city in total darkness. Broken glass from the door cracked under their feet as they went into the office. Both men pushed the heavy desk against the wall under the high window, before adding a chair to make exiting easier.

Karl went out of the window first and dropped to the pavement below. As soon as he had checked it was safe, Anna followed and he caught her as she descended. Nils was next. The darkness and the rain were a shield. They went from doorway to doorway in turn, pressing themselves back when once a patrol went by. The most perilous part was after they had left the shelter of the trees in Studenterlunden, for there were sentries at the Storting. But these must have been huddled up in their capes, rain running from their helmets, and failed to see anything unusual.

With a master key Karl opened the main entrance of the building where Aunt Rosa's apartment was located. Then Anna was alone in the marble-floored lobby and had closed the door behind her. Karl had given her the flashlight and she switched it on to see her way as she crept up the stairs. Wet and cold and shivering, she let herself into the apartment. She hung her dripping coat up in the bathroom. There she dried her hair, which had been sticking to her head as if glued. In the bedroom that had always been hers she tossed off her clothes and fell into bed. She slept instantly.

Anna stayed five weeks at her aunt's apartment. Frida, who had been let into the secret at last, was as delighted as Rosa to have her there. Fortunately Anna had brought her ration card, and managed to alter the name on it to 'Hanna Hanson', but there was so little in the unheated shops, the assistants in coats, hats and gloves, that often the main meal was watery soup. It was Rosa's joke as the three of the them sat down to eat in the kitchen, which was the warmest room, that they themselves were as bundled up as Eskimos to keep warm.

Nils called frequently, always letting his officer acquaintances know afterwards that he had made another duty call on his aunt. He was a welcome link for Anna with the outside world, for, although she never tired of her aunt's company, it was the incarceration that she found tedious. She had to disappear into her bedroom whenever the doorbell rang.

At least she and Nils seemed to regain their old footing and she was always eager to hear the latest war news, which he also shared with Rosa and Frida. On the continent the Allies were continuing to advance, but he always emphasised any set-backs as if to quell their hopes that the war would be over soon. She concluded that his policy was to face one day at a time. After all, he never knew if the Germans would find out that they had a spy in their midst. He was living on a razor's edge even more than she.

It was from him that she and Rosa first heard of a new

274

development in Norway itself. In Hitler's desperate need for extra troops on the Eastern Front, Norwegian youths were being rounded up and sent there as untrained and unwilling recruits.

"Hundreds of them have already fled into the mountains," he added, "and with their ration books withdrawn its hard to get them fed."

One evening when they were on their own, Rosa having gone early to bed, Anna sat back in her chair as she challenged him sharply.

"Frida saw you at the harbour yesterday. She said you were watching food supplies being loaded aboard a German ship. Couldn't you have done something to prevent it?"

He looked at her despairingly. "I could have stopped the supplies at source, but I can't risk the Germans becoming suspicious about me. Do you think I like people going hungry? Rations have been cut to almost nothing in Germany too." He let his head drop into his hands where he was sitting. "How is this whole mess to end?"

She went went to drop down on her knees at his side and put her arms about him. "Don't, Nils! I shouldn't have said what I did. Especially when I'm leaving Oslo tomorrow. I don't want us to part at odds with each other."

He raised his head, looking even more depressed. "Where are you going?"

"Back to the west coast. A radio operator is needed."

He was startled. "Do you know what you're saying? The German detector vans can pick up a signal in no time at all. It's a cat and mouse existence."

"Not where I'm going."

"The mountains? No! You can refuse the assignment."

"But I want to go. I've been shut up here too long. Edvin got in touch with me yesterday. Karl has been in Oslo again and we'll be travelling on the same train, but not together.

I've been sent a bottle of brown hair dye and a fresh set of identity papers in another name. Luckily Aunt Rosa stored my ski-clothes and boots with all else I left here and so I'll be well equipped."

Her satisfaction with the entire project exasperated him. Although Karl seemed to be constantly disrupting their lives, he had never stopped believing that it was only a passing phase for her. When it came to the crunch, she would be drawn back to him as if to her roots. His fear was of any harm coming to her, more than ever now with this new and deadly task she was undertaking.

"I wish this bloody war was over!" he exclaimed bitterly.

"That's everybody's dream at the present time," she said sympathetically.

In the hall before leaving, Nils made one last appeal to her. "Think this project over carefully," he implored. "Let me find you still here when I come again."

He saw the answer in her eyes. Pulling her to him he kissed her with a desperate fervour as if it might be for the last time. For that reason she responded with affection, being as fearful for his safety as he was for hers.

Leaving Rosa next morning was just as hard. After Frida's tearful goodbye it was a relief that Rosa held back tears with a smile as she had always done. She had not been told why her niece was going away with dyed hair and darkened brows, clad in warm ski-clothes with her pre-war rucksack, but she knew it meant danger.

"*Farvel*, my dear Anna," she said fondly as they embraced. "Keep safe and well."

"I will. You, too." Anna gave her a final hug and paused again by the stairs to give a little wave. "I'll be back."

Rosa remained by the door until her niece's footsteps had faded away to be followed by the thud of the closing street door.

Chapter Twenty-Five

Anna arrived in Bergen after a tiring journey of several hours. She had not seen Karl, who would be on another part of the train. As it came to a standstill she saw two SS officers on the platform and became anxious when they began scanning the disembarking passengers.

There was no reason why they should be waiting for her, but it was impossible not to fear betrayal at all times. At the moment she was wedged in by passengers behind and those waiting to take their turn in getting off. It was not until the person in front of her alighted that the SS officers sighted their true quarry farther down the platform, and one shouted out as they moved swiftly in that direction.

"*Achtung*! Stay where you are!"

Anna sprang down from the train in time to see Karl dashing across the platform to leap down on to the tracks. Immediately there seemed to be storm-troopers appearing from everywhere to swarm down after him, the officers in the lead, revolvers in their hands.

Swiftly Anna edged her way across the platform, some passengers having begun to run in their haste to get away from this potentially dangerous situation. She was in time to see Karl bolting along at the side of another stationary train before disappearing between two wagons. In horror she heard gun-shots ring out.

A departing businessman jostled her, muttering some advice. "It's not wise to hang about, *fröken*. Keep going."

Somehow Anna forced herself to leave the platform with everyone else. In the station she pretended to be choosing a newspaper from a rack while waiting in an agony of mind to discover whether or not Karl had managed to get away.

Finally bystanders began moving aside to let the returning stormtroopers through. Anna caught her breath in shock as she saw Karl in their midst, being prodded along by rifles. He was ashen-faced and supporting his limp left arm across his chest with his right hand, the sleeve blood-soaked. She thought he would not see her, but he must have been watching out, for he sent a single deep glance under lowered lids that conveyed a warning and his own farewell.

Afterwards Anna remembered nothing of walking to the hotel where she and Karl had stayed when they had first come to Bergen together. She checked into the hotel room that had been booked for her, dropped her rucksack on to the floor and sat with her head in her hands. For the first time she felt close to despair.

When a knock came on the door, Anna knew it would be Lars, whom she was expecting. She had not seen him since the last time she was in Bergen. He guessed at once by her lack of colour and strained expression, that she had bad news.

"What's happened?" he asked, closing the door behind him.

"Karl was arrested after a chase at Bergen railway station. He was wounded." She told him all she had seen.

He shook his head gravely and swore, thumping a fist on the end of the bed by which he stood. "I never thought they'd get Karl! He's evaded them so many times."

"Where do you think they'll take him after the interrogation?" she asked tonelessly, refusing to consider that he might not survive it.

"Who can say?" Lars went along with her wish to keep

the worst at bay, although he knew that such a prize captive as Karl would be subjected to the most sadistic of treatments. "There are so many patriots confined in camps these days that a few months ago another was built not all that far from Oslo. Recently most of our men arrested have been sent there."

"I've heard of it," she said tersely. "Already it's becoming as notorious as Grini."

He hoped she had not heard much about its commandant, Oberst-Leutnant Horwitz, a brutal sharp-faced Nazi, who had openly expressed a wish for a proper concentration camp in Norway with a gas chamber in which to get rid of obdurate prisoners. "If Karl should survive interrogation and be sent there," Lars said, wanting to do what he could for Anna in her distress, "I might be able to find out. The Resistance has a contact in an ear specialist at a nearby hospital. Horwitz has become his patient, hoping that damage to an ear-drum on the Russian Front can be corrected. The doctor keeps his own eyes and ears open when he visits Horwitz at the camp. He's even come away with a message or two at times that are smuggled to him."

"Then I must hope for that."

They talked about Karl's arrest for a while longer, trying to work out how he could have been betrayed. Anna wondered if he had been followed from Oslo by a Quisling, who had travelled in the same carriage and then identified him by a signal to the waiting enemy. "Otherwise how could he have been known to them?" she concluded.

Lars nodded. "That's possible. After all, if the Germans had been on to his whereabouts in Oslo they would have arrested him before he could board the train." He regarded her sympathetically. "We shan't discover the truth of it unless Karl knows and can tell us one day."

She was grateful that he was trying to boost her hopes for Karl's survival. "You're right, but that won't stop me trying to remember anything that might give me a clue." Taking a grip on herself, she took a deep breath. "Do I leave here tomorrow as planned?"

"Yes. You'll be OK?"

She looked at him squarely. "I will."

Anna suffered a restless night. Whenever she dozed it was only to awake with an image of Gestapo interrogations in her mind that came vividly from all she had heard during her time in Norway. The beatings, the pulling out of fingernails, electric shocks, the sadistic means of keeping a captive's sleep away, the burning with cigarettes and hot irons. Once she sat up on a scream and clapped her hands over her mouth in fear that she had been heard, but the hotel remained quiet and nobody stirred.

She collapsed back on to the pillow and found release in tears. Only then did she sleep for a couple of hours until her alarm clock rang. It was like waking up in a wastepaper basket for, with bed-linen worn out and impossible to replace, many hotels had had to resort to paper sheets and pillowcases. Anna's constant tossing and turning had caused hers to rip. She went to bath and dry herself with the towels that were of paper too.

Anna rode out of Bergen on a bicycle that Lars had brought to the hotel that morning. He gave her a message for London, which she was to send out later on the radio-transmitter that would be waiting for her at the cabin. The bicycle had wooden rims instead of tyres, for the enemy had long since taken those throughout the country in a shortage of rubber. It made a bumpy and uncomfortable ride, but it was her only means of transport to a small village not far from Bergen. There she went to the friendly house of a lawyer, Stein Holstad, who would pass any message received from her to the Resistance. He was not at home, having already left for his Bergen office in his wood-fuelled car, but Anna was greeted by his wife, Mary.

She was a thin, energetic woman in her fifties, who was already dressed to accompany Anna to the mountains.

"I'll keep you provided with all you need, Anna," she said. "My nephew will be your main contact. There's a policeman in the area who always phones a warning if there's any enemy activity around."

"So you've been involved with something like this before?"

"We still are. With the help of several farmers in this valley we get food to three of our local lads hiding in the mountains from conscription by the Germans to the Eastern Front. Naturally it's very basic fare, as yours will be. There's an escaped Russian prisoner-of-war with them too, whom we were feeding on his own before that."

"Shall I be anywhere near them?"

"No, I'm afraid life is going to be very lonely for you from now on."

"I'm prepared for it."

She and Mary left unobtrusively for the mountains. The Holstads' house, surrounded by woodland, was on the outskirts of the village and there was nobody to see them go.

The early November air was crisp and clear, the only snow in the heights. Anna found it invigorating to exert her energy in the climb and all the way and the going was comparatively easy. When the ground levelled out to a valley below two peaks, she saw the cabin that was to be her first retreat.

Mary stayed only long enough to unload the food she had brought in her rucksack. When she had left, Anna took up the suitcase already deposited there and set it on the table to snap it open and reveal the short-wave radio transmitter inside. She had been assured by Mary that the Germans never came into these mountains, but if they picked up a persistent signal they would investigate, however much they disliked the high territories. For that reason she could only stay so long in this cabin before moving to another. Only Mary and others involved in helping her would know her whereabouts.

Anna's first task was to uncoil the wire attached to the transmitter and fix up the aerial outside. After checking that all was in order, she paid more attention to the cabin itself. It was typical in being much like the one in which she had stayed overnight with Karl. She guessed it was either Mary or her daughter who had filled a shelf with books. There were also a pack of cards with which to play patience and a delicately-carved chess set with a board if she wished to play against herself. Mary had told her that it had been made by the Russian prisoner-of-war, who also made wooden toys to pass the time. One of them lay on a cupboard. Anna picked it up by its handle and smiled as a circle of chickens with a hen pecked at the round board as a weight on strings was swung underneath. Putting it down again she wondered if the Russian had amused his own children with such toys.

Beside it in ugly contrast was the revolver she had placed there. She turned from it and went into the bedroom to unroll the sleeping bag she had brought with her.

Now she was ready to transmit the message that Lars had given her earlier that day. She sat down at the transmitter and put on her headphones. The next moment she was tapping out the communiqué in Morse, the tap-tap becoming the only sound in the room. She did not have long to wait before a brief acknowledgement of receipt of the communiqué came through.

After washing the dye out of her hair she listened to the news from London on a little radio normally hidden in a toffee tin, which she would be able to take with her every time she moved to another cabin. She heard that the Allies had taken their first German city and there were advances on all fronts.

Mary's teenage nephew, Roald, arrived in the early evening and gave the pre-arranged knock on the cabin door. He was a strong-looking boy.

"Do you have cats' eyes?" she asked jokingly as she admitted him, for it was dark outside.

"Only a thick mist or a blizzard can stop me getting about in these mountains," he replied confidently. "I've been coming up here all my life. It's our family cabin." He was carrying a can by its handle and set it down on the table. "It's milk for you. My dad is a farmer."

After that everything became routine. It was not every day that a communiqué was passed on to Stein Holstad, but whatever Anna received she transmitted at irregular times to avoid her signal being easily located. Sometimes urgent Resistance matters had to be passed to fellow radio-operators with whom she was in contact, but mostly it was about enemy shipping, particularly U-boats leaving their Bergen hide-outs and aiming to add to the toll they had taken of Allied lives and shipping.

The days passed slowly. Karl was constantly in Anna's thoughts. As yet she could not hope to hear if he was in a camp or whether he was still under torture. She refused to believe that he might have died at the Gestapo's hands. Surely she would know if he no longer breathed? How had he been betrayed?

It was a puzzle she returned to time and time again, even though she realised the futility of it. Her thoughts kept going to the problem like the tongue to a rough tooth. Being unable to solve anything or find the answers to her own questions brought such a restlessness on her at times that she had to get out of the cabin, whatever the weather. It was either to walk or later, when the snows came, to take a turn on skis. If it kept her awake at night she would draw back the curtains and look out at the Aurora Borealis filling the sky with swirling patterns as if the old Norse gods still rode across it.

Stein Holstad came himself on the evening that a detector van had been sighted in the valley. "It's time for you to move on. Leave here at first light."

Anna was well laden when she set out on skis at dawn the next day, for the transmitter, pushed into her rucksack, was a heavy weight. She had left no trace of her presence in the cabin and there would be no clue to help any search for her. A light snowfall did not trouble her and it gently covered her tracks as she followed her compass and memorised directions to her next destination.

For the rest of the winter Anna moved from place to place in the mountains, and had begun writing short stories to pass the time. She had no high opinion of their merit and saw them only as a mental exercise. She burned them each time before moving on to another location. As with the first cabin she had occupied, all the rest were on slopes low enough to be easily accessible to her contacts in the valley.

Once she received a short note from Lars with the latest communiqué. He had written that Karl was in the Horwitz concentration camp, but he knew nothing more. Before reading on, she closed her eyes briefly in overwhelming relief that Karl was still alive, no matter what his physical condition might be. She willed him to hang on to life as she had done in her thoughts and heart and prayers throughout the long weeks of isolation. Only snowstorms forced her contacts to stay away, but usually it was never for more than two or three days.

As spring came, bringing again cobalt blue skies and sun-sparkling snow, Anna knew from the BBC bulletins that it could only be a question of a short time before the Allies brought the war in Europe to a close, for the enemy was falling back on all fronts. How things would go in Norway she did not know, for it had been Hitler's boast that he had turned it into a fortress and it could be defended from Allied attack for a long time.

On the last day of April news came through on the toffee-tin radio that Hitler had committed suicide in a Berlin bunker. It meant that the war in Europe was virtually over. Only Japan remained to be defeated, and the fate of Norway was still in the lap of the gods.

A few days later when Anna was back at the first cabin she had occupied, her replacement arrived. He brought her the news that she had to go down to the Holstads' house where Lars would be waiting for her.

After packing up her belongings and burning the last of her manuscripts she went back down the forested slopes to the valley. Among the trees the tiny wood anemones gave a new and tender whiteness to where the snow had lain and, below her, the fields were turning green.

Mary Holstad welcomed Anna back again and left her on her own with Lars.

"You're wanted for the most important and dangerous venture you'll ever have to do, Anna," Lars said, after they had settled down to talk. "I told you once that the Resistance intended to keep you in mind for anything special and this is it with a vengeance."

She gave a slight smile. "What a relief! I won't mind what it is after being cooped up all the winter. Shall I be alone or working with anyone?"

"You'll be partnering your friend, Nils. He's ideal for the role as he speaks fluent German and we're lucky to still have him. You haven't heard, but just recently he had a narrow escape on his own in an air-crash near the coast when flying from Sweden to England. He still limps a bit, but that's all to the good as far as the sortie is concerned. He'll be masquerading as a top-ranking officer, wounded

285

months ago on the Russian Front, who has been posted to take command of the Horwitz Camp."

She gasped. "Karl is there!"

"That's right." Lars paused significantly. "If he's still alive, Anna."

She nodded tautly. "I realise that. Where do I come in all this?"

"You'll be Nils's mistress. At the rank he's holding, nobody will dare question your presence. You'll remember I told you that Commandant Horwitz had ear trouble? Our specialist in that field has falsely told him that he must have an immediate operation if his hearing is to be saved."

"But why?"

"You'll remember that I said Horwitz was a sadistic devil? He has had the whole camp set with explosives and has vowed that, if Germany surrenders, he will order the blowing up of the entire camp in a final show of Nazi power. As the surrender can happen at any time, it's vital that we get him away from the camp. If not, it will cost the lives of eight hundred men."

She sat stunned. "Dear God!"

"The second-in-command is no less a dyed-in-the-wool Nazi and we can't count on his not carrying out the order in Horwitz's absence. It's taking too much of a chance for Nils to go it alone. He'll need armed support if things shouldn't go well and you'll give him that."

"But Nils has moved so much in Nazi military circles that he could be recognised by someone. As for his speaking German, I know he used to spend some of his holidays in Germany, but he will still have a Norwegian accent to give him away."

Lars shook his head. "He'll be disguised and he has no accent. Right from the start when he first volunteered for the Resistance, he gave his full background. He's totally Norwegian in his loyalties and outlook, but he was born in

Germany. When that country was starving after the Great War, he came to Norway with other children under the Nansen scheme for care in private homes until fit to go home again. His foster parents adopted him as he was an orphan, but those trips he made to Germany were to visit family."

"I never knew that," Anna commented quietly.

"Apparently his adoptive parents wanted him to grow up as a Norwegian boy, and that's what he wanted too. They even moved from where they were living to Molde in order to give him a completely new start. It's why he's been such a useful agent, letting the Germans know his origins while working all the time with us. He could have been shot as a spy at any time. Now's he putting his life on the line once again, as you are, and everything depends on complete cooperation between the two of you if a mass murder is to be averted."

Anna left on the Oslo train in a smart suit, a hat and a hip-length fox fur coat, all suitable attire for the mistress of a Nazi *Generalleutnant*. She had more such clothes in a suitcase, including two silk dresses that bore the label of *Christina*. She did not question where any of the garments had come from, for the Resistance seemed to be able to get whatever was required. They had even managed to get her a First Class seat on the train. The other occupants of the carriage were all officers except for one man in plain clothes who might have been of the Gestapo.

There was some conversation until she pretended to bury herself in a book, but she scarcely took in anything from the pages. Instead she was mulling over why Nils had never confided in her about his origins. Naturally he wouldn't have even thought about it when they were children, being her senior and paying her little attention, but she would have expected it during the time when they were both so close, sharing thoughts and hopes and love.

Yet, looking back, she recalled how he had openly enjoyed being important among his friends, always the one whose company was most in demand on every occasion, ever the unchallenged leader of the pack. Maybe it was satisfaction in truly belonging, which was understandable in somebody orphaned young in violent times. Perhaps it was also why he had been driven obsessively to excel, needing to be the best and always to dominate. Even as he had dominated her, albeit in a loving way.

She turned her gaze unseeingly out of the window at the passing scenery. More and more memories flooded into her mind and brought questions with them that she could not answer.

Chapter Twenty-Six

It was mid-morning and raining when Anna arrived in Oslo. Carrying her suitcase and with an umbrella up, she walked to the Grand Hotel on Karl Johan Gate and on the way glanced up eagerly at the windows of her aunt's apartment. To her concern she saw that all the blinds were drawn.

Taking a cautious glance about her to make sure she was unobserved, Anna crossed the street and entered the building. She pressed the doorbell of Rosa's apartment. If her aunt was unwell, it would not be fair just to walk in and give her too much of a surprise.

Nobody answered the door. Anna inserted her key and let herself in. As soon as she entered she sensed that the place was empty. Going through the hall into the drawing-room she stopped on the threshold in dismay. It had been ransacked. The priceless ikon had gone from its case, the Antoinette clock, the rare ivory collection and all the other treasures had vanished. Dark squares and rectangles on the panelled walls showed where the paintings had hung.

Darting into Rosa's bedroom Anna saw that the safe was open and emptied. Her eyes went to the bed. It had not been made. Had Rosa risen to face the intruders or been dragged from it?

She had begun to tremble so much that she scarcely knew how she reached Frida's room, but that had not been touched. Here the bed was also unmade and so the raid must have taken place in the early morning. In her own bedroom nothing had been disturbed.

Anna knew she must leave as quickly as possible. Until she saw Nils, there was nobody she could ask for any information without risk to herself and the task she had come south to carry out. Hastily she went on to the hotel.

Nils arrived at noon and came up to Anna's room. He was in the greenish-grey uniform of a *Generalleutnant* decorated with the Iron Cross. He had dyed his hair brown and was wearing dark horn-rimmed spectacles that quite changed his appearance. There was a long scar down his cheek from his air-crash. Heedless of his disguise, Anna threw herself into his arms, certain that never before had she been so glad to see him.

"What happened to Aunt Rosa and Frida?" she cried in anguish.

He held her close. "How did you find out?"

"I went to her apartment this morning."

He sighed. "I'm sorry you had to learn about it that way. I'd hoped to break the news to you myself. Fritz gave me a full report. He'd been unable to prevent the arrests. It was found out that your aunt had been in contact with you, who are wanted for the train's sabotage, and Christina. For all we know, Christina may have revealed that under Gestapo pressure."

Anna's face whitened. "Aunt Rosa would be the last person to blame her in those circumstances." She told him of the looting that had taken place.

He shook his head slowly. "I didn't know anything about that and neither did Fritz or he would have told me. It must have happened after the arrest and it doesn't sound the work of a common thief." He frowned thoughtfully. "Maybe I can guess what happened."

"What do you mean?"

"I know from Fritz that some of the Nazi officers are getting desperate with a German surrender drawing so near. They need money and plenty of it to get away and escape retribution. Quite a few of them have talked of keeping the flame of Nazism alive for time to come and they need funds for that too. Maybe some of them remembered the priceless contents of your aunt's flat from a previous house raid. More than one person must have been involved to get so much away."

"When did Aunt Rosa's arrest take place?"

"A few days before I left for Sweden."

"Where did they take her and Frida?"

"They didn't take Fru Johansen anywhere." He kept her in his arms as he leaned back to look sympathetically into her agonised face. "She collapsed and died within minutes of the intrusion."

She stared at him, her eyes dilated with grief. "I should have been there!"

"You would only have been arrested too without being able to help her. Be thankful that, unlike Frida, she escaped the miseries of Grini."

Anna buried her face into his shoulder and her voice was torn. "I don't know how to bear this."

Nils cupped her head in his hand. "If it's any comfort to you, I arranged a funeral and burial just as you would have wished it. You'll be able to take flowers to her grave one day."

"Thank you!" Anna folded her arms tightly around his neck, pressing her cheek to his. "I'll always be grateful to you for that," she declared emotionally.

He kissed her brow. For the first time in his life he had been patient and it had paid off. She was returning to him at last.

A military car was waiting outside. When Anna and Nils came out of the hotel, her suitcase had been stowed away, and a sergeant saluted as he held the car door for them. When he was back behind the wheel, he glanced at her in the mirror. "Hello, Anna, Remember me?"

"Yes, of course, Olav," she replied. "You were at my first briefing in Bergen just after I'd arrived."

"That's right." He was driving the car out into the traffic. "Horwitz went into hospital three days ago, which was when we had to move in. About now he's on the operating table, although nothing will be done to him. I'm driving you to the camp now."

"Are you fluent enough in German to convince everybody there?"

"No, but all has gone well so far. I told them I was a Czech conscripted into the German Army, and some barbed wire pronunciation covers my own accent. That convinced them."

Anna turned to Nils with what was uppermost in her mind. "Have you seen Karl?"

"No, but I found his name on the list of prisoners marked for the most severe treatment. Even worse was a letter from the Gestapo headquarters in Oslo ordering his execution tomorrow. I cancelled that immediately."

"What reason did you give your second-in-command?"

"I said that I still believed it possible to get information out of Karl by my own methods, but not if he kept passing out through weakness. He was to be given medical treatment to get back his strength."

She nodded gratefully. Olav spoke up from the driver's seat. "If the worst happens and Reichskommissar Terboven decides to carry on the war from here after the German surrender, we'll still get Karl away with us somehow."

"What do you think will happen?" Anna asked.

Olav answered thoughtfully. "It's impossible to guess. He has a large territory that hasn't been overrun by an Allied advance and half a million battle-ready men under his command. As a violently-minded Nazi, it might be a matter of pride that he'll choose to fight on. We'll just have to hope for the best." He changed the subject. "What do you think of Nils as a *Generalleutnant*? His scar makes everyone think he was at Heidelberg."

Nils laughed. "It's too recent for that, but it's taken as a war wound. I'm only thankful that I escaped serious injuries in the air-crash or, what was worse, meeting a watery end by going down through the ice with my aircraft. It disappeared in minutes. Fortunately I was alone." His expression became bitter. "But I had important cargo aboard and there was no chance to save it."

"What brought you down? Engine trouble?"

"No. Normally the homeward run to England is made over the Baltic, but if there are rogue German patrols in the area or bad weather conditions, an alternative route is taken back over Norway and the west coast. I ran into some unexpected anti-aircraft fire and managed the landing on the lake, but that was it."

"What happened then?"

"One of the young men hiding from the German recruitment drive heard the Mosquito come down and came from a cabin to look for me. I know there are many of them in the mountains, but I could have been a hundred miles away from any help."

There was much else to talk about and Nils prepared her for what to expect at the camp. "Our quarters are outside the perimeter, but we're getting near now and you will see the camp as we pass by. It's not a pretty sight."

"I'll be prepared," she said.

Yet, when they came upon it in the depths of a forest, it was even worse than she had expected. It covered a large area with many rows of long, grey huts, a bleak obscenity of a place with a large courtyard, surrounded by high wire fences and tall look-out towers in which she could see guards with machine-guns. As Olav drove past she caught sight of a large courtyard, in which about thirty prisoners were lined up, all in dark loose shirts and trousers, some with drooping heads, others swaying on their feet with weakness. Pity overwhelmed her.

"That's a returned work-party," Nils said, following the direction of her gaze. He did not add that they had been digging graves for those who had died in the past twenty-four hours or that the forest around was full of the graves of patriots who had been shot. But she guessed.

Ahead lay the barracks, the officer's mess and other military buildings. Olav drew up outside Horwitz's quarters. There was a great deal of saluting and clicking of heels from officers and other ranks in the vicinity when Nils got out of the car. He returned the salutes as he escorted Anna into the building and past the guards at the entrance.

"I want to show you the lay-out here first of all, Anna," Nils said, giving his hat and gloves to an orderly. As he led the way, she saw through a doorway that Horwitz had enjoyed comfort during his stay. There were large leather-upholstered chairs, some antique furniture and bright woven rugs on the pine floor. Crystal decanters full of various wines and spirits stood on a side-table.

In contrast the office was totally functional with the usual large desk and filing cabinets with a Nazi flag draped across one wall and a coloured photograph of Hitler on another. A door on the far side led to the outer offices. Nils took her across to a table in front of a window facing the camp. On it stood two acid batteries with a firing switch.

"As you can see," he said, "everything is set up and connected to the charges laid throughout the camp. The guards have orders to run for their lives if a klaxon gives a certain series of signal blasts."

Anna gave a nod, knowing that for safety's sake the two batteries had to be connected to each other with a short length of zigzag wire before the firing-switch was pressed. "Couldn't you get rid of this now?" she asked, flicking her hand towards the batteries. "You could say that you've decided to counter-command Horwitz's plan."

Nils shook his head. "I can't do anything that might arouse suspicion. I've already gone against the Gestapo in ordering that Karl's execution be postponed. When I arrived unannounced the second-in-command here, Oberleutnant Ulman, found it difficult to accept that Horwitz hadn't mentioned that somebody else would be taking over. I had to say it was a last-minute decision from the High Command."

"When shall I meet him?"

"I've invited him to dinner with us this evening. He's a dangerous man and I need to keep an eye on him."

"Be careful then. Shall we get a chance to talk again privately? There's so much I want to ask you."

"Why not now?" he suggested. "After you've seen your room we'll have a drink together."

An orderly showed her upstairs. Her room was very military and spartan. It reminded her of her WRNS quarters after she was commissioned. Hurrying to the window she saw the view was of the forest and not of the camp. She pressed her palms against the pane and rested her forehead against it. All she wanted was to run to the camp's wire fence and shout to Karl that she was here, but that was impossible.

Downstairs again, she went to the room with the leather furniture. Nils was waiting for her, a glass in his hand. "What would you like to drink?" he asked, indicating the decanters on the side-table. "I'm having a whisky. It's Scotch. God knows how it came here, but I suppose Horwitz must have confiscated a good hoard of it some time ago. From what I've seen of his style of living, he has a taste for the luxuries of life."

Anna thought it obscene that Horwitz could have considered his own comfort when prisoners in his charge were starving and dying. "I don't want anything of his." She sat down in one of the leather chairs and looked straight into Nils's eyes. "Lars told me about your German origins. Why did you never tell me?"

Nils looked surprised, but not in the least disconcerted. Casually he perched his weight on the arm of another chair. "I wanted to many times, Anna. Not when we were children, of course, but later when we became inseparable. But by that time Germany was out of favour everywhere outside its own territories, and Britain and France were facing the possibility of war. You wouldn't have been able to understand how I could still love the country of my birth without it in any way affecting my loyalty to the land of my adoption."

"You should have tried me!" she protested.

"I didn't want to risk any divisions between us." He shrugged ruefully. "I didn't know then that war itself would keep us apart for a time."

"I hadn't expected it either," she said in a quieter tone, able to accept that he had wanted no dissension between them. "Tell me about those visits to Munich in your school holidays. The rest of us were always told it was to improve your knowledge of the language and that you stayed with a schoolmaster and his wife and family."

"That was correct, but it wasn't known that he was my late father's brother. The reason was that my adoptive mother wanted nobody to know I was not her own child, but then she was a very possessive woman. Her husband understood and he knew I needed to grow up free of maternal manacles. He also thought I had a right to know my own people."

"Early on you used to bring back snaps you'd taken with your box camera," she said reminiscently, remembering how she had envied those who had been with him. "Mostly of children of about your own age swimming or diving or on picnics. There were lots of their pets too. There was one of you with a parrot."

He raised his eyebrows. "You remember that? Yes, there were plenty of good times. My uncle was a beer-swilling, humorous man and I liked him. I suppose I knew from what was said that he was in the Nazi Party, but it meant nothing to me then. It was the same with his sons being in the Hitler Youth, which seemed no different to me from the Boy Scout Movement. My German origins enabled me to take part with my cousins in the competitive sports, and sport was everything to me as you know."

Anna nodded. "I can see how it must have seemed all right to you when you were a boy. After all, the rest of the world didn't sound any alarms at first, but what about later on?"

"I'd come through it all unscathed, although by that time all my German friends were Nazis and I had begun to see what was really happening there. It made me realise the urgent need for a stronger government here that would be prepared for whatever might come in the future. That was when I began to have political aims myself and, of course, I was outspoken with my radical ideas, which didn't please a lot of people, including Fru Johansen."

Anna experienced a renewed stab of grief at her aunt's name. "I think you made amends for that in what you did for her recently."

"I hope so. Perhaps she would have been more tolerant in the past if she'd understood my concern that Norway had continued too long following its own ways on the fringes of world affairs. Not that I had foreseen the violence that was to come, the King's defiance or the bloodshed. As soon as the Resistance was formed I volunteered and told them everything, just as I've told you." Nils put aside the glass he was holding and leaned towards her. "You and I belong to two nations, but," he added vehemently, "Norway will always come first with me."

"I think I'll always be equally divided," Anna answered, as she stood up. "I'd better dress for dinner as if this were an evening like any other for the officers of this camp."

"But it's already been different for us in more ways than one. We've had a talk that we should have had a long time ago." He rose to put his hands on her shoulders and kiss her lips softly, restraining himself from taking her mouth as he would have wished. As he drew away from her, he saw that her eyes were closed and her lashes wet with tears.

He kissed her lids. "What's the matter?" he asked tenderly.

She looked up at him. "Being here. Our talk. Karl in that dreadful place. Losing Aunt Rosa." Her voice was choked. "For a moment I felt lost."

"You can never be that with me." He went with her to the door, his arm about her waist, and watched her go upstairs before returning to his whisky. He felt anxious about her.

At the head of the stairs and out of Nils's sight Anna had halted, gripping the newel post as if her legs might give way. A dreadful suspicion had laid hold of her while Nils had been talking and she could not drive it away. When he had kissed her she had felt as if she were saying farewell to all the dreams and joys she had shared with him in the past.

Drawing herself up, she went into her room and closed the door, leaning back against it for a few moments. She had unpacked when up here before and spread on the bed was the black georgette dinner gown with a *Christina* label that she had put ready to wear. Going across to it she pushed it aside and sat down, trying to cope with everything that seemed to be falling into place.

She herself had sparked it off unwittingly by remembering his collection of childhood snaps. It had led in her own mind to others he had taken as a young man of harbours and inlets of the coast and fjords with an expensive German camera he had brought back with him. All of them would have been helpful to those planning the invasion that had come from every vital point along the whole coastline.

There was so much more coming back to her now. She recalled how she would have been caught in that first Bergen sortie if Nils had not seen her with Karl and feared that she might be involved in it. He had been able to warn them of the German guards being trebled at the factory only because he had alerted the enemy to the forthcoming sabotage raid in the first place!

Then there was the time she had met him in Tresfjord Church. He had said he was hiding after an act of sabotage had gone wrong, but most surely he had been responsible for that failure or else the Germans would not have released him so quickly. All of it had been planned carefully to avoid his becoming suspect to the Resistance.

Her thoughts raced on. He had waited until she had left the Alesund hotel before giving away her friends to the enemy. Again to protect her he had tipped off the Gestapo about the patriots at the next hotel with whom she was to have carried out further Resistance work. Finally she herself had told him that Karl would be on the Oslo to Bergen train! Involuntarily she pressed the back of her hand against her mouth as if it were still possible to hold back that deadly information that had been given on trust. She had thought she knew Nils through and through, but she had never known him at all.

Automatically Anna went through the procedure of getting ready for the evening, which she dreaded now more than ever. She almost wept with angry frustration, her nerves strained, when she found the back of the dinner gown almost impossible to hook up.

Nils's voice came from outside the door. "Are you all right, Anna? You've been a long time."

"I can't fasten my dress," she answered fiercely through her teeth, wanting him to keep away, but he came into the room.

"I'll do it."

She was already turned away from him, the ivory 'V' of her back exposed, her shining hair white-gold in the light. His ever-present desire for her gripped him. Instead of hooking up the dress, he slid his hands into it, cupping her firm round breasts and rediscovering her responsive nipples as he kissed the nape of her neck lovingly.

"I've waited so long for us to be close again as we were before." His voice was heavy with need. "We're together again, my darling. I couldn't live without you. You're in my blood, my bones, my very guts! How lovely you feel!" A groan of yearning escaped him. "I want to kiss your breasts and every part of you."

"No, Nils!" she protested sharply, wanting to scream at him in her rage at all he had done to betray a country that had made him one of its own. His breath was warm as he nuzzled her neck, one of his hands sliding further down her body to hold her between her legs. She tried to jerk away. "Let me go!"

He was deaf to the warning in her taut voice, elated that she was in his embrace, knowing her sensuality and confident that she would melt under his caresses as she had always done, now that they were alone and beginning again. "I love you more than ever!"

He swept her round and his mouth drove passionately into hers as he held her arched against his demanding body. With his free hand he pulled her gown to her waist and tugged it over her hips until it tumbled about her feet. As

300

he caught her about the thighs to carry her with him to the bed, she resorted to methods she had not wanted to use.

He released her instantly with a shout of excruciating pain and staggered back to thump against the wall. "Why the hell did you do that?" he yelled furiously, shock and disbelief on his agony-contorted features.

She went to rescue the gown from the floor. "I didn't want to hurt you!" she gave back, her fury equal to his, "but it's time you faced facts. I don't know any more than you if Karl will live after all he's been through, but even if I lose him I'll go on loving him for the rest of my life! Neither you nor anyone else can ever take his place! Now leave me alone!"

He glared at her in his rage before he went, slamming the door behind him with such force that the whole building seemed to shake. She stared at her own stark, white face in the mirror. He had finally accepted that he had lost her.

Anna waited until she heard the dinner guest arrive before going downstairs. She had not attempted to hook up the dinner gown again and had put on a short green dress that was easy to fasten. In her fish-skin handbag she had her gun, never knowing when she might have to use it in an emergency.

She saw Nils before he saw her. He was pouring a drink for the *Oberleutnant*. He turned with the glass and their eyes met. His were as cold and hard as Arctic ice.

Anna felt a great quaking fear strike at her. Suppose Nils intended to let the destruction of the camp go ahead? He had betrayed so many. Maybe he had volunteered for this sortie to make sure that it happened, and that Karl, in particular, with all the other prisoners who had fought against the Nazi regime were wiped out together.

"Come in, Anna," Nils said in an expressionless voice. "I'd like you to meet Oberleutnant Ulman."

The officer was a large, overweight man with a broad

face, narrow, dark eyes and a fleshy mouth. As the introductions took place he clicked his heels, bowed to Anna and kissed her hand.

"It's a pleasure to be in your company for the evening, *fraulein.*"

Anna, having been used to making conversation with German officers at the Alesund hotel, knew how to talk to him on non-controversial subjects. Nils contributed, but did not look fully at her at any time. His hostility seeped towards her, but Ulman was unaware of it.

Dinner was served in the *Kommodant*'s dining-room on a table laid with white damask, lighted candles and fine Norwegian silverware. Anna kept her handbag with her and put it on the floor beside her chair. Outwardly she appeared relaxed, but she was alert to every nuance in the men's voices, as if seeking clues to what might have been plotted between them without her knowledge.

Ulman was enjoying himself. There had been certain indications that he was winning favour with the new *Kommodant* and that could lead to promotion. If Reichskommissar Terboven continued the war from Norway, he hoped that this man would stay on and Horwitz be invalided home. As for this evening, there was good wine to compensate for the rationed food and a beautiful woman, whom he believed he had impressed.

It was as he was about to take up his wine glass again that there came a commotion outside and the camp klaxon blared out the arranged signal. His glass tipped over, flooding the table with red wine, and he sprang to his feet to rush and pull the black-out back from the window. Every floodlight in the camp was blazing.

"The war must be over!" he gasped. "The lights can only mean that Reichskommissar Terboven has decided to surrender too!"

302

As if to confirm what he had said, the door was flung open and a young officer rushed in, despair in his face.

"The Fatherland has surrendered unconditionally, *Herr Kommodant*! Armed civilian men with armbands have been seen from the lookout tower advancing on the camp! The Resistance is coming in already to take over!"

Nils had not moved and did not even turn his head. "My orders are that every man lay down his weapons and there is to be full co-operation with the Norwegian in command."

"Yes, sir." The officer rushed out again. Cheering was beginning to resound from the prisoners in the camp.

Anna tilted her head back in thankfulness. She was full of joy. The fragile hour in which Norway could still have been held in an iron first was over too. Karl was safe! As soon as the Resistance arrived she would go to him!

She looked at Nils and then rose slowly to her feet in growing concern. He still had not moved and sat staring fixedly at Ulman, who had turned away from the window to face him. Neither of them noticed that she drew her gun from her handbag and held it down at her side.

Ulman, sweat standing out on his forehead and upper lip, became agitated and showed his fear. "Don't look at me like that, *Herr Kommodant*! I won't do it! Not now the Resistance is almost here! There'd be retribution! They'd shoot us both! God knows what they'd do to us first!" He was gripped by panic.

Without warning Nils leapt up from his chair, causing it to crash backwards, and threw open a door to get to the office. In horror at what he might do, Anna rushed after him, Ulman at her heels. She reached the office to find Nils already at the batteries.

"No!" she shrieked in desperate appeal.

He looked at her fully for the first time since she had come downstairs. "Get out, Anna!" he ordered tersely. He

303

turned back to the batteries. She raised her gun and fired deliberately at his shoulder.

The impact of the bullet jerked him away from the table, and he half turned towards her, astonishment in his face, before another bullet from Ulman's revolver hit him in the chest. Anna uttered an agonised cry. As she would have darted forward, Ulman flung her out of his way. She fell against the desk, her flailing arm sending papers fluttering from it. She regained her balance as Ulman stood by the table, glaring down at Nils, who lay sprawled on the floor and groaning, red stains darkening his tunic.

"You bloody fool, *Herr Kommodant*!" Ulman exclaimed contemptuously, turning his attention to the batteries. "I had to stop you to save myself, and you didn't have the sense to realise it!"

They were his last words. As he was about to tear free the short length of zigzag wire that had been vital to the operation, the door from the outer office burst open. The newcomer with the Resistance armband, seeing him at the batteries, fired instantly with his Sten gun.

By now Anna had reached Nils and she dropped to her knees beside him to wrench open his tunic and see if there was anything she could do to stem the flow of blood, but she saw at once it was useless. Outside there came the singing of the National Anthem from the liberated prisoners in the camp.

Nils spoke with effort. "Don't . . . leave me."

"I won't." She wiped away a trickle of blood from the corner of his mouth. In spite of everything, she could never have abandoned him at this time for the sake of all that had once been. As he tried to speak again she took his hand and lowered her head to listen.

"I . . . was dismantling the . . . batteries."

She leaned back, staring down at him. "Dear God!" she whispered in deep distress.

His gaze was riveted on her face as if he would take the image of her with him. "Anna . . ."

Blood filled his throat, his eyes closed and his head fell to one side. A huge sob convulsed her and she raised his hand to press her lips to it and hold it to her. She did not see Lars, wearing his armband, enter the room with a rifle. He took in the scene at once and came to crouch beside her.

"I'm sorry, Anna. Nils was a brave man."

"I made a terrible mistake," she said brokenly. "I thought he was about to destroy the camp. I shot him in the shoulder and then Oberleutnant Ulman fired too."

Lars knew she was confused. He had been told where to find her by the man who had caught the *Oberleutnant* red-handed at the batteries. One of her shots must have gone wild in the exchange of gunfire that had taken place here. He'd make sure she was never questioned about it, especially as a bullet in any healthy man's shoulder was most unlikely ever to be fatal. It was Ulman who had been guilty of Nils's death.

Straightening up, he took off his jacket and laid it over Nils's face. Then he took Anna by the elbow and raised her to her feet. She turned to him as if in a daze.

"Listen to me," Lars insisted to gain her full attention. "We've found Karl. He's been put on a stretcher and we're getting him off to hospital with some of the very sick men we came across in one of the huts."

"Where is he?" she gasped. "Can I stay with him?"

"Yes, I'll take you to him now."

Anna broke into a run as soon as she saw the stretchers being lined up. One requisitioned German ambulance was already driving away with a full load. Karl had just been lifted up to be placed in another, almost full, that was waiting when she reached him.

"Karl, I'm here!"

He looked thin and ill and haggard, but love warmed his

eyes as he saw her bending over him. "I told Lars I wouldn't leave without seeing you," he said, his voice faint, his spirit unbroken.

She took his skeletal hand tenderly into hers and kissed it, her own features transfigured by joy. "Partings are over, Karl. I'm coming with you."

She climbed up into the ambulance after him. The doors were shut and they were driven away.

Chapter Twenty-Seven

In the quiet forest glade where she was seated, Anna, having looked back over two decades to the Occupation, let her thoughts dwell finally on how the whole of Norway had burst into rapturous celebrations on that Liberation day. She smiled on the memory of a large placard in a shop doorway, '*Closed because of Joy*'.

Reichskommissar Terboven had been among the first Nazi leaders to commit suicide. Yet there had been no violence against those who had imposed a reign of terror for all those long years. Neither were the collaborators assulted. Only Quisling received the death sentence and even that was regretted afterwards, for Norwegian law had abolished it years before the war. The resolve to forgive and not forget had taken root early on and had prevailed ever since.

Neither Greta nor Christina survived their imprisonment, but Emil and Margot came through it. Her fiancé returned home with his squadron, having been a pilot since his escape, and they were married shortly afterwards. Frida also lived and had become mellow in her old age. As for Magnus, he had stayed on in Sweden and had become a scientist committed to space research.

Anna's thoughts went to Karl. He had eventually regained his health with only the scars on his body to show what he had been through. Yet there were times still when she had to wake him from nightmares in which he thought himself under Gestapo torture again.

Now he was in Washington at an international oil conference, for the discovery of oil in Norwegian waters was going to make Norway richer than Midas. He had no idea that she had never been entirely free of Nils. It went back to that moment when Lars had covered Nils's dead face with his jacket and she had been struck by doubt. Had Nils told her the truth? But then he would never have lied to her in his last moments. She suffered terrible grief. Karl did his best to console her. It was shortly before their marriage

"Anyone could have drawn the same conclusions as you from his strange behaviour that evening," he said consolingly. "As you've said, you'd had that quarrel, which would have upset him in the first place. He also knew that the lives of hundreds of men were hanging in the balance. Naturally he was under a great strain and he had to dismantle the batteries in case any other officer stepped in."

"But I shot him!" she wept.

"You did what seemed right at a dangerous moment, but your bullet wouldn't have killed Nils as you knew. Ulman did that and would have done, whether you'd been there or not. Although it's now known that Ulman was shot by mistake, such things happen in war. Put the whole matter out of your mind. You were not at fault in any way."

His words of reassurance should have enabled her to get everything into proportion. Although she got on with living, having three children and loving Karl in a passionate and caring marriage as well as taking up a writing career, every so often the memory of pulling the trigger would come back to her. Nils had said she would never be free of him and he held her now by regret as once he had done with love.

With a sigh, Anna stood and brushed some dry grass from her trousers. It had done her good to rest for a while.

She'd had a hectic time in London seeing her publishers and her agent. After a few books that had done moderately well, her latest, an historical novel, seemed to be taking off, and there was talk of it becoming a best-seller. Yet she had cancelled important appointments to be here today. Nothing could have kept her away.

Without haste and with rising trepidation, Anna left the forest and saw the lake lying wide and blue before her. The size and grandeur of its setting reduced the large number of spectators around it to a mere sprinkling. She took up a place on the east bank, not far from the land-based crane. There was a lot of activity on board the shallow-drafted working-boat with its own crane ready for action and she asked a fellow spectator what was happening.

"Divers have gone down again to inflate the parachute-bags on the lifting-frame that's attached to the aircraft, which has lost a lot of rivets in the initial work. It will be touch and go whether it hangs together on the way up"

He broke off as the water began to churn like a maelstrom by the working-boat. Then the vivid yellow parachute-bags burst through the surface in fountains of spray. The Mosquito was safely free of the rock ledge!

The dive-master was busy issuing fresh orders and the last bags went into place. Below the surface the aircraft, slung under the frame, began its slow journey to the east bank of the lake where Anna stood. As the working-boat came alongside the land-based crane was able to take over and almost leisurely began its work.

Anna clenched her hands together, her heart pounding. This was her own fragile hour, in which liberation from Nils would be lost until the end of her days if this salvage attempt came to nothing. It was a conviction that had gripped her from the moment of reading about the salvage attempt in that London newspaper. A curious hush had descended over the whole scene, emphasising the noise of the crane as it winched its burden slowly up through the water. Anything said by the working-boat crew could be clearly heard, their desperate concern adding even more drama to the scene.

Now the water began to hiss and bubble. The dive-master gripped the rails and his voice was harsh with tension. "She's there! And she's holding!"

The general suspense was almost palpable. A dark shape had begun to shiver below the surface and soon there was a more violent stirring of the water. Anna gasped as slowly, almost majestically, the Mosquito speared the water like a rising whale.

Up and up it came, hung with fronded weeds, water cascading from every section, with the port wing gracefully extended as if ready again for flight, and the starboard wing, although badly damaged, still in place. A great cheer resounded around the lake, every camera recording with the TV and film crews the spectacular rise of the fighting machine that had lain hidden for so many years.

The tank had cracked in the lifting, and fuel mingled with the water that was pouring down to form oily blue patches that swirled about on the lake's surface beneath the suspended aircraft. Slowly again, the crane swung the Mosquito over and down on to a specially constructed platform. In its camouflage colours, which had barely been affected by the pure water, the aircraft lay like a great tired bird spreading its wings in the warmth of the evening sun.

The dive-master was the first to spring up on the platform and others followed. The whole team was in exuberant spirits after the number of setbacks encountered before this moment of triumph. Champagne corks began to pop and every member of the team held their glasses high as they were photographed by the media and public alike. The dive-master gave a quick TV interview. Then hot food was served to the team, for there were hours of work ahead for them yet.

The last of the spectators drifted away. The TV and film vans had already gone. Only Anna still stood on the bank. The policeman, whom she had spoken to when she had first arrived, detached himself from conversation with another member of the force, and came across to her.

"There won't be anything more to see now, *fröken*. The divers will be going down again to try to retrieve any scattered components and that salvage work will go on for several days. If you want to see the aircraft depart, that will happen tomorrow when it's transported to a hangar at Gardermoen airfield to await restoration."

"Someone has climbed into the cockpit. I'm waiting to see if the cargo is still there and intact." She was remembering Nils's angry frustration at having failed to get it to England.

"How do you know there might be something on board?"

Her gaze was on the aircraft. "I knew the pilot."

The policeman left her to go and speak to the dive-master, who listened and then looked across at her.

"Come and join us," he invited.

As Anna had expected, he knew who had been flying the aircraft and everything about the flight, but he was interested that she had been given an account of the crash by Nils himself. "I've been told to expect a sealed box on board," he said, "with contents that are still Top Secret. It has to be handed over to those two government officials waiting over there." He jerked his head in their direction.

"Who's in the cockpit now?" she asked.

"A veteran pilot of 331 Squadron. He's taken a battery up there with him."

There was a sudden triumphant shout from the cockpit and everybody looked up to see the navigation lights on the port wing blink and settle into a steady glow. There was a burst of applause from those gathered around. It was as if the plane had taken life again.

The pilot looked out. "I've found the box, but there's another here too."

The dive-master went back on to the platform to take the first box from him and hand it down to the government representative, who had come forward. The pilot was having trouble with the second box and raised it up with difficulty. One of the team came to help the dive-master receive it, but its weight took both men by surprise and it crashed down to bounce off the edge of the platform and smash open against a rock, spewing out its contents amid disarrayed straw and other padding. In a moment of terrible revelation Anna stared at Rosa's jewelled ikon sparkling through some straw.

Rushing forward, she picked it up and gazed at it, ignoring the excitement of those around her. All too clearly she was remembering that Nils had spoken about those Germans desperate for funds to keep the flame of Nazism alive for the future. He had given her no inkling that he had been including himself! It was he who had instigated the raid on Rosa's apartment! He had seen the chance to take a fortune in easily transported goods safely to England where it could be banked away to provide political funds in the future. With Rosa and Frida gone and, using a master key, he could have looted at leisure. His Nazi officer friend must have been his confederate and perhaps it was he who had taken everything else.

All she had suspected of Nils had been true, including that last vengeful attempt to eliminate Karl, no matter how many other lives would have been lost. At last she knew for certain that she had not been mistaken in believing that Nils's finger was already on the switch.

It was her shot that had prevented the catastrophe. Even Ulman's bullet would have been just too late. Then Nils in his last moments, all rage gone, had still tried to hold her to him with a lie. He had been as fanatically obsessive about her as he had been with Nazism.

She did not hear a taxi-door slam or see Karl as he came running down the bank to her.

"Anna! What's happening here?" He stared incredulously at all the *objets d'art* being collected up, knowing enough about antiques to recognise the value as well as the rarity of the tiny Japanese lacquered boxes to the carved jade and ivory. Somebody had taken a rolled up painting from a container that was unmistakably a Degas. Others were looking at a Munch. "Where did all these things come from?"

"They were Aunt's Rosa's," Anna replied in a choked voice. "Nils must have betrayed her for his own ends. Just as he destroyed others throughout the Occupation. He was a traitor, Karl!"

"My God!" Karl breathed, tight-faced, and drew her close to him. They turned together as the dive-master gave an exclamation.

"Look at this, everybody!" He had picked up a leather medal-case stamped with a gilded swastika. Opening it, he revealed a medal awarded to Nazi Norwegians for exceptional service to the Third Reich. It was dated 1942, the year in which the Resistance had suffered some of its heaviest losses.

Karl took Anna's hand and pressed it encouragingly. "Tell him."

She explained, hesitantly at first and then her voice gathered strength as the shadow across her life began to slip away. All there listened intently.

"There is something to Nils Olsen's credit," she said in conclusion. "In spite of his Nazi ideals he was instrumental in saving the life of a Jewish child. That is all I wish to remember about him."

Before leaving the lakeside Anna handed back the ikon. Although Rosa had bequeathed everything to her, except for a life income to Frida and the Oslo apartment, her legal claim to these particular treasures would have to be established.

"How did you know I'd be here?" Anna asked as she and Karl went up the bank on their way to the road, his arm around her shoulders.

"My colleague heard a news item about it on the radio. I left him as deputy and caught the next flight out of Washington."

"I'm so glad you came," she said thankfully, resting her head against his shoulder.

When he had paid off the taxi that had bought him from the airport, they strolled along to her hired car. He kissed her before opening the door. "Is it back to Oslo now?"

Suddenly she wanted to be completely on her own with him. "Not yet. Nobody knows that we've returned from abroad sooner than expected. Let's drive to Molde and be at the country house for a few days."

He nodded approval. "That's a great idea! I can't remember when we last had time to ourselves." Briefly he cupped her face in his hand as he had first done on a snowy quayside and they exchanged a smiling look. "So let's go," he added softly.

He took the wheel and Anna did not look back as they drove away. She felt wonderfully released. No longer held by the past she could look wholly to the future. Soon she would present the ikon to the Hermitage.